JERUSALEM INN

Martha Grimes is a native of Garrett County, Maryland. She is a university lecturer in English in Washington DC and divides her time between England and America, where her series of Richard Jury mysteries have enjoyed great success.

Also by Martha Grimes

The Man with a Load of Mischief
The Old Fox Deceiv'd
The Deer Leap
The Anodyne Necklace
Help the Poor Struggler
The Dirty Duck
I Am the Only Running Footman
The Five Bells and Bladebone

Jerusalem Inn

Martha Grimes

HEADLINE

To Pamela,
a paradigmatic friend

Copyright © Martha Grimes 1984

First published in Great Britain in 1987
by Michael O'Mara Books Ltd

First published in paperback in Great Britain
by HEADLINE BOOK PUBLISHING PLC

"The Wise Men", from *Living Together: New & Selected Poems*,
© 1973 by Edgar Bowers, is reprinted by permission of
David R. Godine, Publisher, Boston.

ISBN 0 7472 3036 6

Printed and bound in Great Britain by
Collins, Glasgow

HEADLINE BOOK PUBLISHING PLC
Headline House
79 Great Titchfield Street
London W1P 7FN

CONTENTS

THE WISE MEN

Far to the east I see them in my mind
Coming in every year to that one place.
They carry in their hands what they must find,
In their own faces bare what they shall face.

They move in silence, permanent and sure,
Like figurines of porcelain set with gold,
The colors of their garments bright and pure,
Their graceful features elegant and old.

They do not change: nor war nor peace define
Nor end the journey that each year the same
Renders them thus. They wait upon a sign
That promises no future but their name.

— EDGAR BOWERS

My sister! O, my sister! — There's the cause on't!
Whether we fall by ambition, blood or lust,
Like diamonds we are cut with our own dust.

— THE DUCHESS OF MALFI

ONE

A MEETING in a graveyard. That was how it would always come back to him, and without any sense of irony at all — that a meeting in a graveyard did not foreshadow the permanence he was after. Snow mounding the sundial. Sparrows quarreling in the hedges. The black cat sitting enthroned in the dry birdbath. Slivers of memories. A broken mirror. *Bad luck, Jury.*

It was on a windy December day, with only five of them left until Christmas, that Jury saw the sparrows quarreling in a nearby hedge as he stood looking through the gates of Washington Old Hall. The sparrows — one attempting to escape, the other in hot pursuit — flew from hedge to tree to hedge. The pecking of one had bloodied the breast of the other. He was used to scenes of carnage; still he was shocked. But didn't it go on everywhere? He tracked their flight from tree to hedge and finally to the ground at his feet. He moved to break up the fight, but they were off again, off and away.

The place was closed, so he trudged about the old village of Washington in the snow now turning to rain. After three o'clock, so the pubs were closed, worse luck. Up one village lane, he found himself outside the Catholic church. *Feeling sorry for yourself, Jury? No kith, no kin, no wife, no . . .* Well, but it *is* Christmas, his kinder self answered.

This depressing debate with himself continued, like the fighting sparrows, as he heaved open the heavy door of the church, walked quietly into the vestibule, only to find he'd interrupted a christening in the nave. The priest still intoned, but the faces of the baby's parents turned toward the intruder and the baby cried.

His nasty sparrow-self cackled. *You nit.* Jury pretended to be in a brown study before the church bulletin board, as if it were important to convey to the people down there that the information posted here was absolutely necessary for his salvation. Nodding curtly (*as if they care, you clod!*) at nothing, he turned and left, Unborn Again.

That sparrow-self was with him in the church cemetery, sitting on his shoulder, pecking his ear to a bloody pulp, telling him that no one had *forced* him to accept his cousin's whining invitation to come to them at Christmas ("*But we never see you, Richard . . .*"). Newcastle-upon-Tyne. What a bloody awful place in winter. *A nice walk amongst the gravestones, that's what you need, Jury . . . and in the snow, too. It's snowing again. . . .* Peck, peck, peck, peck.

That was when he saw her, stooping over one of the headstones, brown hair damp with rain and snow, its strands blown by wind from under the hood of her cape. Old willows trailed veils of wet leaves across his path. Moss crawled up the headstones. The place was otherwise deserted.

She was some distance from him and very still. Stooped over the stone, she reminded Jury of one of those life-sized monuments one occasionally sees, even in the smallest and simplest churchyards, permanent elaborations of grief, hooded and dark and with hands clasped.

Hers were not. Hers appeared to be noting something down in a tiny book. Either she was so absorbed in studying the markers that she didn't notice him coming down the path, or she was merely respecting his privacy.

He put her at somewhere in her late thirties, the sort of woman who wore well. She was probably better-looking now than she had been when she was twenty. It was one of those faces that Jury had always found beautiful, with its stamp of sorrow and regret as permanent as graveyard sculpture. Her hair was much the color of his own, but hers had red highlights that were visible even here in the gray gloom of a wet afternoon. He could not see her eyes, obscured by the hood of the cape. She was bending over a small stone sculpted with angels whose wings had crumbled in the weather.

Jury pretended to be studying the headstones, too, as he had studied the bulletin board. As he was trying to think of an appropriately funereal introduction, she put her hand to her forehead and then on the gravestone as if she were steadying herself. She looked ill.

"Are you all right?" Immediately, his hand was on her arm.

She shook her head as if to clear it and gave him a slight, embarrassed smile. "I just felt faint. It's probably all of this stooping over and getting up too fast. Thanks." She hurriedly shoved the little book and the pencil she'd been using into one of the big patch-pockets of her cape. The cover of the notebook was metal — gold, and not cheap. The pencil was gold, the cape cashmere. Nothing about her was cheap.

"You're not writing a book on epigraphs, are you?" That was properly banal, he thought, irritated with his own clumsiness. If she'd been a suspect in a murder case, he'd have got on nicely.

But his suggestion didn't seem to throw her off. "No." She laughed briefly. "I'm doing a bit of research."

"On what? If you don't mind — listen, are you sure you're all right?"

She swayed a little and put her hand to her head again. "Well, now you mention it, I don't know. Dizzy again."

"You should sit down. Or maybe have a brandy or something." He frowned. "The pubs are closed, though. . . ."

"My cottage isn't far, just the other end of the Green. I don't know what the vertigo is. Maybe this medicine . . . I'll be showing you scars next —"

"That would be nice." He smiled again. "Look, at least let me walk you to your place."

"Thanks, I'd appreciate it." They walked back through old Washington, which Jury saw now as a gem of a village, with its two pubs and tiny library across the Green.

"I have some whiskey; perhaps you'd join me?"

Again, Jury — congratulating himself on his devil-may-care originality — said, "That would be nice."

They passed the larger of the two pubs, called the Washington Arms, creamed-washed and black-shuttered. Her cottage lay at the end of a narrow, hedged walk. Its small porch was high-pitched, as was its tiled roof, above a lemon yellow door like a glint of winter light.

It was not sunny inside, however; the mullioned panes were too narrow and too high to allow for much light even on the best of days. She switched on a lamp. Its stained-glass shade made a watery rainbow on the mahogany table.

"We haven't even introduced ourselves," she said, laughing.

It was true; on their walk they had talked so much like old friends, they'd forgotten the mere detail of names.

"I'm Helen Minton," she said.

"Richard Jury. You're not from up here, are you? The accent sounds like London."

She laughed. "You must be quite expert. I can only tell the difference between Cornwall and Surrey and these Geordies up here. I don't think I could absolutely pick out London as such."

"I'm from London."

"I'll ask you — please sit down, won't you? — I'll ask you what everyone asks me: what are you doing up *here?* London might as well be Saudi, and yet you can get there in three hours on a fast train."

"I'm on my way to Newcastle."

As she was taking his jacket — heavy suede, but no proof against the winds up here — she looked at him speculatively. "You don't sound too happy about it."

Jury laughed. "Good Lord, does it show?"

"Mmm. It's too bad Newcastle only makes people think about coal. Most of the collieries are shut down. The city it-self is really quite lovely." She shifted the jacket to her other arm, not hanging it up or anything, just standing there. She was looking at him out of gray eyes only slightly darker than his own, the color of pewter or the North Sea.

"We're not far from the sea here, are we?"

"No. It's a few miles away, the coast of Sunderland." She tilted her head, still looking at him hard. "Do you know, we've very nearly the same color hair and eyes?"

Casually, he said, "Do we? Now you mention it, yes." He smiled. "You could be my sister."

His smile had the effect opposite the one it usually had. She looked immensely sad and moved suddenly to put his coat away. "Why are you going to Newcastle, then?" she asked, carefully arranging the jacket on a hanger.

"Visiting my cousin. For Christmas. I haven't seen her in years; she used to live in the Potteries. They moved up here hoping to find better work. What an awful irony."

Helen Minton hung up her own coat on a peg and said, "Is that your only family?"

Jury nodded and sat down. He didn't feel he had to wait to be invited. He offered her one of his cigarettes. She held back a curtain of reddish brown hair as she bent over the flame. "Now that's really odd. I've a cousin, too. He's my only relative. He's an artist, a very good one." She indicated a small painting on the opposite wall — an abstract of a sort — intense colors and sharp lines.

Jury smiled. "We seem to be all kitted out in much the same way. Hair. Eyes. Cousins. I like your house," he said, sliding down more comfortably in the deep armchair, smoking.

"How about that whiskey?"

"Marvelous."

As she was measuring out the drinks with the seriousness of a child who must make no mistakes, she said, "It's not my house, really. I'm only just renting it." She handed him his glass.

"I'll ask you what they all ask you: what are you doing up here?"

Holding her glass in both hands, she said. "Nothing much. I came into some money, enough to live on pretty well. I'm just visiting. I think this is a beautiful little village, the Old Town. I'm doing some research on the Washington family."

"Are you a writer?"

"Me? Lord, no. It makes something to do. We get a lot of Americans, of course, though not much of anyone around this time. It's an interesting family: it's from the manor and the village they took their name. And several hundred years later Lawrence built Sulgrave Manor. Have you been in the Old Hall? Of course you couldn't have today: it's closed. You must come back. I've been helping out over there on Thursdays, as their regular person is out temporarily — and I could show you around. . . ." Her voice trailed away. "But I expect you'll be busy with your cousin, and Christmas."

He shook his head. "Not that busy."

"I could show you around," she repeated. "It's owned by the Trust, you know. My favorite room is the bedroom, upstairs — " And she looked toward her own ceiling and blushed rather horribly. Quickly, she went on: "There's a kitchen and sometimes I make people tea, though I expect I'm not supposed to. But there are one or two people who've come back several times — "

With a straight face (but smiling like hell to himself at her attempt to quick-talk herself out of the bedroom) he said, "After you show me the Old Hall, would you like dinner?"

"Dinner?" She might never have eaten it before, she seemed so surprised at the invitation. And then immensely pleased, her embarrassment forgotten. "Why — yes. That would be nice." She looked toward another room, inspired. "We could have it here," she said, arms outspread, as if discovering in Jury's invitation enormous potential.

He laughed. "I certainly wasn't meaning for you to cook. Aren't there any restaurants?"

"Not as good as my cooking," Helen said quite simply. "All of this talk about dinner is making me ravenous. I made some sandwiches before I went out. Would you like one?"

Jury had had no appetite for days. Suddenly, he was starved. He wondered if it was food they both wanted, too. He smiled. "I would, thanks. Can I get us a refill while you get the sandwiches?"

"Oh, please do. The drinks table is just there. I'll be back straightaway."

He collected their glasses. Jury glanced around the room that was growing more shadowy with the gathering darkness outside, though it was only four in the afternoon. It was a pleasant room, furniture slipcovered in an old rose print, the fire lit. The fireplace smoked, he noticed. He was sitting close to it and looked above the mantel at a framed print of the Old Hall. The wallpaper for three or four inches all around was the slightest bit lighter.

Helen came back in with a silver tray on which sat a plate of sandwiches and an assortment of condiments. Everything from Branston pickle to horseradish to mustard to pepper sauce.

He laughed. "Good Lord, you do like your sandwiches done up properly."

"I know. Isn't it awful? I've this terrible weakness for hot food. There's an Indian restaurant in the New Town where we could go." She spread mustard and horseradish on her beef and topped it off with a bit of pickle. Taking a large bite, she said, "I think I'm probably flammable by now. Want some? It's fresh horseradish. A friend of mine put it up." She held up the small earthenware pot.

"No, thanks. I like my sandwiches neat, if you don't mind."

They ate and drank in companionable silence for a few minutes, then she sat back on the couch beside the lamp, tucking one foot up under her skirt. "Where do you work?"

"In Victoria Street." He had wished the question of his work wouldn't arise right away; it had a way of putting some people off.

"Doing what?"

"Police work. I'm a cop."

She stared at him and laughed. "Never!" He nodded. Still, she shook her head in disbelief. "But you don't —"

" 'Look like one'? Ah, just wait'll you see me in my shiny blue suit and mac." She was smiling and still shaking her head, tilted so that the stained glass threw colored rivulets across her face and hair.

"I'll prove it by asking a few astute questions. Ready?"

It was a game and she made herself comfortable for it. "Quite."

"Okay. Why are you *really* here? Why are you so unhappy? And why'd you take the picture down over the mantel?"

At the first question she had looked sharply away. The third brought her eyes sharply back. "How — ?"

"The fireplace smokes. It's the wallpaper; it's lighter all around the frame. You're not getting through my grilling very well. You look guilty as — " Jury stopped smiling. He had certainly not meant to upset her. Her face was flushed now, not with the lamplight's reflection but with her own blood.

All she said was, "You *are* observant."

"It's my job; it's a weakness. Names, dates, places, faces . . . some I wish I could forget. . . ." *But not yours,* he would have liked to add. "Look, I'm sorry. I wasn't meaning to pry — "

"No, no. That's all right. As far as being unhappy is concerned — " Her laugh was strained. "It's Christmas, I expect. It depresses me. Terrible isn't it? But I suppose it has that effect on a lot of people. One actually feels *guilty* for not having a family about, as if one had carelessly lost them." She talked to her glass rather than to Jury. "I suppose we're so obliged to be happy, we feel guilty when we can't — " She shrugged it off.

"Usually I put in a special request for Christmas duty and get through it all that way. You see some of the things I've seen on Christmas and it makes you realize you're not the only one who has a rough time getting through it." *The old woman, frail and birdlike, who'd hung herself in her closet,* he did not add. "It's therapeutic." *If you like that sort of therapy.* "If you've no plans for Christmas, have dinner with us. My cousin would love it. Give her something else to speculate about except where her alcoholic husband is and whether her kids will end up punks and dye their hair purple."

"That's awfully nice of you. But, I mean, I'm a stranger. I couldn't intrude on family — "

"Come on, now. You're not going to go all Father Christmasy–sentimental on me, are you? After what you just said?"

They both laughed.

"Speaking of *him,* I've got to get some Christmas boxes ready for the school. Bonaventure School. It calls itself a school but it's really more of an orphanage."

"You're doing your share of charity work, certainly."

Quickly, she put in: "Oh, don't give me any credit for *that*. It fills up time." Vaguely, she looked over his shoulder at the window where snow hissed against the glass.

And why, Jury wondered, would she need to fill up time? His question about her happiness had gone unanswered. Reluctantly, he put down his glass and got to his feet. "I expect my cousin is wondering where I've got to. I'd better be going."

She walked with him to the door. When she opened it, he saw snow blown by wind ruffling high hedges and bowing small trees. It was mixing again with rain.

Helen pulled her sweater sleeves over her hands and wound her arms about her waist.

"You'd better go back inside," said Jury, turning up his jacket collar. The wind knifed through suede and sweater.

But she seemed not to notice her own discomfort, saying: "You're not dressed for this weather. Haven't you an overcoat?"

"It's in the car."

Having walked beside him to the gate, she looked up and down the street for the car. "Where?"

There was suspicion in her tone, as if he might be intending to hoof it to Newcastle, dressed as he was. He smiled in the gloom at her standing there, feet planted firmly together in dark shoes with button straps. She was wearing lisle stockings and looked old-fashioned, like a woman one sees in Art Nouveau posters.

"The car's in front of the pub. And you're getting wet." He remembered the moment in the cemetery. "What's causing the dizziness?"

Wind whipped her hair. "It's probably just some side effect of medicine. It's nothing, really. A very minor heart thing. You'd better go." Shoving a strand of hair from her mouth, she asked anxiously, "Will you be back?"

A gust of snow had pulled at her sweater collar and he

reached up and drew it together, drawing her, at the same time, a little closer. "Now, you know I'll be back."

They looked at one another for a moment before she smiled and said, "Yes, I expect you will." Through the gloom, she ran back up the walk and inside, waving to him from the door before she closed it.

Jury stopped there on the pavement for a minute or two, shoulders hunched into his jacket. It was the damned wind, cold as hell. A light switched on inside the house; he saw her at the window. The mullioned panes, the rain, broke her face into watery squares like a dream-image.

He waved again and started off for his car realizing that the depression had lifted like the nasty sparrow flying from his shoulder. The snow was up over his shoes but he scarcely noticed it. The roads would be hell, but he hardly cared. Jury started to whistle.

Yet he felt uneasy. The farther away he got from her cottage, the more the feeling grew.

That was when he first thought it: that a meeting in a graveyard was not the best way to begin an attachment. The sparrow fluttered near him, but he shook it off. The next time he saw her, he would certainly find out why she was unhappy.

The next time he saw her she was dead.

TWO

1

JURY didn't have to listen to his cousin to know that New-castle, that all of Tyne and Wear, spelled frustration, poverty, unemployment, the dole — a depressed and depressing place to be, although that's all she talked about on his first evening in the walk-up flat, she sitting there knitting wool as drab as her hair and eyes, occasionally pushing back stitches to look out at the slow fall of snow through which Brendan would never make his way home, slipping and sliding after drinking up the dole money. Brendan was her out-of-work husband, a bold-eyed Irishman, the only one Jury had ever met without a hint of humor to him.

Not much to be humorous about, of course: *The joke-shop, we call it,* his cousin had gone on, talking about the unemployment office, with all of its little cards detailing jobs that had somehow magically been filled just the moment the out-of-worker inquired about them. *One ad for a job to work down the mine last week, and over a thousand applicants. . . . The government got them up here, you know, all those factories, by promising them subsidies for a couple of years.*

Then they go pull the rug out from under you. Brendan was one who had slipped on the rug. Not his fault.

And Jury believed it, really. It was just that he had never liked his cousin much. Jury's infrequent visits, his telephone calls, his little presents of money when she was on the emotional skids — all were done out of affection and respect for her father, the uncle who had taken him in after his mother had died. He didn't like his cousin because she had always lived beyond the fringes of reality, in that child's never-never land where slippers were glass, or if merely shoes, then the elves should come in at night to stitch them up.

God knew, she told Jury, the kiddies needed shoes. Here a sidelong glance at Cousin Richard, and shoes went down on his mental list of Christmas gifts.

The kids, however, were bored by shoes, and knew a soft touch when they saw one; they could sniff out the promise of presents like a whiff of North Sea air. So they put up with shoes the next morning in order to get to the real stuff: a doll, the Jedi ensemble, coloring books and sweets and a huge lunch. The kids, who were a lot better out of their mother's way than in it, all had absurdly fanciful names like Jasmine and Christabel, the sorts of names you give your kids when you don't have enough confidence they can get by with being just plain old Marys and Johns. They all got on fairly well, considering the crowded stores, the littlest one's exploring instincts, and the oldest one's determination to live down her name — Chastity: she picked up looks as if she were picking sailors off ships.

He wasn't sorry that afternoon as he drove over the Tyne Bridge — that gateway to Geordie-town — to see Newcastle in his rearview mirror — a great gray stone mass of rococo roofs, elaborate chimneys, deserted wharves — piled up on the bank behind him and receding farther and farther into the distance as he drove toward Washington.

2

By the time Jury came in sight of the Green, two police cars from the Northumbria station had beat him to it: they were parked inside the gates in the court reserved for those who had some official connection with the Old Hall. Apparently, police did at the moment. The moment he saw them, Jury stopped the car and left it where it stood next to the Green.

Bunched outside the gates were a group of villagers excited enough about this development that some had forgotten their coats, in spite of the snow. Their sweatered arms wrapped around them, they speculated and waited.

Jury shoved his way up to the gate and flicked his I.D. at a constable who tried to bar his way. The constable's apology was lost in the winds, with the name of the sergeant inside.

It was Detective Sergeant Roy Cullen, and the wad of gum he was talking around was no help in understanding him, mixed as it was with Cullen's Sunderland accent. He introduced Jury to Detective Constable Trimm, who with no gum had an even thicker accent.

When he walked in, Cullen had been coming down a flight of stairs, and Trimm had been talking to a black-haired woman with a handkerchief pressed against her mouth. He wasn't getting much from her except headshakes.

"Victim's name was—" Cullen consulted his notebook "—Helen Minton." He raised his eyes. "Upstairs. What's the matter, man, y'look . . . the M.E. isn't come yet. Don't touch—"

Jury didn't wait to hear how he looked or what he shouldn't touch. It was a short staircase, one turning; it felt endless.

• • •

The bed she lay on in that room which had been her favorite was covered in brocade. Her brown hair, the red highlighted by the two flickering candlesticks, had fallen across her face. Her legs were half on, half off the bed, one arm thrust up toward the headboard, one over her waist, the hand dangling down. On the floor directly beneath the hand was a small vial, some of its capsules spilled on the floor. The rope that ordinarily stretched across the room to keep visitors at a safe distance had been moved. Jury went closer to the bed. The bed itself was interesting: its headboard was paneled, with a hiding place for pistols, in case the sleeper feared to be taken by surprise. The hinged lid of the foot was a receptacle for rifles.

He looked at the pills on the floor: the medicine, perhaps, she thought was having unpleasant side effects.

Jury felt a cold draft as the old panes rattled; had the mock-candles not been fixed with tiny, wavering electric lights, one might have thought they had gusted in the wind, as her hair looked wind-blown, lying in strands across her face, partly obscuring it. With his finger he drew the hair back. How long had she been dead? Not very; the skin was cool, but not cold. Death had heightened the pallor, made her face whiter against the dark spread and the reddish brown hair.

Wake up. Blindly irrational, he told himself mistakes had been made before. Maybe now. Snow drove against the panes, piling up on the sills. Seeing her lying here in this room full of history, this mysterious and dramatic setting, he could not get over the notion that it was just a stage-set mockery of death. She would open her eyes and smile and plant her feet on solid ground. *Get up*, that part of his mind ordered her.

But the dead don't rise, despite the season.

• • •

The woman downstairs, the one with black hair and wadded handkerchief, had been joined by a heavyset man in a sheepskin coat who by throwing his weight around was trying to give the impression of not being afraid. Americans from Texas, he was saying.

"Lissen, all's we know is we come in to see the house. Nobody on board to sell tickets, well, we didn't think nothin' a that. So we just wandered around, and then Sue-ann here — " his hard-knuckled hand was clamped on her shoulder, whether steadying her or himself was hard to say " — she went upstairs. Then the screamin' started. Sue-ann said — "

Jury knew this wasn't his case and he shouldn't get in Cullen's way. He asked Cullen, a tall, laconic man, if he could put a few questions to the couple. Cullen nodded, his expression impossible to read. "Perhaps your wife would just tell us herself, Mr. — ?"

"Magruder. J. C. Magruder of Texas." Texans, his posture suggested, were all big and square-shouldered. He proceeded to square his. "We been here now near an hour, Sue-ann and me — "

"Sorry. Mrs. Magruder?"

Sue-ann Magruder dragged the handkerchief away from her face as if she were removing her only source of oxygen, and yet without having disturbed her careful makeup job. Only a few tiny dots of mascara showed on the white linen. Jury had seen enough hysterical women to know she was ready for another bout in the ring at the sound of the bell. "I imagine it looked, when you saw the room, well, almost unreal."

That's what Sue-ann said, and went on to explain: "She was so still, so *still*, I thought maybe it was a . . . mannequin, or something. . . . Well! Where *was* everybody?" At the threat of another spurt of tears, Constable Trimm looked at Jury with ice in his eye and said, "We've owt better t'dae thin this. Gae back doon t'the station and get a statement — "

Magruder interrupted. "Station! We ain't goin' to no *police* station, mister. Look, all's we are is tourists. We ain't got nothin' to do with this. We been up to Edinburgh and just thought it'd maybe be interestin' to see where old George's folks was born — "

"Ya're a bit off there," said Cullen, trying perhaps to defuse the man's objections with a history lecture. "It was his great-great-grandfather born here. Now, we won't keep you long, sir, that's a promise. Just a formality. Constable." Cullen snapped his head in the direction of the couple and Trimm went about gathering Sue-ann's purse and coat — and Sue-ann herself — together. An approaching ambulance, with no consideration for Sue-ann's delicate senses, bleated through the streets. Jury heard it split up slushy ice as it stopped outside the gates. Reluctantly and somewhat vocally, Magruder departed with Trimm, mumbling about the American consulate.

Cullen turned his attention to Jury. "Scotland Yard's interested in this woman?"

"Not Scotland Yard. Me. I'm sorry if I seem to be intruding on your patch. You can toss me out anytime." Jury smiled. "You look like you're about to."

In truth, Cullen didn't look anything of the kind. His stock in trade was making sure no one knew what he was thinking; he just stood there chewing gum, one of those cops whom people tended to underrate and who Jury bet was smart as hell. But now Cullen was in a bind: on the one hand it *was* his patch and no one had invited this rabbit Jury into it; but on the other — Cullen said it, overcasually: "And why're you interested? Something parsonal, is it?"

"I knew her."

Cullen's face didn't change, but he chewed the gum a little faster. Jury knew the sergeant could see a trade-off coming.

"I'll be a monkey's," he said without expression. "How well? When's the last time you saw her?"

Jury studied the walls, frowning as if he were concentrating very hard, trying to get his mind to bring up that vital fact. He said nothing. The crew from the ambulance and the medical examiner came through the door and were motioned upstairs by Cullen.

Cullen stuffed his notebook into his pocket, waved Jury on, and said, "Ah, come on to the station, then, when we're through here. I'll give you a cup of coffee; you look knackered, man."

3

CONSTABLE Trimm was dealing with the Magruders at the Northumbria police station — a big, square, spanking new building of concrete and glass built in the environs of an equally new shopping center with a euphemistic name and a swarm of shoppers, parking lots and cars. Jury couldn't understand what sort of custom could have supported its load of shops, big and small. To see it here bang up against the vast network of motorways and all of this but a mile from the Old Town's village Green made Jury think of a dinosaur feeding on a leaf.

Sue-ann was still getting heavy mileage out of her hankie. Her husband appeared to have wilted a little, once inside the station.

A constable walked in and put the vial of pills on Cullen's desk. Cullen held it up to the light, rattling the pills, then looked down at the report. "Fibrillation. Cardiac arrhythmia. This stuff controls heart rhythm." He looked at Jury. "What was the matter with her heart?"

Jury shrugged. "She said the medicine was having unpleasant side effects."

"It did that, all right."

If it was meant as a small joke, Cullen wasn't smiling.

"The medication was supposed to *control* the heartbeat, not set it off."

Cullen read the page before him, tossed it aside, and said, "Maybe an overdose — "

"No."

About to fold another stick of gum into his mouth, Cullen stopped. "And how d'ya know that?"

"Given the date on the bottle and the directions, she was supposed to take them only when needed. Hardly any missing."

"Not suicide, then, that what you're saying?"

"I knew that, anyway."

Cullen's eyebrows did a little dance of mock-surprise. "You people in London have second sight?"

"No. We hear voices." He was losing his cool; he couldn't help it. But it was stupid to get smart with Cullen. He smiled. "I knew it because I was supposed to meet her there, at the Old Hall. We were going to dinner later. Anyway, if it was suicide, why the hell choose that public place?"

Working on his fresh gum, Cullen sat back and put his feet up on his desk. "Well, we'll know more after the autopsy. She'd not been dead long. A few hours at most. How long did you know her, then?"

Jury knew if he told Cullen he'd only met Helen Minton yesterday, what information he had to give would be considered negligible at best. "A long time," he said.

He felt he wasn't lying.

And he had heard enough from Helen Minton about her life — that the only remaining "family" was an artist cousin; that she was up here doing "research" on the Washingtons; that she did charity work for this school—to make it sound as if he'd known her for years.

"The orphanage," said Cullen.

During the time they had been talking, Cullen was accumulating a neat little dossier — his men bringing him first this, then that report — on Helen Minton. Jury would have liked to see it, but didn't ask. What he did want, he said, was to work on the case with Cullen.

Cullen grunted. It was probably a gesture of sympathy. He picked up the phone on its first ring. He listened, said, "Aye," put down the receiver. "Nothing to work on, much; even the neighbor — name's Nellie Pond, the local librarian — didn't know her except she'd rented that house a couple months ago. According to this — " he went on, holding up a report " — the Pond woman says she heard a fight going on at the Minton cottage about a week ago."

"I see. Well, if you don't mind, I'd like to ask a few people a few questions. Okay?"

Cullen's gum-chewing changed into another rhythm, a slower one, as he regarded Jury with suspicion, a look that suggested Jury might be holding out on him. "What people? What questions?"

Jury smiled. "When I find the people then I'll think up the questions."

The gum-chewing resumed its former rhythm as Trimm walked into the room and said, "They knew nowt enough t'put in yer eye, the Magruders. He's a clot-heed, if iver — " Trimm stopped, trying to hide his surprise — or disgruntlement — at finding that Scotland Yard had still got its big foot in the door of the Northumbria station. He had a round face, with quick, dark, and darting eyes like minnows in a fishbowl. Trimm, Jury thought, was not quite up to the mark in the brains department. Cullen was.

"Will you let me know the result of the autopsy?" Jury asked.

After a brief moment of studying Jury's face with a stare

that just missed cracking the cranium and getting to the brain cells, Cullen nodded. Trimm was obviously annoyed.

"As long as you let *me* in on any little secrets. There's the Chief Constable, of course. But I guess he'll go along with it." Cullen folded his arms, sticking his hands under his armpits. "Last time we got anybody important here was when Jimmy Carter planted that tree on the green with a gold shovel. Then some lads stole it. The tree, not the shovel. So they went and planted another." Cullen's mouth crumpled into something that vaguely resembled a smile. "Besides that there's just the football and the lock-ins at the locals. You like football? Sunderland's in Division One. Newcastle team's in Two."

The spark in his eye suggested Death might be the underdog here, like the Newcastle football team.

THREE

1

THE priest had his missal clenched in his hands as he stopped on the snowy walk between the parish house and the church. His lips moved silently, either from a sudden desire to pray or to hold a conversation with a mangy cat that slunk, belly close to the ground, beyond his reach, suspicious of heathen and Christian alike.

"Father? My name's Jury."

From under steel-rimmed spectacles, the little priest looked up at him, then down at the cat. It was a dirty white, much the color of the priest's thin spray of hair, which stood up on his head like the comb of a cockatoo. The cat was watching the priest, who had taken a cube of cheese from beneath his cassock — taken from a dusty pocket, apparently — which he flung in the cat's direction. The cat snapped it up and then slunk on, weaving around a headstone.

"I don't know where they come from nor where they go," said the priest, scanning the darkening sky for signs of stray animals or angels. "That one's been around for months. Never know it, it's so distrustful. Mr. Jury, you said?" He held out his hand. "I'm Father Rourke."

"It's Superintendent, to be exact." He handed the priest his card.

"Scotland Yard, is it?" Father Rourke's eyebrows fluttered up like tiny wings. After listening to Trimm, his accent sounded determinedly Irish to Jury. County Kerry, he said, when Jury asked. Jury wondered if the blue skies of Kerry had faded from the priest's eyes in the daily wash of innumerable confessions.

"Helen Minton," said Father Rourke unhappily, when Jury told him why he'd come. "Yes, I heard. News travels fast in a village. Come in, come in." He led the way to his door.

The cottage was comfortable enough, if somewhat overstuffed. After the priest went in search of the housekeeper to get them some tea, Jury sat down in a lumpy chair whose cretonned roses had faded into its dull background. On the table beside him lay a stack of journals. He picked one up: *Semiotique et Bible.* He looked inside, felt intimidated, returned it to its place.

Father Rourke had returned as Jury put it down and said, "You're interested in the structuralists, Superintendent?"

Jury smiled. "I don't even know what they are."

"Aye. Well, it's just another way of interpreting the Gospels. They're more concerned about the way in which the mind finds meaning there than in calling them 'true.' If you know what I mean."

Jury smiled. "Haven't a clue. What does it mean, exactly?"

The priest pursed his lips in a smile. "Perhaps that nothing means much, 'exactly.' " He pointed to the journal Jury had leafed through. "Semiology is more or less the study of signs." He searched through some pamphlets, causing a small landslide of papers, found a pen, and proceeded to draw on the back of one of his journals. He held up his drawing, nothing more than a square, with crossbars like a large *X* joining the corners. "The semiotic square. We live by contraries, don't we? Life, death. Thought, nonthought. We *think* by con-

traries." To each corner he added a letter, the same letter —
M. "I'd say you, of all people, might be able to appreciate the
notion." Again, that small purse of a smile, that cut-glass
gaze. "One might finally arrive at some paradigmatic model
which would be universal enough to take in all possibilities."
Father Rourke tore off the back cover of the periodical,
handed it to Jury. "A structure that might simplify thought."

Jury laughed, folded the thick paper in quarters, and put
it in his back pocket. "Father Rourke, you're doing anything but simplifying *my* thoughts. And what's the *M* stand
for?"

The priest looked amused. "Really, Superintendent. *Mystery,* of course. Fill it in. It's but an interpretation of signs."
He shrugged. Simple.

"This is the way of interpreting the Gospels you favor,
then?"

The priest folded his hands over his stomach and seemed to
search the room for approaches. "No, for me, it's the psychological. Dreams, visions — are not they like miracles and par-
ables? And so much that is Freudian. One only has to read
some of the chapters of Paul's Letter to the Romans. And the
Prodigal Son, now isn't that ever a working out of the Oedipal myth? If one studies the text, notices the omissions, the
slips, the gaps — " His old eyes sparkled like Waterford glass
as he smiled at Jury. " — a policeman should appreciate that.
You're used to it — the little discordancies in suspects' state-
ments, that sort of thing. Why if I hadn't been a priest a tall,
I'd have been a cop, now wouldn't I? Not a very good one;
you've been letting me ramble and I'm sure you didn't come
for a lecture on biblical methodology. You want to know
about Helen Minton."

"Yes."

The tea had been brought in by a dour housekeeper who
now stood frowningly with her hands folded beneath her big
white apron, perhaps to see if the scones (small flat ones like

pancakes) met with the Father's approval. Jury guessed he was used to this ubiquitous watching at the porch, for he merely thanked her and waved her away, and she too slunk off like the mangy cat.

"Helen Minton," he said again. The priest put jam on a scone. The wash-blue eyes were still shrewd as they looked at Jury. "It was her heart, I heard. You don't think so."

"No, I don't think so." He looked at the pale violet pattern, nearly faded away, inside his teacup. Like the priest's eyes and the violets, the whole room bore signs of fading — the flowered cretonne, the curtains with their sprays of brown ferns which did not match the slipcovers — the room a busy, untended garden going to seed. And outside, Jury had seen the moss that clung to the stones of the cottage creeping up the sides and mixing with the ivy, unrestrained. Something seemed, like the cat, to creep and hover and wait. It reminded him of the headstones that Helen had been so intently examining when he first saw her.

He told Father Rourke how he had met her (but not that it had been only yesterday, feeling that might disqualify him as "friend").

"Why would she do that, Father? She said she was interested in the Washington family."

"Well, I doubt that, you know." The priest buttered another scone and munched it thoughtfully. "She said that to me, too. But I didn't believe it."

"Why?"

He sat back and scanned the inner air as he had the outer. He did not answer the question directly. "She never came to the services, you know, though she came often to the church. That old cat out there . . . Now, it'll not have much to do with me, the way it slinks away like a snake. Yet it followed Helen everywhere. You can tell a lot that way. But who am I talking to someone like you about people? You know more than I ever will."

Jury smiled. "I doubt that. Then what was she looking for?"

"It's records, you see, those headstones. And she asked to see the parish register. She was looking for someone but probably it hadn't anything to do with the antecedents of George Washington." Father Rourke folded the last bit of jammed scone into his mouth. "Would you be caring to have a look round the churchyard? Perhaps there might be something — "

"I think I would, yes."

He was sure it would be fruitless, one of those tasks that the policeman in Jury felt addicted to performing. Still, he went back to the small headstone with the weathered angels with the crumbling wings. "She wrote this down, Father. I noticed she had a small notebook."

In his clumsy boots — the snow was thick here — the priest knelt down and wiped his glasses. " 'Lyte. Robert.' It's near worn away, the dates." He stood up. "I do remember, somewhere in the whole Washington chain, there were some Lytes." He shrugged. "Well, perhaps she was doing just what she said."

"Was she Catholic?"

"No. Not anything, she said." He sighed and looked up at the darkening sky. "Be dead dark in a bit. More snow coming, they say. 'Twas even worse near Durham, and that's but a few miles or so away."

"She never mentioned a cousin?"

The priest shook his head. "No one, no. But I didn't know her, you see. I wonder if anyone did. She'd only been here a short while. Well, I hope you find what you're looking for, Superintendent." He paused and held out his hand. "Might I have my drawing back for just a moment?"

"Sure." Jury reached in his pocket, handed it over.

Father Rourke took out a stubby pencil, did some erasing,

and then made a brief mark on the page. He handed it back. "An *H*, Mr. Jury. At one corner. Now all you need to do is fill in the other three. Think of the mystery in its simplest terms."

Jury looked up at the spire of St. Timothy's. He didn't want to comment on mystery. He said, "I wish we had you on the force, Father."

· The priest's faded eyes clouded over as he too looked at the spire. "I wish He did too. Good-bye, Mr. Jury."

Father Rourke walked away.

As Jury started toward the gate, the last of the sun sent a dazzling stripe across the snow, elongating his shadow. Two shadows. Jury looked back to find that the white cat was following him.

He was glad Father Rourke hadn't turned to look back.

2

"He's an artist, a very good one."

Those had been Helen Minton's words about her cousin. A constable positioned outside told him the lab crew had come and gone.

Without removing his coat, Jury started going through drawers, searching for anything — the small, gold notebook, letters, anything. But there was nothing in the desk except for a few bills and a checkbook, some scattered pictures, some writing paper. One of the snaps looked fairly recent — at least good enough to use for identification — and he pocketed it.

He went through the cottage that way, finding that she was a neat person, without being oppressively tidy. A sweater slung over a chair; a few dishes unshelved . . .

Jury went back into the sitting room. Under the staircase

was a storage space with a little door. He opened it. In the
dim light from the parlor lamp, he saw among the Welling-
tons, gardening tools and old paint cans, a portrait. He took it
out, sat down, and studied it.

It was of a much younger Helen Minton. In it, she was sitting on a trunk beneath the eaves of an attic, staring out of a
tiny window through which the sunlight flooded, illuminat-
ing only the figure, keeping the rest of the room in shadows.
It was a beautiful painting. Jury took it over to the fireplace,
positioned it in front of the one of Washington Old Hall. The
borders of Helen's portrait exactly fit the empty square.

At first he thought there was no signature, but then he saw
it in the corner, buried in the shadows along the attic floor,
and faded as the name on any tombstone. The name had been
dashed on like an afterthought, and was little more than a
straight line. The first letter might have been a *P*.

He looked at the abstract painting on the other wall and
found the same signature, also unreadable.

Jury took the slip of paper from his pocket on which he'd
written down the information from the tube of pills that had
sat on Cullen's desk. The chemist was in Sloane Square. Presumably the doctor was somewhere near there, too. He
wished they'd put doctors' names on bottles; it would make
things easier. But Cullen would have all of that information
soon enough, either from the estate agent who'd rented her
the house or the chemist in Sloane Square.

Jury looked again at the portrait, at the *P* in the corner.
It made him think of Father Rourke's paradigmatic square.

3

The tiny village library was located between the two pubs,
the Cross Keys on the corner, and the Washington Arms. The
wind had finally died down and the snow had stopped.

Overcome suddenly by a sense of lethargy, Jury had sat down on a bench supplied for bus passengers and was looking across the Green. He lit a fresh cigarette from the coal of the old one. He would have to take a real vacation in the summer; he hadn't had one in years. Visit his friend Melrose Plant at Ardry End, maybe. He wondered if Plant fished. They could go up to Scotland, maybe do some fishing. He studied the coal of his cigarette. *You don't know how to fish, you clot-heed,* as Trimm would tell him. Jury got his exercise flatfooting it all over London, and his fun dropping by the occasional pub with the occasional woman. The pubs he visited with greater frequency, the women with less. Those casual affairs that everyone else had, where nobody's heart ever broke, seemed to have eluded him. He was always picking up pieces. So he had better not dwell on that subject, or he'd be stopping here all day.

He dropped his cigarette in the snow and tramped across the Green to the library.

It was the sort of room that made you want to stand around in it and read for the rest of your life — stand, because the library was too small for strategically placed chairs and tables. All of the living space was taken up by the shelves of books, the books on trolleys, the books tilting in stacks on the floor. There were browsers aplenty, old people and schoolchildren, and none (one suspected) strangers. As Jury approached the half-circle of desk directly inside the front door, two very small children whose chins barely reached the counter were settling their books there. They crossed their arms over them as if someone might snatch them. The little girl was giving Jury an appraising look. He winked. She hid a smile by ducking her head below the edge of the counter.

When one of the librarians turned to him, he said, "I wondered if I could see Miss Pond." He handed her his card, startling her into upsetting a little pile of book tokens before she answered.

"She's reshelving some books. I'll get her." She made a quick escape, letting the hinged countertop drop behind her.

Presumably it was Nellie Pond with whom she returned. She was very pretty. She had incandescent red hair, a bright sheet of it around her shoulders. Her skin was pale and so clear he almost expected to see his reflection there.

Jury introduced himself. "I'd like to talk with you, if you have a moment. As a matter of fact, if you have several moments, I'd like to take you for a drink. The pubs are just opening."

After she had retired behind the counter, he noticed there were one or two surreptitious glances in a cracked mirror under it. Jury had that effect on women — they went quickly for combs and lipstick. Nellie Pond wore only a dab of pink, which didn't go with the flaming hair she couldn't keep her hand from smoothing. "Well, I . . . well, that'd be nice. I was about to leave, anyway." From a peg she plucked an old, brown coat and he helped her on with it.

"It's about Helen Minton. The Northumbria police were asking you, I believe." He put down a half-pint of lager and lime for Nell and a pint of McGowan's for himself. The sandwiches looked a bit dry around the edges, but she devoured hers almost immediately.

"Aye. Poor Helen. Canny lass, she was."

They were sitting by a small hearth in which a fire blazed, which enhanced the general air of conflagration about Nellie Pond's person. Her hair absorbed the firelight, and it sparked her amber eyes. The flames cast shadows and lights upon her high-cheekboned face.

"Did she ever talk about anyone round here? Or anyone at all, for that matter. She seems to have been something of a loner."

She chewed this question over along with her cold beef sandwich, ruminatively. She drank the way she ate, with rather alarming intensity. She was finished with both sandwich and lager while Jury was just getting started. He got up and ordered another of each.

"Only about the villagers in general, no one special." She was more interested in inspecting her fresh sandwich than in this bit of news.

"Didn't it surprise you, the way she died?"

"Oh, aye, it surprised me. Being found in that bedroom in the Old Hall."

"Were you a particular friend of hers, Nell?"

That she liked the sound of her name on his lips was clear. She stopped eating and gazed at him. "Well, no. I don't think Helen had particular friends. She didn't talk much about herself."

"You said something to the police about an argument — a 'row,' you said, you'd heard coming from her cottage about a week or so ago."

"Aye. Fairly yelling, the man was — "

"It was a man's voice?"

"Oh, aye. I couldn't hear hers, really. But Helen always was pretty quiet. Had a low voice, soft-like. Well, I went to the window, to look out — it was dark — "

Jury had his notebook out, which seemed to make her slightly nervous. he smiled. "Don't worry; this is just routine."

She seemed to believe it. "It was after eleven, I know. Tuesday week — "

"Just last week, then."

She nodded. "Anyway, he walked up the path from her cottage and turned toward the Green."

"What did he look like?"

She shrugged. "Too dark to see. Sort of tall, I think." She was looking at Jury as if to make comparisons; she looked somewhat overlong at him, judging from the blush. "It was blowing up fierce, like today, so he was hunched over. Had on a dark coat and a cap. He had to hold it down against the wind." Nell was looking at her wristwatch. The black band was frayed.

"Time for just one more drink?" He took advantage of her hesitation to fetch two more drinks and another round of sandwiches. She looked appreciative. "I don't know how you eat like that and look the way you do." Jury smiled.

Nellie Pond reddened slightly, but was clearly not offended. "Metabolism, I guess. Mum's the same way."

"Was there anything about the man you saw which looked familiar?"

She shook her head. "I never did see Helen with a man. I never heard her talk about men, except in a friendly way."

"Didn't that strike you as odd? She was beautiful."

Nellie was halfway into a sandwich round by now, and looked at Jury again over its rim, wide-eyed. "I never thought of her as — " She shrugged. To each his own tastes. Then she asked, "Did you see her, then?"

"Yes." A small log sparked and split and rolled from the grate. Jury shoved it back with his foot.

Nellie Pond lowered her voice. "What we heard was she took some pills. An overdose of something."

Jury neither confirmed nor denied this. "There's going to be an autopsy tomorrow. The exact cause of death hasn't been established. Had she ever been married, do you know?"

The question surprised her. "Helen? Oh, I don't think so. But, then, like I said, Helen didn't talk about herself." Eating her third sandwich round, she reflected. "There's a person might know something: woman Helen met in Shields. An hotel there, called the Margate. Don't know whyever she'd want to go there."

Jury took out his notebook. "What was her name — this woman's? Did she tell you?"

Nellie nodded, polishing off her sandwich. "Dunstun — I think. No, wait, I'm a liar. Dunsany, that was it."

"Ever talk about her family?"

"She hadn't one. Except, I think, this cousin. I think she mentioned he lived in London. Helen was from London. Had a house there. It doesn't take that long, does it, on these high-speed trains they've got? There're businessmen in Durham that whip back and forth like it was nothing. I've never been," she added wistfully, looking at the crumbs on her plate as if they were her lot in life.

"Aside from this Margate Hotel, did she go about much?"

"Well, I don't know. Durham, of course. Everyone goes there, it's so nice." She frowned. "Spinneyton. Now that was a bit odd. . . ."

"Where's that?"

"Not far from Durham. Run-down little place out in nowhere. But she wanted to go to a pub there, she said. And that was funny, as Helen didn't go much to pubs. I mean, whyever would she want to go to this one? Workingman's place. Scruffy. Fights and lock-ins. Jerusalem Inn, it's called."

FOUR

As if showing through frosted or dirt-streaked windows, the lights of Bonaventure School glowed dimly, but in only a few of the downstairs rooms. There was an untenanted air of hush and vacancy about the house and grounds. Jury could see up the dark drive to a mass of square stone beyond high iron gates.

The headmistress, whom he had phoned from the pub after Nellie Pond had left, had not been eager to have routine — meaning, probably, her evening meal — upset.

In the stone pillar of the gate was a bell and a tiny brass plaque that said *Please ring*.

"Want to see a trick?"

Jury looked around. The voice cut through the cold air like crystal, but its owner was nowhere to be found. The question was repeated and Jury looked up. Up in that tree, just inside the locked gates. The bare branches were still thick and hid her in the dark. She started down, monkey-wise.

Seven or eight, he would have put her at, as she stood with her fingers wrapped around the iron bars and said, "Well, *do* you?"

Jury thought for a moment. "Sure. If it's a good one."

The uncertainty of his acceptance seemed to please her. Probably, she had expected No. She would have taken Yes, unimaginative as that reply would have been. But that her trick was being measured off against other unknown and even better tricks made it pleasantly risky.

"It's good." She closed her eyes and chanted to some wood goblin. In the dim light cast by a single lamp he could see that her lashes were long and pale, like her hair; they rose and fell like moth wings. She had the dirtiest face in living memory. "Now, you close yours."

"Close *mine?* But if I close my eyes, I shan't see the tricky part."

She debated. This cynical stranger had no belief in wood goblins. "Then turn your back."

"All right." Jury turned and listened to the clatter behind him. "May I turn round now?" he said after a full, unmagical moment.

"No." She was grunting a bit. "It's a long trick." Finally, she allowed him to turn. She was standing now outside the gate. The loosened bar was back in place.

He expressed proper astonishment and she smiled. Her teeth were white and even, except for the odd missing lot here and there.

"I can get out when I've a mind. I do, too. No one knows. Are you going to tell?"

"Certainly not," said Jury.

She nodded. There was a chance for him and the goblins after all. "Ring the bell and they'll let you in."

Jury did; there was a buzz. She took some pleasure in pushing the gate inwards, refusing his help. Once inside this castle's fastness, she pushed the gate back. From her pocket she pulled a dirty little screw of paper and looked into it. He thought she was counting. Then she held it up to him. "Want one?" It was said with the magnanimous look of one who is being generous against one's will. "Not the green, though. That's my favorite."

"You choose." Carefully, she rolled one jelly baby out of the much-handled packet and into his palm. "The black ones. I don't like them."

He thanked her as they started the trek to the school. "What's your name?"

"Addie," she said and ran a few yards, as if ashamed to be caught giving away information.

But she stopped and let him catch her up when he said, "I'll bet you twice as many sweets as are in that bag that I know what Addie stands for."

She stopped chewing and stared. "You can't. No one *ever* does!"

"Umm. Well, if it's that hard, give me four guesses." He knew she'd never go along with that.

"*Four?* That's too many." She gave him a look that added, *unreasonable fiend.* "Three." *Take it or leave it,* the look said now. She was not, apparently, at all concerned with her own end of the bargain.

"Okay. But it's going to be hard."

"I know. Go ahead."

"Adelle."

"No!" She danced away from, backwards.

"Adelaide."

"No!" She was wringing the neck of the paper screw in her excitement.

"Annabelle."

Addie squinted up at him. Was he mad? " 'Annabelle'? There's not a 'd' in *that!*"

He shrugged. "Stupid of me. I guess you win."

But Addie was not sure. Her forehead furrowed as she was brought near the edge of supreme sacrifice. But how could one take advantage of such a great nit? Victory was near . . . still . . . "I'll give you one more!" she fluted.

"Another guess? That's decent of you."

Her decency acknowledged with a tense little nod, she held the sack tight in both hands, wringing its paper neck. Whose neck would be wrung if her own largesse were to be her downfall was anybody's guess. "Adeline."

Her No rang through the frosty air, all triumph. "It's Ariadne!"

"What a beautiful name." He remembered a line of poetry — the wind that tangled Ariadne's hair.

Its beauty was bypassed. "When do I get my sweets?"

"Soon as I can get some. Tomorrow, maybe."

They were at the front door now, which was opened by a girl in her teens, thin with ash blond hair. She started to say something to Jury and saw Addie. "Where you bin? Git yersen in; go on, naow, dee as yer bid," she added in her thick Geordie accent.

Addie took off round the side of the house, spewing up snow.

Taking her mission quite seriously, the girl said to Jury, "Mistress's waiting."

Miss Hargreaves-Brown was waiting, that was clear. Her hard-knuckled hands clasped on her well-organized desk, she made it appear she'd been stopping here most of her life, forced to suffer other people's lateness and general inefficiency. When the teenage girl led Jury into her office, she looked long and elaborately at her watch.

Had it not been for Addie, he would have been spot-on half-past six, the time set for their appointment. But thinking of Addie, and looking at Miss Hargreaves-Brown, he fancied it was worth being five minutes late. "Sorry, Miss Brown. I — "

A condescending little smile. "Miss *Hargreaves*-Brown," she gently corrected him.

He had known, of course, her name, and had deliberately

truncated it to see her reaction. The way she stiffened suggested Jury had been close to ravishing her of her most prized possession: not her maidenhood but her name, what she hoped would be taken as a measure of the genteel and moneyed class. Jury apologized, showed her his identification, offered her a cigarette which she refused, and took the moment to look her over. Miss Hargreaves-Brown was in a limbo between middle and old age, dateless. She could have been a young seventy or an old fifty. He bet the dress she wore — dark wool and silk collar and cuffs — was her best. A lady, he imagined, of slender means. Certainly, her salary for running Bonaventure School couldn't be much. Her accent was not North, but South, and he wondered what *she* was doing in Tyne and Wear.

Everything about her was spare and tucked-up, from the neat chignon to the handkerchief in her sleeve. Jury could almost hear her exhorting her little charges to waste-not-want-not or to remember that cleanliness was next to godliness. He wondered why God should favor clean people.

Jury had told her over the phone why he wanted to see her, and it was to Helen Minton that she now alluded. "Unfortunate woman," she said, making it sound more like a judgment than a sympathetic response.

"She brought the children things, I understand." When Miss Hargreaves-Brown nodded, Jury went on: "Did you get to know her well?"

"No. I don't think Helen Minton was the type anyone got to know well, really."

"Why do you say that?"

"She was — secretive, I thought. Yet *she* asked questions." Hardly fair, her tone implied.

"What sorts of questions, Miss Hargreaves-Brown?"

"About the school, the children."

"But as it's an orphanage, that wouldn't be surprising, would it?"

Miss Hargreaves-Brown sat back in her chair as if Jury had
given her a body-blow. "Bonaventure is *not* an 'orphanage,' " — the word was gristle in her mouth — "but a *school*.
It's perfectly true that many, well, most of our children are
underprivileged and come from either broken homes or —
true — have no parents. We are endowed both privately and
by the government. We have proper teachers. Admittedly,
we are somewhat understaffed — "

Which probably meant fifty percent up to the mark, Jury
thought.

" — and some of our teachers don't have Cambridge degrees — " As if neither did police, so who was he to question?

" — and it takes quite a sharp mind to administer, if I do
say it myself." Here she pulled the handkerchief from her silk
cuff and patted her upper lip. It was as if Jury were not police, but social services.

"I'm sure it takes a great deal of wisdom and experience,
Miss Hargreaves-Brown. Sorry I was misinformed."

She rose, pushing back her chair. "Perhaps you'd like to
see it."

It was with reluctance that Jury accepted this invitation.

Bonaventure School was one of the last places that Jury
wanted to see. The stone frontage had been familiar enough
to him; the cold corridor leading from the headmistress's office a foretaste of other cold corridors to come, other rooms
lined with bunk beds, all in military order.

As she told him with some pride of the small economies she
was able to practice to keep down costs, Jury's thoughts were
on just such a school as this, in which he had spent several
years of his childhood after his mother had been killed by one
of the last bombs that fell on Britain; after the uncle who had
so kindly taken him in had died.

They were walking down a hallway of institutional beige,
off which long rooms debouched to right and left, cheerless

chambers of neatly made beds, corners of gray blankets tucked under in the way of hospitals and barracks. Beige, gray and headmistressy brown, the colorless world of an old daguerreotype.

She whirled him through the rounds: "They've just had their evening meal. Breakfast's at seven. . . ."

All's right with the world, he thought grimly.

In one of the rooms sat a boy on his bunk reading a book. He was hurried away by Miss Hargreaves-Brown to evening chapel. Jury's own bed, long ago, had been in a corner — for which he had been grateful, as it allowed him to look at his corner of wall and paint mental pictures on it. Beyond earthly things, adventurous things, wild rhinos and elephants and treks through the bush. He had been going to be a big-game hunter and had wound up a policeman. There weren't too many openings for big-game hunters.

They walked through the washed-out world of Bonaventure, down another corridor, differentiated only from the last by a need of paint, and she was talking about herself: ". . . extremely difficult place to run. Why just the *heat* . . ." Her hands were still folded before her, as if in supplication for funds. ". . . been teaching at a quite good public school. This post was open and although I was young for it, I convinced them that I was — am — very public spirited. . . ." Jury made some appropriate comment and wanted a cigarette, even a drink.

"Did you not like Helen Minton, then?" Jury asked, as they sat in more comfortable if slightly worn chairs by a cold fireplace, once again in her office.

Her sandy eyebrow rose. "Like her? I hadn't thought about it one way or the other. Milk?" She had offered him coffee.

"No thanks, just black, please."

To the teenage girl, the same one who had brought Jury to

the office, the headmistress said, "You may *go* now, Lorraine."

"M'um," murmured Lorraine, nodding. But she showed some reluctance to comply with this order, twisting a long strand of hair, gazing hopefully at Jury, waiting for he knew not what, so he smiled that same smile he had bestowed upon her when she had placed the tray between them. That seemed to have been it, for she left them.

"How old is she?"

"Sixteen. *Some* of our children are, admittedly, orphans. Lorraine has been here all of her life. A little backward; we have a hard time teaching her. It's not the first time. Some sad cases, we've had."

"I can't imagine you've had many happy ones."

She ignored that. "Some are simply day students. They, of course, go home in the afternoons."

"You wouldn't know if Helen Minton had any enemies?"

"Why no. I mean, I can't imagine she *would*. Whatever makes you ask that?" With head cocked and eye narrowed, the headmistress asked, "You're not suggesting there was something *unusual* about her death?"

"I would certainly think being found in the bedroom of Washington Old Hall 'unusual,' wouldn't you?"

"She was ill. It must have been that her heart, at that moment. . . ?" Miss Hargreaves-Brown shrugged.

"How long was she here?"

"Upwards of two months, I believe. Don't think me unappreciative . . ."

As she undermined the value of whatever small tasks Helen Minton had performed, Jury interrupted: "Did she say nothing else about her illness, or about any part of her life which might . . . well . . . throw some light on her death? You might have known her as well as anyone around here. Helen Minton seemed to be more or less alone."

"*You* knew her, Superintendent?"

"Slightly."

"Then you've some *personal* interest in all of this." The headmistress said this is a tone of disapproval, as if police had no business being personal.

Jury agreed, in a way. "Yes."

She tucked a wisp of hair into the chignon, and said, "I don't know anything else about Helen Minton. She was from London, that's all I know." As an afterthought, she added, "She was quite attractive. I mean, I suppose some would find her so." She did not look at Jury as she said this, but drank her coffee.

Perhaps she did not know any more, but Jury still had the feeling she was holding back. She would, however, remain adamant, he knew, in her denial.

"Thanks very much, Miss Hargreaves-Brown. You've been kind, letting me take up your time this way, when I know how valuable your time must be. I'll be going now."

Lorraine showed him out, lingering in the dark doorway.

As he walked down the long path away from the Bonaventure School he looked toward the gates. There was a buzz and he pulled back the iron gate, which closed behind him.

"Good-bye!"

He turned round. It had come — of course, how could he be so dim? — from the tree. Up there, mostly hidden by the thicket of branches, was the dark little figure like the ghost of childhood.

Jury waved.

"Good-bye and God bless," said the Tree.

"Good-bye."

". . . and God *bless!*" called back the Tree.

"God bless," said Jury, before he turned away.

FIVE

I N THE dark, he could barely make out the signs. Jury had
turned off the A-1 onto an arterial road and seemed to
have driven for miles with only that waste of a moor to his
left. Maybe he'd misunderstood the directions he'd got at the
petrol station. Politely, Jury had extricated himself from a re-
play of the tales of all of those unfortunates who had gone for
rambles on the moor and had (the petrol attendant would
have him believe) never been heard from again.

The road was narrow, patched with ice, and recently
plowed: small cliffs of snow hemmed it in on either side. Up
ahead was a sign of life: a man tramping along without either
hat or overcoat. Hardy lot up here, thought Jury, stopping to
roll down his window. "Do you know a Jerusalem Inn round
here?"

The small man's face cracked in a smile. "Why aye ...
atwixt here an' t'chorch, dede aheed, 'tis."

"You going that way, then?"

"Aye, near there binoo."

It would be easier to take him than talk to him, Jury
thought, as he opened the door. "Hop in."

The little man scuttled in and smiled at Jury. He hadn't bothered to put in his teeth, and his watery blue eyes were glazed, as if the day had iced them over, but more likely he'd had a few at home before starting out for the pub. His hands were wrapped around what looked like a giant onion, something out of a cheap sci-fi flick. As they headed north, he kept it propped on his knees like a suitcase.

"What's that?" asked Jury.

The man blinked at him. "A leek, mate. Aye, myed a canny job o' it this yeaer; won, aa did. Wowd a doon laest yeaer oney aa hed one o' me bad torns. Bad abed, aa was. Cud do nowt. You be froom t' South?"

Jury smiled. The question was rhetorical. It was not a compliment.

The Jerusalem Inn was a square, stucco building with a sign as plain as the rest of it, a board with the name in wide black letters stuck on the side like an afterthought and lit by a weak overhanging lamp.

Where the custom came from in weather like this, Jury couldn't imagine, but they were there, perhaps a dozen of them, seeming as permanently fixed as the sign.

Dickie (Jury's traveling companion) set his leek and his money on the bar and asked Jury what he was drinking. A lager, Jury said, as the publican approached. He had the rubicund face of an angel or a drinker, skin pulled tightly against the bones.

It was four days before Christmas and the Jerusalem Inn was certainly ready: decorations abounded — old strings of lights, waterfalls of tinsel, dusty rings of holly, and a life-sized creche in the nook beside the fireplace. A desultory game of pool was going on between a thickset fellow dressed largely in tattoos and a leather vest and a wiry, black-haired man with a gold ring in his ear. Fashion, more than sexual persuasion, Jury assumed. To the right of the pool table was a

square table of a video game, which a young man was playing. Beneath a bit of mistletoe, a shark-faced young woman
was in the process of kissing a tall, ungainly fellow, and a long
process she was making of it. But their performance had to
give way to the leek, which had (Jury had finally figured out
from Dickie's lengthy blether as they drove along) taken first
prize in the yearly leek-growing contest.

Several people came over to clap Dickie on the shoulder.
"An' you'd a won last year, too, Dickie, if you'd oney
cleaned it up a bit." There were drinks set up, and all apparently on Dickie, though Jury thought it should have been
the other way round. Jury doubted if Dickie had two pence
to rub together most of the time, but he was clearly the soul
of generosity. A lack of pence probably went for everybody
here.

The Jerusalem Inn, beneath its Christmas finery, was a
workingman's pub. It was a relief, in a way, after the wax-
work pubs of the West End — the red plush, the converted
gaslights, the gold-leafed mirrors, the whole creaky panoply
of Victoriana. Nor did it have the countrified collection of
pewter and brass and eternal hunting prints hanging above
cretonned cushions. There were long benches against the
walls, one of them occupied by a trio of silent elders who
looked as if they could have taken part in the Nativity scene
to their right beside the fireplace.

Around the horseshoe bar in the room's center, the faces
reflected, pretty much, their lot — a futureless existence of
the dole. Some, Jury was sure, railed against it; others accepted it grimly; and some — the younger ones — took the
dole as a way of life, what they'd been born to. Work and the
weather provided conversation.

Jury knew that he had been carefully scrutinized (like the
leek) by everyone here, yet not an eye had he actually seen
turned in his direction. After the leek and the lovers settled
themselves down, people went about their business, conver-

sations undertaken in the hushed tones of pilgrims before the service begins. One crusty character sat with a cane and a dictionary, talking to no one, occasionally *hemming* as he turned a page and tapped his cane on the bare boards. Another man in a hooked anorak sat reading a book, a nervous whippet beside him. The pool players went back to their game.

The publican was hovering with the drink Dickie had bought him, obviously curious about Jury. "You from round here, then?" he finally asked.

"No. London."

The publican pretended surprise. "I guess you get two blocks from Harrod's, it's like outer space, innit?" He smiled to take the bite out of the joke. Light glinted from his glasses.

"Do you get much custom way out here?"

"Oh, aye. You'd be surprised. There's Spinneyton, that's down the road, where most of them are from. Not much money but the dole; collieries are mostly shut down, wharves at Newcastle mostly empty." He shook his head philosophically. "Me, I'm from Todcaster. Only had this place six months. Hard to get accepted by this lot. You know, clannish." He whispered this last, as if London and Todcaster formed a bond between them, and then went down the bar to collect glasses.

As he waited for the publican to finish his business, he walked over to inspect the Nativity scene. The eyes of the three old men slewed around to check his progress. Did he *look* like a cop? Jury wondered. He sighed as he checked out the animals, in a bad state of repair. Among the fake ones — a goat with a missing leg, a lamb without a tail — slept a real terrier with one eye ringed in black, making up, perhaps, for the thin display.

Only two of the Three Kings were there, and they could have done with a fresh paint job. Mary was there, and Joseph.

But there was nothing in the straw they were bending over.

Something tugged at his sleeve, and a small voice said. "I had to give it a wash."

Jury turned and looked down to see a girl of six or seven staring up at him, her eyes the same clear, almost glassy brown of the doll's she was holding. It was a big doll with painted hair of faded red. It could have passed for either a boy or a girl child. Right now it was clothed in what Jury suspected was one of the little girl's old dresses. The waistline came to the hips and the hem hung over the doll's toes.

Seeing Jury did not comprehend her remark, she inclined her brown head toward the manger. "It was dirty."

"Oh," said Jury. He looked at the dress. "Is it a girl, then?"

Looking toward the straw, she frowned, as if considering her error. "Right now it is." She smoothed the old dress, obviously used to its being a girl and wishing it didn't have to do double duty during the Christmas season.

Through a door at the rear walked a pretty, youngish woman with a tray full of glasses. When she saw the child, she shook her head, came to the creche-side and whispered, "Chrissie! Put the baby Jesus back, lass. How many times must I tell you?" Her hair was the color of her daughter's, but without the luster; her face was a memory of the little girl's.

"I had to give it a wash," said Chrissie, querulously.

"Put it back." The woman looked at Jury, adults in league, shook her head, and sighed, "Bairns." Then she moved behind the bar and started shelving the glasses.

Sadly, Chrissie undid the dress, making sure she kept the doll turned away from Jury so that he couldn't, presumably, see it naked. Having undressed it, she climbed over the rope meant to protect the ensemble within, replaced the baby, and climbed back again. The whole scene now met with her frowning disapproval. "It looks dumb." Her pudgy arms were folded, old-woman-wise, across her chest.

"Well," Jury considered.

Since he didn't agree straightaway, she said, even more decisively, "It looks ugly without its clothes."

Jury drank his lager and said, "It doesn't look like the baby Jesus, I agree. What happened to the other one?"

"It got broke in the fight. They're always fighting in here. Smushed." She made some sort of wet sound, obviously enjoying the noise. "So they made me put in Alice. It's a girl." Covertly, she looked at Jury to see whether he would contradict her.

"That's too bad. But I expect you'll get her back again after Christmas." She nodded. Jury went on: "The thing is, Jesus wouldn't be wearing a dress."

She scratched her elbows. "He wore sheets. I've seen pictures."

"That's when he was older. Swaddling clothes, that's what you need."

"*What?*" It was the most harebrained thing she'd ever heard of.

"Swaddling clothes. Old rags, I'd say, would do it. If you've got an old piece of cloth your mum doesn't need, you could tear it up and kind of wrap strips around Alice." He pointed his glass toward the chipped and broken actors in this drama behind the rope. "They were poor. They'd nothing better to dress him in."

Chrissie looked down at her own dress, faded and sprigged and, like her doll's, too big for her, an obvious hand-me-down. "They come to the right place, then." She turned and ran through the door, probably to search for the swaddling clothes.

Jury bought the publican — Hornsby was his name — a drink by way of softening him up before he showed him his I.D. and the snapshot of Helen Minton.

Having settled Hornsby in more of a mood for a chinwag,

the man turned out to have nothing much to say. He scratched his neck and shook his head. "Never seen her, man — uh, Superintendent." Hornsby showed the picture to his wife. Mrs. Hornsby drew her long hair behind her ear, as if that somehow might help her eyesight, and squinted at the face in the picture, half-lost in the shadow of a tree. Mrs. Hornsby was clearly not a woman to jump to conclusions, which could have meant she had a mind that had to pull its load slowly like a yoked ox, or else she was a very careful thinker.

She looked around the inn at each of the patrons, as if some clue would assert itself in their separate presences. Indeed, she did seem to be trying to fish for some memory as she looked from the three old regulars to Helen's picture, and from the pool table to the picture, and from the Nativity scene to the picture. She bit her lip and Jury was sure she was going to confirm her husband's words, but she didn't. "She was in here Tuesday week, let's see, must of been eight, nine o'clock. She asked for a Newcastle Brown Ale and I kind of laughed and asked her did she know how strong it was, and then *she* laughed and said, Yes, she'd had it before. I knew she wasn't from round here, because of the way she talked — talked like you, see — I thought probably from London. I liked the way she stood at the bar and didn't seem to mind the Jerusalem's not the Ritz. Then she watched the pool for a while and Clive" — here she inclined her head toward what must have been a room in the back — "bought her another drink. She talked to the bairn a bit, Chrissie — " Mrs. Hornsby's face split in a smile that vied for brilliance with the tinsel hanging above her. " — and then she bought Clive a drink. I don't think she wanted the third one; she hardly touched it, but she knew it was the thing to do. Well, a woman doesn't have to, but she did, and I liked that. She talked to Robbie" — and here she looked toward the tall young man Jury had noticed at the video game machine.

"Robbie's kind of — simple." It seemed to pain Mrs. Hornsby to say it. "But he'd do anything to help a person. We give him a room here, and a bit of money to keep the place clean." She frowned. "Sorry it's all I remember about her."

Jury stared at her and her husband patted her on the shoulder and said, "Canny lass is Nell. Never misses a trick."

"If every witness were like you, Mrs. Hornsby, we'd have London cleaned up in no time."

Mrs. Hornsby blushed furiously and tried to drag her eyes away from Jury but found, apparently, that there were worse things to look at in this world. She smiled her transforming smile again. Jury bought her a drink.

"Clive might know something." She pointed toward the door her daughter had just run through. "There's a match going on in the back room. He's playing. And Marie probably talked to her; Marie usually does with anyone new. Cadges fags and tells them her hard life."

Marie turned out to be the shark-faced woman, not bad looking, but the sort who made you want to take your money off the counter. You couldn't blame them, he supposed, for gathering around. Anything to break up the monotony of pool and darts and workless days. Even police business was better than the joke-shop, as long as the business didn't interfere with their lock-ins. Jury bet most of them were falling-down alcoholics. Drink was all they had and the dole money paid for it.

"She was living in Washington, she said." Marie accepted a cigarette with alacrity and leaned partially against the bar and partially against Jury. For a drink, Jury imagined she could come up with something of questionable reliability. He bought her a Carlsberg, but it didn't loosen her memory.

Jury disengaged himself from the tangle of regulars and went over to the video game and sat down opposite Robbie, whose slack face he thought bore the traces of malleable handsomeness, the puttylike quality of looks not fully formed, wavering on the other side of the table like a reflection in water. "You're Robbie?" The boy smiled. He seemed to be in his late teens or his early twenties. The eyes were dull, but the manner very friendly. Jury showed him the picture and Robbie ran his hands through his brown hair, dull like his eyes, as if this were some sort of test he had to pass. "You remember this woman?"

His answer was a stuttered, "Yu-uh-es." And he nodded his head up and down several times, apparently pleased that he could remember.

"What did she talk to you about?" After a moment during which his eyes roved the room, not in the purposeful way of Nell Hornsby's, but in the painful manner of one who can't do what is expected of him, Jury tried to jog his memory, but gently. "I just wondered if she mentioned her name, or something. Or why she was here. No one else seems able to remember much."

That was an obvious relief to Robbie. He looked down at the screen, watching the colored ghosts whiz out, followed by Pac-Man.

"Want to play?" asked Jury, fishing some coins out of his pocket.

Robby nodded. "Aa — 'm not ver-r-r-y g-good," he said, despondently.

"Me either."

Robbie chased Jury all over the board, ate up all of his ghosts, and was generally beating hell out of him, when Hornsby called across the room that the Superintendent was wanted on the telephone.

When he heard Deputy Assistant Commissioner Newsome on the other end of it, Jury was sorry he'd told the Northumbria station where they could reach him.

* * *

Not that he had anything against Newsome, a disarmingly laconic man, but he didn't care for the DAC's message. "Look, I'm not criticizing. But Racer's kicking up a fuss because you're supposed to be on vacation up there and now here's the Chief Constable calling up wondering why Scotland Yard . . . you know what I mean."

"I cleared it with Cullen."

He could almost hear the shrug in Newsome's reply. "Why don't you just come back and make the Chief Superintendent happy, eh?"

"My appearance has never made him happy. Okay. I was coming up to London anyway tomorrow. I'll catch an early train." Hornsby, who had taken in every word, Jury was sure, while shining the same glass several times over, informed him there was a fast one from Newcastle at 8:30.

Jury told Newsome he'd take the 8:30 and hung up.

Nell Hornsby was polishing glasses and watching Robbie, who was having a turn at the pool table, playing by himself. "Awful sad, that boy. Mum dead, dad gone off. He was at the Bonaventure School."

"Bonaventure?" Jury turned to look at Robbie.

"That place in old Washington. They call it a school. More of an orphanage, I call it. When he turned sixteen he had to leave. They can't stay there after that. Figure the kids can earn their keep. That's a laugh, when even the men can't in these parts."

"What's his name? Robbie what?"

"Robin Lyte."

Robbie looked up from the worn green of the pool table when Jury came over with a couple of half-pints and a handful of ten-p pieces. "I'm not much good at pool." He nodded toward the video game. "How about Pac-Man?"

The struggle to reply must have been Sisyphean. The boy's eyes closed, as if lack of visual contact with the world would produce verbal contact. His neck twisted with the effort of getting out a *Yes* and adding a *Thanks* to it.

They played in a silence broken only by Robbie's chuckles every time he won, which he always did.

Jury did not produce the snapshot of Helen Minton, feeling he couldn't force memory. If there were something helpful locked in Robin Lyte's brain, Jury would have to find some other key.

"You went to Bonaventure School, didn't you?" Robbie's face was turned down to the ghosts waiting to gobble another ten-p and nodded. "Didn't like it much, I bet." The boy looked up from the little maze of lights and shook his head. He looked, about the eyes, injured, as if the smudged skin were trying to heal from a blow. Jury shoved more coins in the slot with a force that rocked the table. "I don't blame you. I went to a place like that. Iron cots, bad food, cold corridors. Four years of it. It was after my mother died."

Ignoring the pulsing ghost inviting them to play, Robbie took out his old wallet and the picture. "Mu-u-ther."

The young woman, with blond hair that looked freshly permed, was smiling a trifle pertly, arms linked with two other young womenfriends. Robbie pointed her out carefully as the one in the middle.

"She was pretty." Jury handed the picture back, looked down at the ghost, and said, "Mine was too."

Nell Hornsby called Time and Jury took the glasses up to the bar.

"Might sound daft," she said, "but sometimes I think the lad's the happiest of the lot." She drank off her brandy.

"You couldn't prove it by me," said Jury, before he walked out the door.

II

PUB STOP

SIX

1

I T WAS noon at the Jack and Hammer, and the mechanical smith outside on the high crossbeam began its simulated strikes with a forge hammer. The wooden Jack looked quite fresh in his newly painted trousers of blue and his coat of aquamarine that matched the rather brilliant shade recently slapped on between beams and casement windows by Dick Scroggs, the publican. On Long Piddleton's High Street, already a colorful collection of crammed-together shops and cottages, the Jack and Hammer glowed in winter sunlight.

Things were no less colorful inside where a woman and two men were sitting at a table near a healthily burning hearth. Two of them, taken together, were worth millions, and the other sold antiques to tourists, which amounted to the same thing. This one in particular, with his lavender ascot and jade green Sobranie, was a perfect match for Jack outside, although not as wooden. No less colorful (metaphorically speaking) was the old woman by the fireplace, tippling her gin and mumbling her gums, who sometimes charred for Dick Scroggs, and sometimes didn't. When she didn't, she talked to the stone hearth cat and drank her wages.

"Do you think Scroggs will ever finish tarting this place up?" asked Marshall Trueblood, who owned the antiques shop next door. He looked round at the polished brass and pewter and recently added gamebird prints and plugged another Balkan Sobranie — pink, this time — into a long cigarette holder.

Melrose Plant thought the question ill-advised, considering the source, but was too polite to say so. Plant had always considered Trueblood more of an event than a person. He kept on with his *Times* crossword, occasionally stopping to lift his pint of Old Peculier.

"Oh, I don't know. I rather like it," said Vivian Rivington. "It used to be such a grotty old place. Since the Load of Mischief closed, it's rather nice having — "

Marshall Trueblood shut his eyes in pain. "*Do* stop being so full of bonhomie, darling. I find it quite tiring. Good lord, here's old Scroggs parting his hair in the middle and slapping it down with some odious hair tonic. And he's even doing *meals.*" He sipped his Campari and lime.

"Well, I like it, anyway. It's somewhere to go for a meal if one doesn't feel like cooking — "

Trueblood dribbled ash into a tin tray. "If one wants a *meal,* darling, one goes to London."

"You're such a snob," said Vivian, matter-of-factly.

"Well, *someone* has to be one. Look at Melrose sitting there, who *should* be, and yet is so disgustingly egalitarian. Being a gentleman, darling" — this "darling" addressed to Melrose — "went out with Empire — "

Melrose assumed he meant furniture and not colonialism.

"You're an endangered species, Melrose. And I think it's terribly boring of you — *both* of you — to be going away so close to the Christmas hols, and to County *Durham.* Good heavens, you must be mad. It's near Newcastle and all sorts of roughs prowl the streets and brawl and break beer bottles at football matches. And it snows there."

"It snows here, too. It's that white stuff that was coming down this morning," said Plant, working quickly through two ups and three downs.

"I'm talking about *snow*, darling. Tons of it. *Walls* of it. It doesn't do that here — what's the matter Viv-viv? You look a bit pale."

Her face did look waxen in the firelight. "All that talk about snow. It reminds me of the big one we had years ago. And the murders." She turned to Melrose. "Have you heard from Superintendent Jury lately, Melrose?"

Known him for years and still won't call him by his first name, thought Plant. Mistress Formality. "Phone calls, mostly. Jury hasn't much time to write, I imagine."

Trueblood slapped his hand on the table, jumping the pints and glasses. "Now *there* was a perfectly *divine* man! Stopped by his digs once or twice whilst I was in London. But he's never there. Let's murder someone and get him back here. . . ." He looked around at the old lady by the fire. "Withers, old trout," he called out, "would you be willing to be done in for a lifetime supply of gin-and-it?" He turned back and said, "Not terribly logical, I expect, but . . . like a cig?" He held out his black box of Sobranies to the others.

"No thanks, I don't smoke crayons," said Melrose, getting out a thin cigar.

Mrs. Withersby, hearing the magic word *gin*, shifted gears from her Cinders-by-the-ashes to her social persona, and struggled toward the table, carpet-slippers slapping on bare oak. Mrs. Withersby's idea of "social" did not, however, quite square with the norm, and even as she shoved her glass toward Trueblood, she said, "Gin-and-lager, Marigold. The Pansy Palace'll be thieved one a these fine days, you sittin' over here." She hooked her thumb in the direction of Trueblood's Antiques. She then turned her attention to Melrose Plant, who had thus far bought her three drinks, and her dented face broke, thin blue mouth like a bat trying to smile.

"Oney I must say, this 'un" — she looked toward True-blood, who had gone to get her drink — "at least don't sit about all day in some great lump of house doin' nothin' when others is workin' theirsen to skin and bone."

"Withers, old bean," said Trueblood, handing her her freshly filled glass, "we were all planning a rave-up at Harrogate. Orchestra laid on and everything. Black tie. You could wear your chiffon, the lemon yellow — "

"Piss off, Marigold," said Mrs. Withersby, by way of thanks, as her slippers slapped away.

Trueblood shrugged, examined his perfectly manicured nails, and said, "So *tell* me. *Why* are you going up to the Northeast? You never go anywhere at Christmas; you always sit in your socks and drink Cockburn's port in front of your blazing fireplace. And whatever will dear Auntie Agatha do without her Christmas goose?"

"We could take her along," said Vivian.

Melrose ignored that comment. If Vivian insisted on being idiotic . . .

2

A WORD which might better have been saved for the dear auntie who was now filling the door of the saloon bar in her black cape.

"Agatha, old sweat," said Marshall Trueblood, shoving out the fourth chair with the toe of his highly polished shoe. "Do join."

Lady Agatha Ardry, who disliked nearly everyone in Long Piddleton except herself and the new vicar, especially loathed Marshall Trueblood. To her nephew, Melrose Plant, she had often expressed the opinion that Trueblood should be tarred and feathered and run out of town.

Melrose had replied that they did that sort of thing in her

native America but over here they suffered fools to live. His glance (he hoped) had been full of meaning.

"I see the Withersby person is here. No, thank you." So she stood as she said, "What's all this nonsense about going up to the North now Christmas is coming?"

As if it hadn't come around for years. Without looking up from his crossword, Melrose said, "For once I agree, dear Aunt. It is nonsense." He ignored Vivian's black look.

"Thought so." Apparently this was such good news she plumped herself down in the proffered chair.

But her face fell when Melrose continued: "Nonsense, but true, nonetheless."

Clearly, the announcement whetted her thirst, if not her mind. She called to Dick Scroggs for a double shooting sherry. His parted and oiled head looked up from his newspaper spread on the bar, saw who it was, and kept on with his reading.

"I don't understand this at all. You never go anywhere on holidays. Confirmed bachelor. Set in your ways ... Mr. *Scroggs!*" she called again.

"A bachelor, perhaps, but as yet unconfirmed. Nor, apparently, set in my ways if I'm willing to go to a house party. But since it's Vivian who's asked me —" He looked up and gave his aunt a darling smile, designed to turn her blue. She had always been afraid that something might happen between Melrose and Vivian. That Vivian had got herself engaged to another did little to alleviate Agatha's anxiety, since the other was in Italy. "A weekend in the country. Some sort of artsy soiree. Vivian, not satisfied with suffering on her own, has landed me an invitation to suffer along with her."

Agatha turned her guns on Vivian, neither thanking nor paying Dick Scroggs, who set her sherry before her. Those sorts of things were left up to others. "Why? Plant doesn't do anything artsy. Who's invited you?"

Vivian pulled a letter from her pocket: raised writing on

cream-laid paper. "Charles Seaingham. You know, the critic. He does things on art and books for the papers."

He must not have done much for them, for Agatha denied all knowledge of the man.

"I met him at that little party the publisher had — you know, when my book of poetry came out — "

Always the morale-booster, Agatha snorted. "*That.* Poetry doesn't sell, Vivian, as I've told you. You should write those romances like Barbara Cartland." She took the letter from Vivian's hand and read it through the lorgnette she occasionally affected, thinking it made her look stately and dignified.

Difficult, thought Melrose, for Agatha to look like anything else but a stump. Indeed, as she sat there, solid and square in her dark brown tweed suit, that was just what she reminded him of. Birds could have nested in her hair.

"MacQuade. Who's he?"

"A writer. He won — "

Agatha was not interested in what he wrote or won. "Parmenger? Never heard of him," thereby reducing the man's size to a pea.

"A painter."

"Nudes, probably. Or big squares of color. Never did understand that sort of stuff." She frowned. "This name. St. Leger. *Lady* St. Leger . . . now I *know* her — "

"No, you don't," said Melrose, without looking up from his puzzle.

She frowned. "And just how do *you* know?"

"If you knew her you'd know how to say her name: 'Sel-in-ger', not 'Saint Leger.' As 'St. John' is pronounced 'Sinjen.' "

"And how would you pronounce Saint Francis of Assisi, then? Sinfrenass? I don't know why you people don't spell your names the way they sound."

She thrust the letter back into Vivian's hands, and tried another line of attack: "I would like to know, Vivian, how it is you aren't spending the holidays with your fiancé. *That* seems most peculiar."

"Because, frankly, I just don't feel like traveling all the way to Venice and, also, frankly, I don't get on too well with his family, and —"

"And, also, frankly," said Melrose, "Count Dracula doesn't like Christmas. All those crosses —"

Vivian's face went a fiery red. "Would you *please* stop calling him 'Count Dracula'!" She slammed down her half-pint, spewing up droplets of ale. Melrose thought it quite a display of anger for mild-mannered Vivian, although she had picked up a little Mediterranean temperament in those months in Italy.

Trueblood said, "Actually, Dracula wasn't an Italian, Melrose; he was Transylvanian."

"He traveled a lot, though."

"Oh, shut *up!*" Vivian turned her chair away.

Smiling wonderfully, Trueblood said, "But he *is* a count, isn't he, Viv-viv."

"Stop calling me 'Viv-viv,' and, yes, he *is* a count."

"Foreigner," said Agatha with distaste, forgetting Milwaukee, city of her birth. "He'd have to give way over here, title or no. He's a foreigner."

"Italians usually are, dear Aunt."

Trueblood plucked up a cigarette that matched his ascot, waved the match out as elaborately as a catherine wheel, and said, "*I* found him quite charming."

That was no recommendation, thought Melrose.

Agatha had clearly decided that Vivian was having entirely too much good fortune — what with Italian counts plucked from blue Mediterranean shores and house parties with the literati. "I told you to watch out for fortune hunters. Especially foreign ones."

She had told her nothing of the kind, Melrose knew. Indeed, Agatha was only too happy to get her nephew out of harm's way. "No one who knew Vivian would ever marry her merely for her money," said Melrose, smiling wonderfully.

"I've told you time and again to marry one of your own sort —" Agatha could have bitten off her tongue, that was clear, since Vivian's "sort" was sitting right there doing a crossword. Melrose could see his aunt's mind totaling up the fittings and furniture, the grounds and gardens at Ardry End like an adding machine. She was his only living relative and had no intention of having that number swelled by things like wives and children. Quickly, she amended her statement. "But it's true, you are getting on, and the man does seem a perfectly respectable Italian —"

As if, thought Melrose, she'd known a gondolaful of unrespectable ones.

" — who will probably have the sense to hold on to his title. Unlike Some Others We Know."

Melrose felt rather than saw the look as he filled in five words, one right after another, saw immediately what the others must be in the way of a chess player looking ahead several plays, put his pen away and said, "Tell him to hold on for dear life, Vivian. It will sound quite grand, your being the Countess Giovanni —"

Vivian looked so distressed that Melrose stopped and changed the subject, frowning at Agatha. "Incidentally, how did you know about this trip? We've only just been sitting here planning it ourselves."

"I've come from the house —"

Meaning *his* house, not hers. Hers was a thatched cottage in Plague Alley.

". . . speaking to Martha about the Christmas goose."

Melrose's cook had hinted once or twice something about giving notice if Lady Ardry didn't stay out of her kitchen. Of course, Martha wouldn't leave. Both she and Ruthven had been in service to the Earls of Caverness for what seemed like centuries. "Martha does not like you in her kitchen." He drank the dregs of his beer and said, "I don't know why she'd be talking about goose, anyway. We weren't having goose."

As if this had suddenly become the bone of contention, Agatha sat back, astonished. "Don't be absurd; we always have goose."

"Times are hard. It's to be shin of beef, cold potatoes and Queer-times pudding."

"Where are you having this Dickensian repast?" asked Trueblood. "The Old Curiosity Shop?"

They had their Old Curiosity Shop right there, as far as Melrose was concerned. "That still doesn't explain where you heard about this trip."

"It was Ruthven. That man has *never* liked me. I just happened to overhear him talking to Martha as I was going into the kitchen."

Agatha would have listened at the door of a cage of baboons, if it came to it. "I'm taking Ruthven, too," said Melrose.

Would it be apoplexy? A seizure? Or merely that sputtering out of shooting sherry as she gagged. *"Ruthven!* Plant, what on earth — ! You must leave him here."

Melrose's butler might have been excess airplane luggage. "No, I can't do. You see, it's very complicated. Martha wants to spend the holidays with her relatives in Southend-on-sea. He really has never got on with her family" — here Melrose looked at Vivian, who was studying her hands — "but, being a gentleman, he, of course, wouldn't absolutely *refuse* to go to Southend. So I shall just say I need him."

"You don't need him! What do you need him for?"

"To draw my bathwater."

"Bathwater! You become, every day, a bit more of a snob, Plant."

"Why don't you have a little trip yourself?" Melrose suggested. "Go to Milwaukee or Virginia and visit those

Randolph Bigget people you were running round Stratford-upon-Avon with last year."

"Why not, Agatha?" said Vivian, coming back from her fevered and unhappy reflections of Venetian canals and fat dowager countesses.

"Fine for *you* to talk! Going off at Christmas this way." Rooting through her large bag, she produced a handkerchief and held it to her eyes. "Leave me here to fend for myself." She glared at Melrose. "Who'll cook my goose?"

The last in the line of the Earls of Caverness studied the air above her head and smiled, too much of a gentleman to answer.

3

IT WAS, unfortunately for Melrose, a case of she-who-laughs-last. Agatha turned up on his doorstep — or, to be more accurate, on his Queen Anne couch having morning coffee and telling Melrose that she knew the name had had a familiar ring to it.

"What name? What are you talking about?" he asked crossly. He was still in robe and slippers and had been looking forward to a leisurely read of his *Times* over the breakfast of fresh oat cakes and scones which Agatha was busily consuming.

"St. Leger, my dear Plant. Don't you *remember?*" There was one of those looks and sad sighs meant to suggest he was in his dotage. "Elizabeth St. Leger. Well, I don't know *her* all that well, but Robert — your uncle — "

"I remember my uncle. What's he to do with her?"

"Robert was a great friend of Lady St. Leger's husband — Rudy, I think his name was. Surely you've heard of him? He was a rather well known artist. He's dead. Anyway, Robert — he was always so artistic, you know — "

"I know nothing of the sort. Uncle Bob spent most of his time gambling." And generally carousing about London and the Continent and America where he met Agatha. Perhaps at one time she had been pretty and pert, but he could not for the life of him either remember or imagine it. "And what's all this leading up to, anyway?"

"Simply that Elizabeth St. Leger and I met on any number of occasions and I thought it might be nice to ring her."

Alerted to trouble, Melrose sat up. "And just why did you do that, Agatha?" As if he didn't know.

"Why, as we'd been talking about them — her — I thought it would be simply jolly to renew an old friendship. You should try one of these scones, Plant. They're much better than Martha's usual. It's probably what I told her about the baking powder — "

"Never mind the baking powder. *What* did you and she chat about?"

"Oh, this and that. And the oddest thing is, when I mentioned this Christmas house party and that my nephew was to be there, well, she absolutely *insisted* on ringing Charlie Seaingham — "

She hadn't even heard of the man until yesterday and he was already "Charlie."

" — and *he* insisted that I come along, and, well — " She held out her arms in a hopeless gesture suggesting that, hard as it was on her, she was not one to shirk a request made in friendship.

Melrose sat morosely regarding his aunt as she jammed up another scone and tucked half of it into her mouth. "So what it amounts to is that you've been invited to the Seainghams'."

"I shall not be out of place, after all, amongst artists and writers."

"That's nice. *I* shall feel very out of place."

"*You* do not write, my dear Plant."

He looked up over his gold-rimmed spectacles. "Are you

going to tell me you're still writing that mystery, Agatha? The one about the strange goings-on in Long Pidd, your 'semi-documentary'? That was four years ago. I have yet to see a word." He returned to the *Times*.

"I've decided to do a piece for the *Long Pidd Press*. A column, really. It was after I wrote that scorching letter about the Withersby person's being found flat out on the High, in her cups."

"Mrs. Withersby is seldom out of her cups, but I don't see that's any problem of yours. And the *Long Pidd Press* doesn't exactly tell the news of the world. I'm not all that interested in the vicar's healthy rose plants or exhortations not to throw beer bottles in the Piddle River. What is your column?"

"I thought it might be called 'Eyes and Ears.' "

"That should have a wide audience, since everyone's got two of each."

"Don't be snide. It's to be a sort of sociological study of Long Pidd. After all it is a very *old* village, one of the oldest in Northants, and by interviewing people and keeping one's — well, eyes and ears open — " Here she gave a clever little laugh.

"Gossip, in other words," said Melrose.

"Certainly not! I hope I have better things to do with my time!"

"So do I," said Melrose, snapping his London *Times*.

III

LONDON TIMES

SEVEN

1

THE cat Cyril was sitting on the sill behind Fiona Clingmore's desk, observing the progress of a small bug making its painful way from sash to the brighter environs of glass, all unaware of the fate Cyril had in store for it.

From Chief Superintendent Racer's point of view, it would have been a fitting analogy, thought Jury — Racer would imagine himself waiting before the window, ready to squash Jury the bug.

Fiona Clingmore, Racer's secretary, sat in her usual chair performing her usual pre-lunch ablutions. It was an exhaustive process, which consisted not of merely dabbing on more lip rouge and fluffing up hair, but in revamping the whole model. Her black wool dress had had an extra tuck taken in at the bust, thereby battening down the hatches a little more. He noticed that her usual black ensemble extended today to stylish stockings decorated with tiny black butterflies.

Her compact snapped with a little click, and she gave Jury a brilliant smile. She also crossed her mod-stockinged legs, heaving up her hemline another inch or two. "Well, I think it's a shame, getting you back here from your Christmas hols. How long's it been since you had a proper leave?"

"Brighton when I was five, with my spade and pail. Not to worry. I had to come back anyway. Is Wiggins about?"

She nodded. "Saw him creeping round the halls a while ago. You want him?"

"Yes, I can use him."

She sighed. "Sometimes I think you're the only one that does. Poor Al."

Jury smiled. "Poorly Al, don't you mean?" He looked at Racer's door. "I imagine he expected me two hours ago?"

She grimaced. "Now you'll be keeping him from his lunch at the club. You know how he hates to miss his whiskey and soda spot on twelve."

Other mysteries were negligible compared with Racer's rise to a chief superintendency. There had been a long-standing rumor of neopotism, since someone had discovered that Racer's wife was related to one of the higher-ups. Then had come the rumor he was going to resign. And now some other fishy smell was in the air, one that only the cat Cyril would appreciate — that Racer might stumble up the next rung into a deputy assistant commissionership.

The idea that Racer could find an even bigger horn to blow appalled everyone but Jury, who was used to having Racer roll the stone back down the hill, Sisyphus-like, to land at Jury's feet.

At Jury's feet at the moment was Cyril, who had slipped unobserved into the office to take his princely place on the sill behind Racer's desk. Racer hated the mangy beast (as he called him). Cyril was anything but mangy. He was copper-colored and white-pawed and divided his time between his personal grooming and outwitting the Chief Superintendent.

Racer was just twitching the new coat from his bespoke

tailor off the rack, getting ready to leave for his club. "You!" he said. He made Jury sound like a natural disaster. He slid his smoothly tailored jacket sleeve into the smoothly tailored topcoat and said, silkily: "Isn't it too bad we had to get you back from Glasgow or whatever place your sister lives."

Jury sat down, prepared to stay. That Racer was equally prepared to leave didn't bother him at all. "Cousin. And it's Newcastle, not Glasgow."

"Pity the poor Glaswegians. You were supposed to call in this morning," he snapped. "I'm on my way to lunch."

"This morning I was on the train from Newcastle."

"When you *go* on holiday, why don't you stay away from provincial police? You've been messing about in their business. You know better than that."

Jury looked out of the window, taking his time. Weak sunlight washed over the sill and Cyril, burnishing his fur as he sat there in stately silence, tail lapped round forepaws. On the wall beside the window was the official portrait of the Queen. Jury wondered if Cyril would still be there, glimmering in winter light, when crowns and coronets had sifted down to dust.

"*Well?*" Racer pounced. "I haven't got all day, man."

Jury came out of his dreams of feline grace. "Sorry. I've come across something up in Tyne and Wear which I think needs investigating."

An imitation of a smile played on Racer's mouth. The only thing Racer seemed to enjoy more than his club and girls half his age was cranking out laborious lectures to Jury on the state of the country's police forces, beginning the history around the time of the Peelers and moving on to the formation of the provincial police forces and their advances in the detection of crime. "Even murder, Jury. Yes, even up in the northeast of England, they have police forces. Even Tyne and Wear. *So what are you doing sticking your nose in what's no concern of yours?*"

Jury said nothing. Cyril flicked his tail whip-wise and yawned.

"Well? Well? You've kept me a goodish quarter-hour from my club; what have you got to say for yourself?"

The quarter-hour had been used by Racer himself setting Jury straight on the Peelers, the Bow Street Runners, and the buildings set aside in Whitehall for Scottish kings which gave Scotland Yard its name. "Nothing much, except I don't see how all that's quite relevant."

"Relevant! I just told you, lad! The Northumbria police are fully equipped to deal with a murder — if it is murder — on their doorstep. They don't need *you*." *Who does?* the tone implied, as Racer prepared to leave for his club.

But Jury still sat with catlike patience and lit a cigarette, to Racer's massive annoyance, as it meant Jury was settling in for the long haul. The quickest way to get what he wanted was to delay Racer's lunch. "You see, the way it happened was . . ."

After three or four minutes of Jury's review of the discovery of the body of Helen Minton, Racer interrupted. "All right, all right. No need to give me every bloody detail. Just what is it you want? You know perfectly well we can't go sticking our long noses into the affairs of Northumbria unless they ask for help."

"The sergeant I've been talking to doesn't seem to mind—I don't know about the Chief Constable. Anyway, they may need my help."

"Your help, my aunt Fanny." Cyril had slipped from his perch down a ladder of air and caught Racer's eye. Racer made the intercom throb, ordering Fiona in to get the rat-eater out. Cyril made a circuit of the desk and rubbed up against Jury's leg, purring like a power plant.

"My help," Jury went on, "because I might have been the last person to talk to Helen Minton. I'm waiting for what the autopsy turns up. What I want to do is have a look round Helen Minton's London house."

"A search warrant, that's it?" Racer flicked his gold wristwatch and held it to his ear as if Jury's appearance might have stopped all the clocks from Scotland Yard to Greenwich. "Well, get one then. It makes no odds."

"Probably I won't even need one, if there's anyone in attendance at the house. We haven't located the cousin."

At this point Racer was colliding with Fiona Clingmore, coming in to collect Cyril. Racer did not immediately step back from Fiona, but said with Racer-sweetness, "If I find that ball of mange in my office once more, *once more* — " Here he became more interested in leaning further into Fiona's frontage.

"Well, Cyril's not mine, is he?" She was chewing gum and very nearly splattered a bubble across her chief's face, he was standing that close. "I can't watch his every move, can I?"

Jury interrupted this exchange by asking where Wiggins was.

"In sick bay," said Racer, readjusting his lapels.

Jury sighed. "We don't have a sick bay."

"Don't need one. We've got Wiggins."

Cyril slipped between Racer's legs and planted himself in front of the door to the corridor. He washed his already pristine paw until Racer got near enough to give a kick that Cyril artfully eluded by bounding up to Fiona's desk, where he continued on his paw.

2

"Just two shopping days to Christmas, and I'm sure I'm coming down with something," said Detective Sergeant Alfred Wiggins, the bottom half of his face masked in a handkerchief as if germ-warfare were here. He blew his nose. "And me with my gifts still to buy."

They had parked the car on a curved moon of street off the King's Road and had been walking toward Sloane Square when Wiggins had apparently been reminded of his gift-buying by the spangled windows of Peter Jones. Featureless, starved-looking mannequins were draped in gowns of silver and satiny black, apparently this season's fashionable ensemble. In the next brightly lit window was a Nativity scene, more befitting the Royal Boroughs of Chelsea and Kensington, he supposed, than the poor display at the Jerusalem Inn. The Three Kings were dressed in flowing robes of gold lamé and silky stuff, as if they had come, not to pay homage to the child in the manger, but to call on the girls next door.

"It's my family in Manchester — must be a dozen kiddies between them. I never know what to get kids, do you — I mean, not having any?" Wiggins popped a throat pastille in his mouth. "At least I'm glad to see the shop's got some kind of religious theme to it." The porcelain face of Mary looked done by Peter Jones's makeup consultant.

"If you can call it that," said Jury.

"It is a bit fancy, isn't it? Look at the way they've done up the Three Kings' presents. You'd think Bethlehem had a gift-wrap department." Wiggins sneezed.

Jury said, "What you need is a little myrrh."

Any unfamiliar medication would rivet Wiggins's attention. "Myrrh? I always thought that was some perfume-y thing. You know how allergic I am to perfume." His tone was reproachful.

Jury knew. Sergeant Wiggins was allergic to just about everything except plaice and chips. "It's used in medicine, too, I think. Or used to be. Good for catarrh. And flu." Jury hadn't the least idea what it was good for, but it seemed to brighten Wiggins a bit, to think the Wise Men had had the sense to bring along something medicinal. Jury felt Wiggins's interest in the manger scene was now renewed as he got closer to the window, a little sad perhaps that in there might be some cure, some amulet, some anodyne for whatever ailed him.

"Do you believe all that, sir?" asked Wiggins.

He could have been talking about myrrh or the whole Christian myth. Jury thought of Father Rourke, who spent his life answering questions like that. And he wondered if the window dresser with his magically suspended halos had displayed a certain intuitive sadness by placing the holiday party scene next to the Wise Men, as if it were all one big glitter palace.

When Jury didn't answer, Wiggins added, "It makes you wonder, doesn't it?"

Jury was silent. He felt the loss of something irreplacable, as if a thief had come out of the night, velvet-gloved and softly shod, and taken whatever it was away without Jury's ever having known, and slipped through the square, with its crisscrossed strings of tiny lights.

EIGHT

1

THE pretty maid who answered the door in Eaton Place was wearing a neat, bottle-green uniform, white-cuffed and polished as the brass knocker. But her eyes were red-rimmed, her face pale, her expression woebegone. The presentation of Jury's card did nothing to help her. Yes, she had heard from the police in Northumbria. Behind them the hallway was wrapped in shadows, its gloom broken only by the dull light from the etched glass of a hanging fixture.

Her name, she said, was Maureen Littleton, and she was housekeeper here. Jury was surprised, given her youth. He apologized for the lateness of the hour and the circumstances that had brought them. It might have been better to assume a manner less sympathetic. Certainly Wiggins's getting out his own handkerchief was no help, bringing the housekeeper dangerously near to tears. Jury stemmed a fresh onslaught by requesting a cup of tea.

"Sergeant Wiggins seems to be coming down with something, and I wouldn't mind a cup myself. Perhaps we could just talk in the kitchen?"

Pressed to perform this routine task, she regained her control. The familiar and warm surroundings of the kitchen downstairs were a help, too.

It was her own parlor in which they sat and Jury had let her go about her tea ceremony without question or comment except for the usual dull chat about the weather and how the kiddies would have the best Christmas gift of all: snow.

The tea steamed as they sat in chairs where a coal fire glowed. They sat at a round table and she poured out tea with the ritual silence that she apparently felt it deserved. In the brighter light, Jury saw she was older than he had at first thought, but some of that might have been the result of the old-fashioned hairdo — dark brown hair rolled up all around like a Gibson girl. No makeup and, of course, the severely cut uniform. It could well have been her version of mourning-dress.

"How long have you been with Miss Minton?"

"Well, it's the Parmengers I've been with. Nearly nineteen years. Helen — Miss Minton — was Mr. Parmenger's charge. I was only a girl. I started out as kitchen maid. It was when Mr. Edward Parmenger was alive. Mr. Frederick's his son. The painter. There were four of us servants then." From her expression, it might have been another era. "It was when Miss Helen went away to school."

Wiggins had been about to take out his notebook, but at Jury's brief headshake, put it back and took out a packet of cough drops instead.

"She went away to school. What about Mr. Frederick?"

"Oh, no, sir. He went to school in London."

Maureen Littleton couldn't have been much older than Helen Minton herself. "She was your employer's ward, I understand."

Maureen nodded, the steam from her tea mug — Jury and Wiggins had been given proper cups — rising like river-mist, behind which Jury saw the face lock up in sadness again.

"Did you know Miss Minton's parents?"

"Her mother, I did. Not her father, though."

"Did her uncle seem — fond of her?" Jury watched her look down into her cup, still the loyal servant years after the elder Parmenger's death. Maureen was apparently not a gossip in any circumstances, least of all in these.

"He was a kind of — straitlaced person — "

Read for that, thought Jury, *martinet*, or *termagent*.

" — and didn't show his feelings much, except — "

Jury cued her when she stopped. " 'Except'?"

There was a slight shrug of her shoulders as she poured out more tea into Sergeant Wiggins's proffered cup. "Well, he *would* get a bit angry now and then."

Terrible temper, in other words. But he couldn't get Maureen to go into any details. "Now, Miss Helen. I don't think I ever heard a cross word from her to any of the servants. Not when she was young, and not when she was — " Once again, she had to look away.

"It seems a little strange that the house would be left to Helen Minton rather than his own son."

Maureen did not find it so. "You see, Mr. Frederick — " She waved her hand as if Mr. Frederick's status, both professional and financial, explained itself. "He has his own place. Smallish, it is. In St. Johns's Wood. Near Keats's house. The poet," she explained to Jury, helpfully. "It's got good light, he's always saying. He comes here to dine with Miss Helen. And I've heard him talk about — skylights, or something. He's a grand painter, but I don't know much about that sort of thing."

Maureen was clearly in awe of Mr. Frederick and those other luminaries whose names broke into print for whatever reason. Art, rock groups, movie stars. "They were on good terms, then?"

She seemed simply nonplussed that Jury should think they'd be on anything else. "It'll kill him," she said simply.

That did surprise Jury. It did not seem to have occurred to Helen Minton herself that her existence, or lack of it, would go far toward killing anybody. "Go on," he said.

"With what?"

Maureen was nothing if not literal. He smiled at her. It was a smile that had often turned a woman's literal mind into more imaginative channels. And Maureen was as softhearted as the featherweight sponge cake she had served with the tea. Wiggins was working on his second slice.

"Apparently, you think Frederick Parmenger is — was — very fond of his cousin."

"I do, yes." She poured herself more tea, and Jury too, and rocked and reminisced. From the time Helen had come there they'd been close as two peas in a pod. Find one, find the other. "Until she went off to school, I mean. He was teaching her to paint, or trying to. She never had the knack, much. But him, he was a genius, even from when he was small. I don't mean I was here then. That's what Mrs. Petit — she was cook — told me. 'He's a genius.' "

Whether Maureen or Mrs. Petit understood what it meant didn't seem to matter; the word was enough; it hung, even now, in the air like the smell of good cooking.

"There's lots of pictures of his upstairs. You should see them."

"I'd like to see the house, if it's not too much trouble."

Nothing, her look said, would be too much trouble for him. Sitting there, with Jury talking and Wiggins eating his cake, Maureen had relaxed considerably. Nor had it seemed to occur to her as odd that a Superintendent from New Scotland Yard would be inquiring into the death of her mistress. To Maureen, sudden death meant police.

When Jury touched again on the elder Parmenger her face locked up again.

Jury thought he knew the key to that particular door. "You see, Maureen, I knew Helen Minton."

2

SHE sat up straight. Jury was no longer the policeman in some routine investigation, but like some sailor who'd come from the sea with the remarkable tale that in a foreign port, he'd come upon her long-lost relative. "It was a chance meeting. I didn't know her all that well."

"Aye, she was that nice, she was." She fixed Jury with worried eyes. "Why are you asking questions, though?" It had apparently only now occurred to her that a Scotland Yard Superintendent wouldn't be showing up on the doorstep because a woman had died a natural death.

Jury's answer was indirect. "I wanted to know about her relations with her family — her uncle, her cousin. Or anyone who might possibly have had a grudge against her." This time when Wiggins discreetly produced his notebook, Jury didn't sign him to put it back.

"'Grudge'?" Maureen looked from one to the other, saw they were serious, gave a strained sort of laugh. "It almost sounds like you think she was — " She couldn't get the word out.

Jury did it for her. "Murdered? There's always that possibility, yes."

"That's daft." Her little laugh was far less certain than her words. "There was no one that'd wish Helen any harm." Friendship outweighed formality in her forgetting the "Miss." "She didn't have enemies; she'd hardly any friends, even. I mean, she didn't go out much, nor have people in."

"She had her cousin."

"Mr. Frederick? That's different."

"Do you know where he is? We haven't been able to turn him up. The Northumbria police would like to talk to him."

She shook her head. "He's often away. He goes to France

and places like that." Maureen did not appear to approve of such places.

"When Helen was living here — after her parents died, she got along with Edward Parmenger, did she?"

Maureen didn't answer; she was watching Wiggins scratch away with his pen and quite clearly resented it. Her gaze made Wiggins look up and he laid his notebook aside. Then he said, "Did you make the cake, miss? It's the best I ever ate. I'm careful what I eat, especially sweets."

Hiding a smile, Jury looked away. As a loyal, plodding, and energetic note-taker, Wiggins was invaluable. Lately, he'd been polishing up his charm.

This time it seemed to work, for Maureen was quite happy to replenish his plate, and with his mouth full, Wiggins took up where Jury had left off: "This Mr. Edward Parmenger — I sort of got the idea he wasn't too fond of the girl. What do you think about that?"

Sergeants didn't bother her as much as superintendents, apparently — at least not those who were having their third helping of her cake — and she answered: "Like I said, he seemed a bit cold towards her. But then he was a hard man, to tell the truth."

"Like that with everybody, you mean?" asked Wiggins, pressing the tongs of his fork down on cake crumbs.

"No. No, not exactly."

"Well, then, like what, miss?"

"He didn't like her. Mrs. Petit was always saying how he didn't."

"That's the cook, is it? Or was?"

"Yes. Mrs. Petit — she's dead now — felt sorry for Miss Helen."

Jury smoked and stared at the fire and waited for Wiggins to ask the question, *Then why did Parmenger take her in?*

"Could I have another cup of tea, do you think?" The sergeant's desire to charm answers out of witnesses had its limits.

As Maureen poured the last of the pot, Jury asked, "How old was she? Where was this school?"

"In Devon. It was very expensive." If Edward Parmenger had been a bit tight-fisted with his love, he wasn't with his money, her tone suggested. "About fifteen, I guess. She was there about a year, maybe two. Then Mr. Edward took her out."

"Why?"

She shook her head. "I don't know. I was only kitchen help then. And though Mrs. Petit talked about things, I never did hear. . . . Well, I never thought it was odd, nor anything."

Yes, you did, thought Jury. "You didn't sense some sort of — scandal, maybe?"

"No, sir, I did not!"

Jury had to smile. She was so much younger than the old family retainer — the Mrs. Petit sort, or Melrose Plant's butler, Ruthven. Maureen, he thought, should be walking out, as they used to say, with some young man. She even had *him* thinking in Victorian terms. From the way Wiggins was looking at her, Jury was inclined to think she might make him forget his cornucopia of medicants.

"I'm sure if anything — to put it bluntly, Maureen, if your mistress was murdered, you'd surely want the person brought to justice." He was using Victorian terms himself.

Her back grew ramrod straight. "It's certain I would. But I can't — "

Jury waited, but Maureen was silent. "It sounds as if Edward Parmenger took Helen in without wanting to. Did he feel some obligation?"

"Well, I should *hope* that if my mum were to die — " The girl crossed herself. " — someone would take me in. I don't, now, have many relations left. An old auntie in County Clare." She blushed. The Maureens of this world stuck to business and didn't get off onto their own problems. She cleared her throat and went on in a softer voice. "I only mean that, yes, it was a sort of obligation." She turned sad eyes on Jury. "Helen's da, he killed himself, they said. And her mum died later, I guess of a broken heart."

And the Maureens would also be inclined to romanticize. "So Edward Parmenger took her in, yet didn't seem to like doing it?" Jury leaned over the table, putting his hand on her arm. "Look, Maureen, I know you must feel loyal to the family. But what I'm thinking is that Edward Parmenger farmed out Helen Minton — sent her to that expensive school — because he didn't want her around his own son. They were very close and they were cousins. And she was a lovely girl. Then Helen's father was not a person of very strong character . . ." He waited, not precisely clamping his hand on her arm, but not easing up on it either. Wiggins was dividing his time between his note-taking and giving Jury uncharacteristic dark looks.

She sighed, started to poke the fire up, couldn't reach the log with the poker, not with Jury holding her arm, and gave up. "He was Mr. Edward's younger brother and drank too much and gambled. And he worked for Mr. Edward and — how do you say it — 'cooked the books.'"

Wiggins asked, "So what you're saying's that Miss Minton's Uncle Edward was kind of taking it out on her?"

"It looked that way. And, too, he really liked his sister-in-law. Well, who wouldn't? Helen — I mean, Miss Helen, was like her. Looked like her, too. She was a quiet sort. And it just killed Helen's mother when it all came out about her husband, and there was Mr. Edward threatening to go to law and — " Maureen spread her hands, hopelessly.

Jury said, "So when it ended so tragically, maybe he was salving his conscience by taking in Helen. But he didn't want her about. So he sent her away to school." It wasn't enough, Jury thought.

Seeing her face turn away, Jury felt sorry for her. It was as if some invisible hands had loosened the collar at her throat, the pins in her hair — it had probably been happening all the way through this interview and Jury had only just noticed — for the years dropped away together with the formality. A strand of dark hair now drooped about her cheek, the comb had come loose in the back. Looking into the firelight, she said, "Ah, the pore girl."

"He wanted his son Frederick out of harm's way."

She shook her head wearily. "I'm being that honest with you. I don't know."

It might not have been enough for Jury, but he knew it was quite enough for Maureen Littleton. He got up. Wiggins did so too, reluctantly. Besides looking at Maureen, he had been toasting his feet and forgotten his pad and pen. "Thanks, Maureen. You've helped a great deal. We can see ourselves out."

Immediately, the hair, the white collar, and the set of the mouth got tucked properly in place. The uniform was straightened and a *Certainly not, sir,* although unspoken, hung in the air.

It was a beautiful house, the shadows in the dimly lit hall hanging like the dark velvet draperies at the high windows in the drawing room they passed before reaching the front door. There was a fire ablaze in there too, and Jury saw the small head of a dachshund rise, its nose testing the air for unfamiliar smells.

"It's hers," said Maureen. They walked into the room, and the little dog clambered up heavily, as if its weight or its sorrow were too much for its legs. It had been lying on a scrap of rug by the fire and in front of a leather wing chair. "It won't leave that place. I try taking it down to my parlor to get it to lie there by the fire. But as soon as I'm not watching, it'll just struggle up the stairs and come back. She always sat here

after dinner. My, but she did set store by that old dog."
Maureen looked at the dachshund helplessly. "He's nearly
blind. He's going to die soon." She said it with the certainty
of a doctor pronouncing sentence.

They stood on the front stoop in the dark, Maureen with
her arms wrapped around her uncloaked arms, Wiggins telling her to get back inside before she caught her death, Jury
looking off across the street at the blank frontage of the
Church of Scotland. It was cream-washed and in the night
seemed sickly in its moonlit square. He almost resented its
lack of ornament. No embroidery, no stenciling of stained
glass, just this sickroom pallor. Surely, he thought, with perverse annoyance, the God of the Scots could do better than
that. Presbyterians, he thought, and then wondered with
some shame if he were right. Were all Scots Presbyterians?
Oughtn't he to know? He was furious with himself because he
thought any police Superintendent ought at least to know
that. He sure as hell didn't know anything else that was coming in very useful. It was a point that he felt he had to settle
right now and Wiggins knew all that sort of stuff. "Wiggins!"

Sergeant Wiggins turned, startled, from Maureen, with
whom he had (Jury had heard their conversation filtered
through his own anger) been discussing Christmas dinners.
"Sir?"

"Nothing."

Wiggins resumed his talk with Maureen. "Well, of course,
we police never know. But if I'm here Christmas . . . it'd be
nice. I'm not a fancy eater, I should tell you. . . ."

Jury wondered who was inviting whom to a meal, and he
smiled a little, his annoyance with God somewhat assuaged.

". . . plaice and chips, that's the ticket with me," continued
Wiggins. "I know it sounds awful dull, but — "

"And mushy peas," said Maureen, brightly.

Jury still kept his eye on the church, their debate over the relative merits of whole versus mushy peas again falling away like grace. *Just one lousy stained-glass window, is that too much? Do You have to take it* all *away? How do You expect people to believe in that pale, sick-looking blank front?* Before he realized he was saying it, and still with his back to them, he said, "She was like a sister to you."

The conversation stopped. He heard the intake of Maureen's breath, and turned, even more ashamed. He hadn't meant to say it aloud. It had been in his mind all the while they had talked. Both girls the same age, servant and orphan, pretty and kind and serious. And, he was sure, lonely. "Sorry," said Jury, feeling completely inadequate, turning back to look at the Church of Scotland with renewed anger. *See what You've done!*

He felt Maureen's hand, delicate as the snow drifting down, on his arm, and all of Ireland lodged in her voice now. "It's the truth you're saying; she was. But I swear I don't know what happened. If you're right, and someone did — this awful thing, well, I like to think I'm a good Catholic, but I don't think I'd wait for God to take vengeance. No, I don't know but what I'd kill the killer meself. And that's the truth."

Jury stood staring at the Church of Scotland and thinking things over and growing the more angry because his anger was subsiding. But not his sadness. This doorstep reminded him too much of that other one down the path from the village green in Washington.

"Who the hell," he said, clearing his throat, "eats mushy peas?"

NINE

1

"OF COURSE, I don't celebrate Christmas," said Mrs. Wasserman, as she poured Jury another cup of strong coffee. "You know me ..." And she smiled and shrugged as if her own religion had been bought by caprice during a day's shopping. "But that doesn't mean I don't give presents to others, you know, who *do* observe it."

They were sitting in Mrs. Wasserman's basement flat drinking coffee and eating cake. He was tired after the long visit to Eaton Place; still, he had not been sorry when she had noticed him coming up the walk. Jury did not want to go up the two flights to his empty flat. Maybe he should adopt Cyril before Racer threw the cat out of the window some day; Mrs. Wasserman would love feeding him, as she did Jury, whenever she got the chance.

She had been astonished to find him back, for he had told her he was spending the holiday with his cousin in Newcastle. Astonished and pleased. She depended on Jury for protection. Bolts, locks, chains, bars — many of which he'd helped her install — were no match for a Scotland Yard Superintendent living above you, sitting across from you.

For some moments she had been rocking away, talking about the Christmas season; now she leaned toward him, dropping her voice to a whisper, as if the bolts and bars could keep out not only muggers, but Jehovah: "To tell the truth, I like your Christmas." Jury might have been the one who had thought up the holiday. "All the decorations, the colored lights, to see the Prince turning on the lights of the big tree ... And Selfridge's! Have you seen the *windows?*" Jury shook his head. "You should see the windows, I know you're busy, but you should take a minute. They've done the whole Christmas story, one window to the next, and you walk around the outside and there it is. The Wise Men and everything."

Jury smiled. "They have the Wise Men in Peter Jones. They're really getting around."

Mrs. Wasserman dismissed Peter Jones with a wave of her hand. "Ah! That store ... Just because it's in Sloane Square ... No, no. You've got to see Selfridge's. *Such* windows, Mr. Jury."

He thought of the Wise Men and Maureen and the Church of Scotland.

"Excuse me, but you look a little down. It's this work you do. Here, have some more cake."

He shook his head, smiling slightly. "I guess it is the work. Sorry."

"Sorry? To *me* you apologize?" In mock-horror, she spread her fingers across her large, black-clad bosom. Her hair was as black as the dress and drawn back as it always was into a bun, so tightly pinned he thought it must make her head ache. "To me he apologizes," she said to the empty chair beside Jury, as to a third visitor. She poured more coffee. "After all you've done for me, you don't apologize for being down, no."

"Thanks. But I haven't really done that much. Just helped

out with putting in some window grilles and a deadbolt lock."

She replaced the coffee pot and addressed the invisible visitor again. "Just a lock, he says." Mrs. Wasserman smiled and shook her head sadly, as if Jury were simpleminded. "You have helped me considerable, ever since you came here. Wasn't I afraid even to go on the Underground?" She sipped her coffee. "And one day you'll find Him, I know," she said, complacently, brushing cake crumbs from her broad lap.

With the talk of decorated windows, it took Jury a moment to sort out the Him, and realize it wasn't God she hoped he would find, but her relentless pursuer, the man who she claimed for years had been following her. Jury knew there was no such man.

But he was real to Mrs. Wasserman, some image burned into her brain from the Old War — that's the way she spoke of the Second World War — in the way people do, making distinctions between what was real and meaningful and what was now, today, merely trendy. Vietnam, to Mrs. Wasserman, was a stupid, wasteful skirmish. *None of them got their heads screwed on,* she had said of America, of all of those responsible. But it wasn't the Old War. In Jury she felt she had a confederate, despite the difference in their ages. He had been six, she had been a young woman during the Old War. What she had been forced to endure — she had been in Poland then — he had never asked and she had not told him, nothing beyond a few pictures from her album, but those certainly not of the war. Pictures of the family, and no details. Whatever the source of the Pursuer, he was something that had rooted in her mind and thrived on darkness, like the plant there in the corner that seldom saw light. She kept the curtains drawn, the chains fastened, the bolt thrown.

And it was an enormous consolation to Mrs. Wasserman that Jury appeared to believe her, and had always taken

down the description on the times when she had seen Him.
There had been many times. The description fit every third
man Jury saw walking down the street.

She was talking now — again to the invisible occupant of
the third chair — about how the Superintendent never gave
himself credit. How she had been scared to death even to
leave the flat before he had come to live two flights up.

That was true. Before he had walked with her to Camden
Passage, to the markets and to the Underground, she had
done little more than scuttle once a week to the nearest shops
to buy her food.

Yet, despite the fact she watched for Jury through a chink
in the curtain, and always knew when he was in and when
not, Mrs. Wasserman had a delicacy, a respect for his privacy. Never once had she imposed upon his privacy — as had
his cousin, his mates, with that *what you need's a wife*, or a
girl, a dog, a cat, a something.

". . . in a way, it's depressing." She was still talking about
the holiday. "So much glitter, so much gold." She shrugged.
"Is it true more people commit suicide?"

Jury nodded. "It's true."

She drained her cup. "Well, that's so sad. Too much to expect we'll be happy. Being a Christian, it must be hard."

It was more of a question than a statement, and because
she thought she had said something in bad taste she looked
away.

Jury smiled. "I don't know if I am one. I haven't been to
church since — I can't remember."

"We could go," she said suddenly.

"What?"

She was already on her feet. "Come on. For a few minutes,
it won't hurt you. St. Stephens is just up the street."

Jury couldn't believe his ears. "But, Mrs. Wasserman. I
mean — are you allowed?"

In supplication, she addressed herself to the empty chair,

arms outstretched. " 'Allowed,' he asks. Am I allowed? And who's to stop me, I'd like to know — the police?" She laughed and laughed, feeling this was very rich indeed. As she was pinning on her hat, letting him help her into her coat, she said, "Mr. Jury. After what I've been through in the Old War, after what you've been through in the police? We don't split hairs, do we?"

2

THE telephone woke Jury the next morning. As he reached for it, he saw it wasn't morning at all, but nearly noon. It couldn't be, he thought; his old alarm clock must have stopped at midnight. He picked it up and tried to shake some sense into it, but it went on dependably ticking away, all unmindful of its owner's having missed the morning train to Newcastle.

"Damn," he swore softly into the receiver, on the other end of which happened to be the shell-like ear of Chief Superintendent Racer.

"It's bad enough you sleeping to noon, Jury," snapped Racer, "without swearing at your superiors."

"I was talking to my alarm clock."

There was a brief silence as Racer (Jury knew) tried to sharpen some dull sword in his mind for a perfect riposte.

All he could come up with was, "Get a cat, Jury." There was some mumbled by-play as Racer turned from the receiver. Jury thought he heard a small, but very throaty, growl. "No good, a man living alone. You can have this ball of mange of Fiona's."

"Cyril is much too attached to you. Is that why you called me? To discuss Cyril's and my welfare?" Jury's head was in his hand. Why did he feel like he had a hangover? He hadn't even had a pint at the local. Maybe that's what going to church did to you. Brought all the bile up, all the poison that had dissipated through your system. . . . Racer was letting fly with a few invectives of his own.

"Beg your pardon?"

"I *said* — if you could keep your mind on the business to hand, lad! — this swede from the Northumberland police — "

"Northumbria," corrected Jury. "It takes in Northumberland, Sunderland — "

"I don't need a geography lesson! Ever since you made Superintendent — "

This went on for about a minute, Jury's superintendency lying in the chief's stomach like an indigestible meal. Jury finally cut in: "You were saying about the Northumbria police. Sir."

Racer inspected that 'sir' for gnats, and then said, "Name's . . . wait a minute." Shuffling of papers. "Colin something . . ." More shuffling.

Jury stopped yawning and got his feet on the floor. His head felt like it was down there with them. "Was it Cullen? Sergeant Roy Cullen?"

"Yes, yes, that's it," said Racer, impatiently. "What the hell does he think I am? Your personal answering service?"

Jury was already struggling into his shirt, the phone cord getting in his way. "Would you please tell me what he said, sir?"

"Here it is: something about a woman named Minton."

Racer knew perfectly well what the name was. Because Racer hadn't found her first, he was going to be doubly difficult. "Helen Minton. Autopsy report. He said you'd want to know it. She was poisoned."

And Jury was left staring at a dead receiver.

IV

SNOWBLIND

TEN

IT WAS the snow that stopped them, flying straight into the windscreen like tracer bullets.

"We're lost," said Lady Ardry, who had taken charge of the map and the pen-sized little torch when the first few flakes had appeared. In the rear seat of the Flying Spur, Ruthven was huddled beside her beneath his lap rug.

"Don't be silly, Agatha," said Vivian. "We're not lost at all; we're just slowed down a bit. Charles told us to turn off on this road."

"You can't drive in this blizzard, Plant. You must stop."

Where, Melrose couldn't imagine. It was dead dark at only five-thirty and he couldn't see more than two feet in front of the car. "Are you talking about that place back there with all the picnicking caravaners?" Melrose wiped the misty windscreen with his leather glove.

"There was a place you could have pulled off the road — what's that sign say?" She wiped a circle clear on her side and peered out into deep darkness. "Spinney Moor." With the penlight she traced their progress on the map. "Good

God, Plant, you've landed us slapbang in the middle of a moor."

"Then we're not far from the Seainghams' place. He said it was just north of Spinneyton," said Vivian.

"I loathe moors and bogs," said Agatha, shuddering.

Negotiating a narrow curve, Melrose said, "It's quite interesting, really. You've heard the story of the Spinneyton Slasher? No? Well, the Slasher hacked people to death and sunk the remains in the bogs just around here."

Except for Vivian's *"Melrose!"* and Ruthven's mumbled *"Really, my lord,"* there was dead silence in the back seat, perhaps for the first time since they'd got on the A-1.

"You're only trying to give us all a fright," said Agatha. But her tone was uncertain.

"No, really, The Slasher had a hatchet fetish — "

"Oh, for heaven's sake, Melrose," said Vivian, wiping away the mist that kept re-forming on the windscreen.

Melrose thought of variations upon this theme: *The Spinney Moor Murders, The Spinney Moor Stalker* ... He might submit these titles to Polly Praed for her delectation.

"We just passed a sign that said 'Spinneyton.'" Vivian sighed with relief. "There must be a pub somewhere. Let's stop and call Charles Seaingham."

"Vivian's right," said Agatha. "Stop at the first place."

"I daresay the first place will be the last. Spinneyton doesn't look as if it could sustain the life of the Dun Cow, if this was where it got lost — much less a public house."

"What's a dun cow?" asked his aunt. There was the sound of paper rattling. Mention of even meat on the hoof must have her rooting out another of Martha's sandwiches.

His arms hanging over the wheel, his eyes squinting through a snowblind windscreen, he asked, "You haven't heard of the Dun Cow Creeper — ?"

"Lights! Lights!" shouted Agatha.

"You sound like Othello. I see them."

In the distance, what looked like cottage windows shone like dim stars through the snow. "Seaingham's place is only a mile or two north of the village. If Byrd of the Antarctic could make it, we can." This set up a chorus of complaints, even a mild recrimination from Ruthven, who was more afraid his lordship would catch pneumonia than that they would end up in the squelchy undertow of some Spinney Moor bog.

"If this is a village," said Agatha, her mouth full of sandwich from the picnic basket she had had Martha do up, "bound to be a pub. There always is."

There was indeed, for the lights belonged to a square, squat building, marooned out here in the snow, the cars in its little lot shrouded in snow. As they were getting out of the Spur, the door to the pub opened and someone, with imprecations borne off by the wind, threw someone else out. The one thrown rose, dusted snow from his shirt and boots, and marched back inside.

"Good God!" said Agatha. "What sort of rough place is this?"

Melrose looked up at the blank side of the building where a dull lamp cast a halo of light around the name. "How perfect," he said. "Jerusalem Inn."

"Now *this* is what I'd call a right old rave-up." Melrose lit a cigar and watched the brawl previewed outside continuing inside. It gave the impression of a fight fueled by nothing more than its own violence, a sort of internal-combustion machine that would stop as quick as a car the minute someone took his foot off the gas.

Agatha was clutching her nephew's arm and insisting they must leave; Vivian was open-mouthed; Ruthven's head was shrinking into his collar as a chair flew past him. He seemed to be grappling with the empty space it had flown threw.

Someone was scouting the doorway for the local bobby —

102 ~ JERUSALEM INN

what could he do in this storm, anyway? — as the one black-haired bloke with a ring in one ear picked up a table and made to crash it over the head of a fat man in leather and tattoos before being restrained by a chap in dark glasses and nail-studded waistcoat.

"Ah'll clash yer face, clot-heed," was the thanks the second chap got for this as the one with the ring in his ear broke away.

"Ah, clap yersel doon, Nutter, ya fool," yelled an old man, tapping his cane on the floor three times as if this magical incantation were all that was needed to bring a halt to the affair.

Far from clapping himself down, Nutter was spun around by a big fellow with ginger hair, and bashed in the face. Nutter grabbed this interloper by his red locks and crashed his skull against the bloke's nose. Blood gushed as the big fellow slumped across a bench.

"Git up, git up, ah'll nut yer fuckin' heed off," yelled the one known as Nutter — apparently for good reason.

The man behind the horseshoe bar, whom Melrose took to be the publican, was like a general whose troops had gone wild. Another table toppled to the tinkle of breaking glass from the efforts of two men who were crashing skulls together in what appeared to be a popular local pastime.

There were several nonparticipants, men and a sprinkling of women, enjoying the whole thing from hard wooden benches against the wall as if it were a spectator sport, which Melrose rather supposed it was. The one he had seen in the doorway had wrenched a leg from a table and seemed to be coming in their direction. Melrose clicked a button on his silver-knobbed cane, drew the shaft from the swordstick, and the one coming on seemed to realize his error and turned his attention elsewhere to club a companion with the chair leg.

The melee ended abruptly, as Melrose supposed it would.

Chairs and tables were uprighted, broken glass magically cleared, bottles restored and everyone sitting down to the casual evening of drink.

Several eyes turned toward the interlopers standing in the doorway and Melrose wondered what a sight the four of *them* must have made in this workingman's pub. Vivian in mink (a gift from the Italian count); Agatha in her black cape; Ruthven with his bowler still tucked in the crook of his arm; Melrose in a chesterfield and with that walking stick. They fit in here about as well as a string quartet.

"Have you a telephone?" asked Melrose of the publican. "And a bottle of Remy?"

The publican, a bit pale but none the worse for wear — he was used to it, probably — said, "Phone's just round the bar, mate, on that wall." Vivian went to call Charles Seaingham.

"Well, Melrose, here's a fine place you've fetched us up to," said his aunt, taking her balloon glass over to an empty table by a fireplace. Ruthven accepted a mite of cognac and went to sit on a hard bench, as if that should be the lot of servants. He was soon in desultory conversation with another bench-sitter, refighting the fight.

Melrose waited for Vivian and looked around the Jerusalem Inn. Despite the fight, the spartan fixtures, the plain deal furniture, in its Christmasy decor, the pub was trying to live up to its name.

"What are you drinking?" Melrose asked the publican as he placed a large note on the bar. "And what was that all about?"

The publican, who introduced himself as Hornsby, thanked Melrose for the drink and shrugged his shoulders. "Don't know, man. Happens all the time. Someone got pissed, and let Nutter have it. Nutter'll be on with his blether and then the stupid bugger's that surprised when someone else gives him one." The publican shrugged philosophically, then, looking at Melrose's stick, asked, "Is that thing legal?"

"Not really. Do you know a Charles Seaingham? It's his place we're heading for."

"Mr. Seaingham. Oh, aye. You go through Spinneyton — not much of a trip, it isn't — and take the first road off to the right. But I don't think you'll be getting far in this muck." He went down the bar to draw a couple of beers for the fellow with the tattoos and a tiny man who reminded Melrose of an asp. Soon Hornsby was back. "Bad night. You from the South?"

"Northants."

Definitely "South" from the look on Hornsby's face. Despite the recent doings, there was an air of weary festivity. Dusty decorations had been dragged from boxes. Sellotaped across the big mirror behind the bar were big cardboard letters in alternate green and red saying *Happy Christmas*. Strings of colored lights were hung along the ceiling beams, which were draped with little waterfalls of tinsel.

Melrose saw, however, as he went to join Agatha and Vivian, that the most eye-catching decoration was a large creche, almost life-sized, in the corner beside the fireplace. Cheap plaster of paris and chipped paint, a forlorn display: there were a goat with its ears broken, a lamb with its front leg off, so that it did appear to be trying to kneel. As if to make up for the poor representation of the animal world, a dog of uncertain breed slept between the lamb and the goat. It looked as if it had jumped down from the painting above the fireplace, which announced that Poor Trust Was Dead, killed off by those who did not pay their debts. Mary and Joseph, both with benign smiles, leaned over a boxlike thing filled with straw and empty but for a kitten who had seen its chance and taken it. The kitten had ugly checkerboard markings, which gave its face a gargoyle-like lopsidedness.

He was suddenly flooded with sadness that Mary and Joseph did not know their child was missing. And where was the third of the Three Kings?

"Stop lollygagging about, Melrose, and sit down. Vivian's just rung up Charles Seaingham — "

"He's coming to fetch us," said Vivian. "In this snow, he thought it would be best."

"We shouldn't put him to the trouble. We could probably get rooms here, and go along in the morning."

"*Rooms?*" said Agatha, with her usual perfect timing. "At an *inn?*"

While they waited, Melrose took his glass into the back room where a couple of pool tables — or were they snooker? — had drawn a variety of talents in various stages of drunkenness. The only sober ones seemed to be a handsome young man in a dark shirt and a leather waistcoat who was chalking the tip of his cue and talking to another young man, brown-haired, tall, and with the dazed and slack-mouthed look of the very dim or the retarded.

Melrose watched a player rack up the balls and deliberate for a moment before a break shot that sent the cue ball off the table. He also managed to dribble some beer on the green. An argument started, and before it could gain the momentum of the one in the front room, Melrose left the boozy game in favor of the warmer climate of the front room. There, he was very glad to see the door open, admitting a cloud of snow and a gentleman who must be Charles Seaingham. There was a brief consultation with Hornsby, who pointed to their fire-side table.

Charles Seaingham apologized profusely, as if taking on all responsibility for the weather and complimenting them upon their forbearance. He was a tall, iron-haired man in his late sixties, who would take over, Melrose thought, where the world left off. Although he seemed almost folksy in person, Melrose knew the man was urbane and sophisticated, one whose critical insight was so respected it could blow away reputations like old news clippings. Vivian, thought Melrose, should certainly be flattered that Seaingham not only admired her poetry, but apparently herself enough to invite her to his house. Introductions were handed around, Agatha quick to get in the Earl-of-Caverness stuff, which Melrose scotched, to Charles Seaingham's confusion.

"Well, perhaps we should be going. I've just brought the Land Rover, as it's the only thing that can get through now." As they headed toward the door, he added, "There're only a handful of us, old friends I think you'll like." He laughed. "They'll welcome some new faces. We've been snowed in up there for three days now."

How jolly, thought Melrose.

ELEVEN

1

IT HAD to be an abbey.

SPINNEY ABBEY the bronze plaque on the stone pillar announced. Certainly, "the house" was an extremely modest appraisal of the vast structure whose unaccommodating, cold chambers (Plant was sure) awaited them at the end of a quarter-mile-long, partially plowed drive. The place was huge, austere, deep-windowed, medieval. Tall chimneys, lancet-vented and with conical caps, struck spearlike into the nightsky. Melrose's spirits were not raised by Seaingham's informing his little party that the abbey sites were often chosen for their dismal locations.

They piled out of the Land Rover and, hunched against the snow, all made their way up to a front door that looked as if it could only be hauled open by a couple of Gauls or Goths. It was magically opened by a single butler.

"Marchbanks," said Seaingham, as they were helped out of coats and scarves and boots, "see that Lord Ardry's man is taken care of, will you? And tell Cook we'll be dining in another half-hour." He smiled. "These people need a drink to take the chill off."

As far as Melrose was concerned, the chill was on. The Great Hall, two stories high, contained a huge central hearth and recessed windows that were double-lighted above and shuttered below. A massive Christmas tree, lit by crisscrossed strings of white lights, stood beneath the vaulted ceiling. Once the hall must have served as dining-chamber to visiting lords and their retinues. Now it seemed to serve no purpose other than as a half-acre of tiled flooring and statuary on the way to somewhere else, no doubt equally feudal.

Marchbanks, who was now squaring off against Ruthven, fit the place perfectly. He might have stepped out of one of the niches spotted up and down the walls which held austere busts and forms, most with hanging heads and draperies of vaguely religious origins.

While Marchbanks led Ruthven away, Seaingham whipped the others into action, leading them to another door — this one a large, sliding double-door, its dark wood polished by years of wax and firelight.

There were not really all that many people gathered here, but the room gave the impression of having a rugby-field-ful. Perhaps it was just the way the guests were spaced or — rather in the manner of the statues behind him — draped against couches and chairs and walls. The state of the house-guests, however, was owing far more to inebriation than to religion. The martini pitcher had clearly made its way round several times over, and the whiskey and soda siphons had got a good workout. This salon or parlor held only slightly to the ambience of the Great Hall. The lintel of the palatial fire-place was a frieze bearing some past lord's coat of arms. There were tall windows with transomed lights and stone window seats. But aside from that, the room was all warm elegance: velvet and brocade, green pastel walls, cream ceiling with garlanded moldings. Melrose was quite fond of ceilings: Ardry End was full of Adam ceilings whose delicacy one's eye could trace in idle moments when Agatha came to tea.

From some distant wing came the ragged sound of the worst piano-playing Melrose had ever heard.

Grace Seaingham, Charles's wife, was taking all the ribbons for Perfect Hostess: she managed to hand Agatha and Vivian around without appearing to lay a glove on them. She was on the thin side, with a sort of cool beauty made even chillier by white silk and glass blond hair. Her only jewelry was a mosaic pendant.

The whole lot of them were dressed up, gowned and dinner jacketed. Melrose imagined Ruthven would expire on the spot to see the Earl of Caverness sitting down to dine in tweed. Looking the room over, he felt almost sorry he hadn't worn jodhpurs and a sweater out at elbows. Agatha would be dying a thousand deaths because she wasn't in purple velvet and pearls. His mother's pearls, rather. The Countess of Caverness had not bequeathed her jewels to Agatha. But that made no odds to Agatha. Right now she was wearing an opal of Ardry-Plant origins.

In the course of the introductions, Melrose realized that not all of the evening clothes fit their models quite as comfortably as did Lady St. Leger's, who was clearly born to the purple that Agatha wished she were wearing. Elizabeth St. Leger offered Melrose her hand, fingers twisted a bit, probably from arthritis, not unusual for a woman of her years. She wore a single strand of pearls and her gown was velvet, but gray and plainly cut for her rather stout figure, the sort of cut that would cost a shorthand-typist a year's salary.

That particular allusion was called up by the next lady, Lady Assington (who whispered *Susan* in his ear, as if her first name were a well-kept secret). There was, beneath Lady Assington's expensive 'twenties-style green gown, a typist trying to get out, which was probably what she had been before she'd married Sir George Assington, thirty years her senior, mustached, and a pukka-sahib type. He was (Melrose discovered) a distinguished physician. There had to be some reason for Seaingham's putting up with the wife. When Sir George was introduced he studied Melrose's ear, or the air surrounding it, and then immediately returned his hands to his back and his back to the fire.

It was a good thing the room was plenty warm, or the next guest, introduced as Beatrice Sleight, would have frozen where she stood in what she was wearing. The black gown had a slit back, a front cut to the waist, and a slash up the side, all like arrows pointing Danger. She had an abundance of gorgeous mahogany hair, as polished as the woodwork, stuck here and there with jet and amber combs, one of them topped by a gold dragon, ruby-eyed and sapphire-winged. The combs gave to the hair that tumbled look of one just preparing for bed. Melrose imagined she usually was. Round her neck in enameled mountings were large, square emeralds that looked absolutely black in this light. This elaboration of jewels was in exact contrast to Mrs. Seaingham's pendant: set in the mosaic was the symbol ☧ — the religious chi rho. And Beatrice Sleight was also the opposite of Vivian, who went around like beauty-in-hiding, dressed right now in a plain skirt and a cashmere sweater and looking as comfortable as someone who'd come on a camel.

Beatrice Sleight gave Melrose more of herself than her hand: the only thing between them was her cocktail glass. She was a writer belonging to some sort of genre she seemed to have invented herself: she specialized in the *roman à clef* with the Brtitish peerage as her central target. Two of her books — *Death of a Duke* and *Exit an Earl* — had rocketed straight to the top of the best-seller lists. "Everyone's interested in the private lives of the peerage, aren't they?"

"I wouldn't know," said Melrose, with a smile, before Charles Seaingham untangled him from Beatrice and led him toward a youngish man. This was William MacQuade, the one whom Vivian admired. MacQuade had recently won several awards for a novel that even Charles Seaingham had praised. To say that was to say a good deal. Melrose liked him, as much for his ill-fitting dinner jacket as for his intelligence. Two minutes with him, and he didn't utter one cliché, like "Beastly old blow out there," or attempt to fill Melrose in on his genius.

The tall, brooding type who'd been leaning by the window when they'd walked in turned out to be the painter, Parmenger. He put Melrose in mind of Heathcliff, and Agatha was obviously adding to his moorland gloom. Parmenger merely kept one hand in his pocket and the other folded round a large whiskey and said nothing but "Hullo." He was very handsome, horribly talented, and couldn't care less if Melrose were Lord Ardry, plain Plant, or even this lady's nephew. After introducing them, Seaingham withdrew to talk to Vivian. A man of sense, thought Melrose.

"My nephew, Lord Ardry," said Agatha, re-introducing Melrose and Parmenger.

"Melrose Plant," her nephew corrected her for perhaps the hundredth time in the last few years.

Frederick Parmenger looked from the one to the other with a slight smile on his mouth but none in his eyes. "You seem to disagree on who this is."

Since Melrose knew who he was, the mild insult of *this* didn't bother him at all. Indeed, he inferred that the meeting was the most interesting thing that had happened to Parmenger during the whole of the cocktail hour — an hour extended into two, since Charles Seaingham had had to fetch his last guests from the inn.

"Melrose likes to tell people he's relinquished his title," said Agatha, drinking her gin and bitters, saying it in a way that implied Melrose was a liar.

"Actually, I believe it's *you*, dear Aunt, who likes to tell people I like to tell people — "

She waved him away, a bad-mannered boy. "Stop talking in riddles, Plant." Parmenger, who had begun to be interested in this little family squabble, was now being bored to death by Agatha's talking about painting, and making Parmenger look for a refill with her I-know-what-I-like philosophy.

The piano music — was it the Seaingham's idea of a medieval musicale? — stopped and Melrose was on his way to rescue Vivian from Lady Assington, when Charles Seaingham came up behind him and said, "My dear fellow, here's someone you must meet."

Melrose turned.

"Lord Ardry. The Marquess of Meares." Seaingham chuckled and winked. "We call him Tommy. Family name, Whittaker."

Melrose stared. It was the pool player from Jerusalem Inn.

Tommy Whittaker, Marquess of Meares, stared back. Obviously, from his expression, Tommy Whittaker had also seen Melrose when he'd wandered into the back room of the pub. Tommy looked a little sick.

All Melrose wanted to know was how this boy had got back to Spinney Abbey, changed into black tie, and sat down at (and fortunately had now got up from) the piano, before the Land Rover had arrived.

Tommy Whittaker cleared his throat and said, "I wish people wouldn't introduce me that way."

"So does he," said Vivian, inclining her head toward Melrose and managing to get a little of the Parmenger-tone into the *he*.

"I'm too young to be a marquess."

Vivian, who had decided to be clever after two martinis, said, "He's too old to be an earl. You've something in common."

"I'd be careful, were I you, Vivian. You're the one who made us stop at the Jerusalem Inn — " He stopped, seeing

Tommy Whittaker redden. The blush only made the Marquess of Meares handsomer. He was, indeed, one of the handsomest young men Melrose had ever seen. Girls' hearts must have crumbled like crackers.

Vivian sailed off, steered by gin, to talk to MacQuade, and Tommy Whittaker cleared his throat and said, plaintively, "I say. You *won't* mention you saw me there?"

"I'd take a bullet in the chest first. Only tell me. We barely made it in the Land Rover. Just how the hell did you get here *before us?*"

Tom Whittaker gave him a blinding smile, but before he could answer, Lady St. Leger appeared at his side, supported by a silver-handled cane. "I see you've met my nephew," she said to Melrose, but all the while looking at Tommy Whittaker adoringly. "You were a bit late, my dear. Of course, I know you must practice — " To Melrose, she turned and informed her that her nephew was quite musical . . .

At that point Marchbanks drew open the double doors and announced dinner with as much grace as he could muster, considering dinner was late, and he had had to make room for Ruthven, the butler's butler.

2

THE dining room had mullioned windows of rose and amethyst glass, was oak-paneled and candlelit, and, in its mingling of tones, seemed to throw over the dinners a fine patina of burnished copper.

Thus the voice of Susan Assington was like a scratch upon this lovely surface. "I think," said Lady Assington, "we should have a murder."

She looked up and down the dinner table, crowded with polished plate and polished crystal and tarnished conversation.

"I *mean*," said Lady Assington, tapping a silvery nail against her wineglass, "it's just too *perfect.*" Having captured the entire table for the first time — and they were already on their dessert — she was breathless for a response.

Melrose, seated to her right, asked politely (when no one else took her up), "Why is that?"

"Why, here we are, *snowed in!* Just the sort of thing to bring one's nerves to the boiling point — "

Lady Assington was not one to worry over her metaphors, thought Melrose. But since she appeared to have no nerves at all, boiling was as good for them as freezing, he supposed. Susan Assington's dark hair was cut in the bobbed flapper style of the 'twenties. The gown itself hung and clung at odd angles, as if the seamstress had gone mad in the making, hacking her way with scissors and silk. Melrose noted all of this as she went on about murder, waving her fork about, tipped with the soufflé Grand Marnier that had probably been whipped to a froth in the same dark kitchen as her mind, but with considerably more success.

". . . *twelve* of us, don't you see? You can hardly get away from that, now can you?"

Not if you can count, thought Melrose.

"We're like that book where all those people are fetched up on an island and go killing one another off — "

"Ah, yes. Well, I shouldn't worry. There were only ten of them, but we'll probably find a body stuffed up a chimney or out in the potting shed. No footprints in the snow, of course."

MacQuade laughed and gestured toward the windows behind him. "It's like the Yorkshire Moors out there — dark footprints on all that white . . . just the sort of symbolism I love."

"I'm afraid murder will not bow to your taste for imagery, Mr. MacQuade." Melrose smiled. "How would those nice, black prints have landed there — ?"

Lady Assington shivered. "Oh, *do* stop all this talk of murder——" Susan having forgotten, apparently, it was she who started it. "I don't read thrillers, not really, Lord Ardry." She had suddenly decided to cultivate more literary tastes, looking around Seaingham's table.

' "I do," said MacQuade, leaving Susan Assington to shift for herself. He rolled the wine around in his glass. "I've even tried to write one, but it's no good. I don't have the mind for murder. All of those loose ends one has to tie up . . ."

Melrose thought of Polly Praed, his mystery-writer friend, and said, "Some of them are good. And it's not 'Lord Ardry,' Lady Assington. Just 'Melrose Plant.' "

How stupid of him, he realized, when her widened gazelle-eye fixed on him. If there was one thing Susan Assington loved, it was a title——it had taken her long enough to get one. Susan (née Breedlove, he had discovered in conversation with Beatrice Sleight) had clerked in a milliner's until Money walked in one day. Loss of title far outstripped loss of life on Lady Assington's list.

"But if you're the Earl of Caverness——well, it's clearly 'Lord.' " If there was one book she'd read within an inch of its life, he was certain it was Debrett's. "I don't understand," she said.

Agatha bellowed from her end of the table, "Who *does*? Can you imagine *giving up* being an earl? But, then Melrose always has been a queer duck." She sighed and had a second helping of soufflé from Marchbanks's silver spoon, as she signed to Ruthven for wine. Plant's man had been graciously permitted to second Marchbanks, fortunately for Agatha, who thought she owned him.

Melrose wondered if the visa he had used to cross the border were now found to be invalid, as eyes turned on him, expecting him to explain his queer duck behavior. Not everyone, though: MacQuade smiled one of his rare smiles. Vivian had her eyes turned ceilingward. And Bea Sleight, across the table from him, leaned so far into the candles he was sure she'd melt the combs in her hair. The ruby eye of the dragon glittered.

"It's simple enough," said Melrose, who had no intention of explaining anything, "I didn't want it. Them," he added for good measure.

Tommy Whittaker joined in the conversation for the first time. "You mean you can just — *stop?*" It was as if Melrose had been slave to the demon rum or opium.

"Of course. In 1963 an act was passed that allows us to disclaim our titles. Unless one is Irish. Then one is, unfortunately, in for the long haul."

Beatrice Sleight leaned even farther into the candlelight, probably to show her décolletage to its best advantage. Her tone, when she spoke, suggested that Lord Ardry's motives for giving up those titles that she presumably hated had to be ulterior. "Well, then, why did you?" She went on with heavy-handed sarcasm. "To enjoy all of the advantages of us commoners? I mean, did you want to *vote*, or something?"

"For whom?"

Parmenger laughed, Vivian smiled down at her dessert plate, and Susan Assington drew her sleek hair behind her ear and looked as if she would answer the question if she could.

But Bea Sleight was not for letting Melrose off so lightly. In her book, a belted earl was stuck with wearing it. "The trouble with You People," she said, dribbling cigarette ash in the Christmas-rose-and-candle centerpiece, "is that you simply wink at the decadence of the peerage." Her eye slid from Melrose to Tom Whittaker to Lady St. Leger to Sir George to an appalled Susan Assington.

"No more decadent than the rest of the world, surely," said Charles Seaingham, reasonably, from the other end of the table where he had sat Agatha next to him. (The man really did have strength of mind.) It was rumored there might be a title in store for him, though a knighthood would condemn only Seaingham and not his progeny.

"No? Look at people like Lucan and Josyln Erroll."

Lady St. Leger said coldly, "Hardly *representative* of the peerage. There's always the bad apple in the lot."

Bea Sleight's laugh was unpleasant. "Bad *apple?* That's what you'd call them? You all stick together, don't you? You can go round murdering nannies and running roughshod over everyone — "

"I think we can do without this rehearsal of the indiscretions of the nobility," said Lady St. Leger.

"I'd hardly call Erroll's conduct simply 'indiscreet' — after all, he — "

Melrose tried to lighten the onslaught by offering up one or two examples of mild peer-madness among the nobility — better, at least, than Lord Lucan's murderous tendencies. "I rather like old Poachy — Lord Ribbenpoach is his courtesy title; he's heir to a dukedom or something. He's a bit mad. Gets out in his own woods and poaches his own game. Or so they say."

Charles Seaingham mentioned the trouble they'd had with poachers on their own land, probably as much to turn the conversation round as anything.

"A lot of you are mad — " began Bea Sleight. A murmur from the other end of the table suggested Agatha couldn't agree more. "It's all that inbreeding."

"Oh, really," said Melrose with a laugh. "All that gets us is look-alike noses and protruding teeth." He heard Parmenger, down the table, apologize abruptly for spilt wine. They were on Stilton and port by now (Grace Seaingham refusing to stand on the tradition of the ladies' retiring for this reverential act), and MacQuade, seeming to enjoy all of this immensely, passed the bottle to Melrose, who went on, "Pity that I shall die d.s.p."

His aunt stopped eating long enough to say, with a kind of horror, "If you've not made a *will*, Melrose, you must do so immediately."

Beatrice Sleight laughed. "He means 'without children.' "

Grace Seaingham broke in: "I should think Mr. Plant's title is strictly his own business." She pushed back her dessert plate, untouched.

Melrose smiled his thanks to Grace, and said to Beatrice, "It appears to be your forte, bringing the peerage to heel. Glad I'm not one of them anymore."

"*You* really fascinate me."

Melrose sincerely hoped not.

"I've looked you up in Burke's."

"Already? I only just got here."

Bea Sleight smiled. "Charles told us you were coming. You're in all of them, aren't you? Debrett's and Burke's and *Landed Gentry*."

"You didn't check the *Almanach de Gotha?*"

"I would do. Only it's in French."

"Pity."

The subject of Melrose's titles having arisen, Agatha was only too ready to tell the table, naming all the lost titles sadly and sonorously as if they were a lot of drowned babies: *Baron Mountardry of Swaledale . . . fifteen hundreds . . . Viscount of Nitherwold, Ross and Cromarty . . . Clive D'ardry De Knopf, fourth Viscount . . .*

She droned on. Melrose had the feeling he was listening to an announcer at the Royal Ascot calling off the names of the entries as they slipped into place at the starting gate: *They're off! It's Viscount of Nitherwold leading. . . .* Melrose yawned as the conversation was carried into the historical/political arena of the Wars of the Roses. He studied the pinkish white centerpiece — there were Christmas roses all over the house.

While the House of Lancaster and the House of York battled on around the table (Parmenger wasn't adverse to fighting a war, even an old war, and championed, in his wonderfully perverse way, Richard III), Melrose talked gardening and roses with Lady St. Leger to get her mind off the remarks of Beatrice Sleight.

"Susan brought them," she said, looking at the centerpiece. "Sweet of her. She's quite the gardener, though one might not think it." Lady St. Leger's tone was wry. "Our own gardens at Meares are extensive. I used so much to like to get my own hands in the earth. But now — " She shrugged. "I don't like formal gardens, do you?"

"No, but I can't keep my gardener from trying to punish the hedges into all sorts of shapes."

"Oh, dear. I do loathe topiaries. What an awful thing to do with hedges and bushes."

"I'll bet Aunt Betsy knows more about parks and pleasaunces than Miss Sleight ever will about peers," said Tommy Whittaker, in a low voice.

His aunt smiled fondly. But Beatrice Sleight heard it. "I wouldn't count on it, sweetie."

Her eyes, sparked by candlelight, were quite vicious. Melrose began to think Susan Assington was right: they really ought to have a murder.

3

FIRST the piano, then the oboe. The others in the drawing room, where they had retired with their drinks and cigars, finally, had clearly had their fill of this musical mélange; besides Lady St. Leger, only Grace Seaingham had listened to Tom's recital, sure proof of her saintliness.

Rather fascinated by her pale, madonnalike beauty, Melrose took his brandy over to sit beside her. "Thanks for rescuing me," he said.

Grace Seaingham laughed. "I don't think you need anyone to do that." She looked toward Beatrice Sleight, who was doing everything she could to capture Parmenger's attention. "We've known Bea for years. She can be rather awful." But Grace Seaingham said this in a totally nonjudgmental way, as if they could all be fond of "awfulness" if only they'd try. "Do you know Freddie Parmenger? I mean, have you seen his work?"

"I've heard of him, yes. He's got a show on in London, hasn't he, at the Academy? I must admit to a total lack of grasp of modern art."

"Oh, Freddie wouldn't like *that*." Her crystalline laughter rang out. "He doesn't consider himself modern; he considers himself immortal."

"Is he that arrogant?"

"Arrogance has nothing to do with art, does it? I mean art of the caliber of Freddie or Bill MacQuade. Though one could hardly fault *him* for vanity." Her head inclined toward MacQuade, who smiled at her. Then her look turned to Parmenger, still in his chair, reading. "Look at him refusing to be social."

Considering it was Bea Sleight he was refusing to be social with, Melrose could easily overlook Parmenger's bad manners. Her pretense of interest in his book was quickly rebuffed, and she moved off like a dark cloud to the side of Charles Seaingham.

The look, the way she slipped her arm through his, answered the question of why she had been invited. And Melrose also saw that Grace Seaingham's eyes were locked on the pair of them — Charles and Beatrice — with a look not of anger but of total bereavement.

He couldn't stand that look on such a face and very quickly reverted to her comment on art. "Arrogance has nothing to do with it? You're probably right. Do you allow artists then to operate on a different moral plane — ?" Melrose was immediately sorry for such a gaffe.

She smiled slightly. "I don't think my 'allowance' has anything to do with it, really. Anyway, my own morals probably wouldn't bear scrutiny."

To that surprising statement, Melrose could think of no reply.

Putting down her glass of silvery Sambuca, she said, "Would you excuse me, Mr. Plant. I'm just going to get my cape and go to chapel."

"Your cape? You're going *outside?* Is there no domestic chapel — ?"

She laughed a bit at his distress. "To the Lady Chapel. Don't worry: the walk's covered. It's only just outside the East Wing. There's nothing in that wing, really, except my husband's little study and the gun room. And at the far end, a solarium I had put in. Tomorrow I must show you round."

He looked after her as she went to get her cloak, finding himself unaccountably irritated. He wondered, indeed, what it would be like being married to her. Would all of that goodness — and he didn't doubt it was genuine — wash over and over one through the years, eroding, like the ocean, the coastal shelf of one's outline?

"Despite what you must be thinking, Mr. Plant, I really don't have a tin ear."

Melrose smiled, surprised at Lady St. Leger's rather impish look at him. "The marquess probably just needs a little practice."

"Only a little? You're as kind as I daresay you would be candid, were I a friend." In her lap was an embroidery hoop. She was working an intricate design. "I'm sure everyone thinks *I've* forced Tom into these music lessons. Actually, it's Tom who wants to take them. I can't imagine what he has in mind. But I don't mind playing along with it — please pardon that ghastly pun."

"Both the pun and the piano, Lady St. Leger."

With her eyes fixed on her needlework, she said, "But not the oboe."

"Ah, no. I'm afraid not — but your nephew will no doubt find some appropriate outlet for his talents."

"I certainly hope so. Unfortunately, he shows little inclination to do well in his schoolwork — except, apparently, in ancient history, for some reason. The headmaster of St. Jude's — "

"St. Jude's *Grange?* He doesn't go there, does he?" Melrose was simply appalled.

"Why, yes." She looked at him with bright eyes. "You know it then?"

Indeed he did, though he would sooner have admitted a connection with Mr. Squeers's chamber-of-horrors. Not that St. Jude's starved or beat the boys (and probably girls, now) except intellectually. St. Jude's was one of the greatest anachronisms in the British Isles, where the lineage stretched back from the present lads to their great-great-great-great-grandfathers — an inescapable hand-me-down scholarship. It had high walls and bell towers, and Melrose, during his brief sojourn there, wouldn't have been surprised to find a moat. But it was all facade. There were no keepers, no whip-crackers, no real teachers to speak of. He had been invited to lecture on the French Romantics, and the few freckled and spectacled lads who did attend his black-robed talk were having a simply marvelous time in the back row with rubber bands. The incredible thing about St. Jude's was the way in which it had maintained its reputation for scholarship, when everyone knew that its graduates were only smart enough to count the money in their wallets. The only thing St. Jude's had was an A-1 cricket team and a lot of rich, cricket-loving alumni. Melrose had let out a long breath when he had finally escaped from the school's black-gowned, ivy-hung, crenelated-bell-towered, mullion-windowed atmosphere. He'd sooner be bricked in by Poe than spend a term there.

"I imagine you think me very old-fashioned, Mr. Plant," said Lady St. Leger, who had been talking about young people in general and her great-nephew in particular.

"I'm rather old-fashioned myself," said Melrose, setting aside the Italian liqueur which Grace Seaingham had suggested. She claimed it did wonders for the digestion, especially the coffee beans floating on top. Sambuca con Mosca, she called it.

Agatha, who always wanted to be in on anything new in the way of eating or drinking, thought it looked quite attractive and asked what the *con Mosca* meant.

" 'With flies,' " said Grace, without so much as a grimace. "It's the coffee beans on top, you see."

Melrose disliked syrupy liqueurs and was smoking a cigar to get the taste out of his mouth. They all seemed to have their favorites. Beatrice Sleight went in for the most violent-looking one — cranberry-colored; Grace Seaingham drank this crystal-clear stuff that seemed to suit her, Melrose thought. Agatha turned down the Sambuca "with flies" in favor of crème de violette.

Lady St. Leger was drinking far more sensibly and expensively with her Courvoisier. She was smoking the cigarette he had offered her, holding it carefully between thumb and forefinger in the manner of one who rarely smoked. "Well, it is possible that I overcompensate because Tom isn't my own. His father, the tenth marquess, and his mother both died when he was ten and as I was their closest friend — or *we* were, I should say, but Rudolph is dead now." Her eyes grew misty. They were an elusive, pearly gray, the shade of the Waterford crystal which held her cognac.

"Both at the same time?"

"Yes. They died of malaria in Kenya. They were great travelers."

One would have to be, Melrose supposed, to be enticed by Kenya. Melrose thought longingly of Ardry End and riveted his eyes on Vivian, who was talking to Charles Seaingham. She winked and waved and did not even seem to care that he returned neither gesture.

". . . safari."

Melrose turned to Elizabeth St. Leger. "I beg your pardon? Tom's parents were on a . . . safari?" Melrose slid down in his chair, prepared for the worst.

"Yes. It was during that last one that they died."

"He was ten? It must have been traumatic for him." Melrose felt quite justified in disliking Tom's parents intensely. To be run down, dead drunk, in an open car on a railroad track seemed eminently more honorable.

"It was hard on Tom. The loss of his father, especially, I think. So they left him to us."

The young Marquess of Meares sounded like a bequest in a will. Melrose was almost beginning to sympathize with Beatrice Sleight's opinion of the peerage.

"I felt they were sometimes — frivolous," Lady St. Leger admitted, in a lowered voice.

To say the least, thought Melrose.

"That's why I may be inclined to go a little far, to be a little too strict with Tom. I am very fond of Tom; he's a good boy. The thing is, he's got a name to live up to; one can't just throw it over — oh, I do beg your pardon."

She was, after all a lady. Melrose smiled inwardly, merely inclined his head outwardly in a royal pardon.

Quickly, she reverted to her plans for her nephew which included Christ Church College, Oxford, and a career in medicine, law, or if he *must* be a bit "bohemian" — and here she glanced at Parmenger and MacQuade, who hardly fit *that* description, Melrose thought — music or novel-writing for a while.

Poor Tom Whittaker. His life seemed to have been stamped, signed, sealed and about to be delivered up to the City, with, perhaps, a brief fling in some seamy Parisian street.

"You must think I'm much too strict."

Melrose was a little surprised that Elizabeth St. Leger was quite serious in her wish that he endorse her actions regarding her nephew.

"I'm sure that's not for me to say." Seeing Agatha across the room, Melrose thought that over there was one who would be only too happy to say. "But I am inclined to feel one should live his life as he likes. As it's the only one he has."

"But that's just what Tom's parents did. Although I suppose I've no room to talk: Rudy — my husband — and I used to go on safari to Nairobi. I now think it's ridiculous. No roughing it at all. Good heavens, they even dress for dinner on those jaunts into the jungle. And I think, now, hunting's inhumane. The whole idea of fox-hunting, for example . . . Well . . ." She shuddered.

"Your sympathies lie with the anti-hunters, then?"

"Yes, I must admit they do."

"And what did you think of the New Forest foxhounds that were very nearly put down for killing those two deer. Because of the hunt saboteurs using horns and whistles to confuse hounds. Do you admire that sort of stratagem?"

She seemed a bit confused on that point. "You approve of blood sports, then, Mr. Plant?"

Melrose certainly didn't, but he wasn't up to continuing his discussion of the subject, especially seeing that Aunt Agatha was about to bear down on them.

"I shot an antelope once. Terrible."

Was it mere coincidence that whenever Agatha approached, one thought of shooting something? Aunts or antelopes, it was all the same.

"Your nephew does not seem to me to be frivolous at all."
Tommy Whittaker had taken up a silent watch by the fire.
"If anything, he's much too serious for a lad of his age."

She shook her head. "You're wrong, Mr. Plant. Tom is inclined to be like his parents. Except for his music — at least he takes *that* seriously — "

If only he wouldn't, thought Melrose.

". . . he's quite frivolous."

Again, Melrose inclined his head, prepared to be wrong.
But he doubted he was. "In any particular way?"

She brushed a bit of cigarette ash from her velvet gown.
"He plays pool." Her silvery eyes nearly pinned Melrose to his chair.

"Good heavens," said Melrose, rising in the wake of Agatha's arrival beside them. She settled into his vacant chair as if she'd nested there for years.

"Well, now, Betsy! I see you do embroidery too!"

Too? wondered Melrose, who had never seen Agatha with anything in her left hand but a cup of tea or a fairy cake.

"I liked your book," said Melrose to William MacQuade.

"My book?" The young man seemed mildly surprised.

Melrose smiled. *"Skier.* Surely you remember it. It won the Booker."

MacQuade blushed. His thoughts had clearly been elsewhere, and from the direction of his gaze when Melrose moved up beside him, they had been on Grace Seaingham.
"Sorry. I wasn't trying to be modest."

Melrose doubted he'd have to try; he seemed to be a very self-effacing person. Consistent, probably, with true talent — unlike the author of *Exit an Earl.* "Charles Seaingham certainly praised it. He seldom likes anything. But I shouldn't put it that way; it makes him sound crotchety or merely iconoclastic, when he's simply being truthful. Not much to like in the world of arts and letters these days. It's pretty hard to come up to the mark with Seaingham. I think the last thing he liked was *War and Peace*." Melrose had said it to defuse MacQuade's embarrassment. Must play hell to be in love with the wife of a man who's championed you.

MacQuade laughed. "He's not quite that old!"

"I didn't mean it that way." MacQuade probably wished Seaingham was "that old": the man was getting on into his late sixties, but his ascetic way of life seemed to be keeping him pretty damned healthy.

Unlike his wife, who had the transparent look of a person chronically ill. Her thinness, though attractive, was not that of a woman who wanted the silhouette of a fashion model. He remarked to MacQuade that she reminded Melrose a little of Wilkie Collins's woman in white.

"Yes, she does," said MacQuade, again coloring, as if he were afraid his companion could see straight into his brain. "She oughtn't to be going out in this cold. He oughtn't to allow it — " MacQuade's irritation was gaining momentum.

Melrose tried to smooth this over by suggesting, "Well, if one is of a religious bent, and it *is* Christmas . . ." Though, personally, he couldn't imagine cloaking oneself up to dash out to chapel, even if it was only a few feet away and one were wearing ermine. "Have you known her — then — long?"

"I . . . well, no. I believe I know Grace better than Seaingham himself." MacQuade cleared his throat and cast Melrose such a look as would have given the game away completely, if nothing else thus far had done.

Melrose had retreated to the bookcases and a volume of French poetry, not to read, but to watch Frederick Parmenger and Bea Sleight. She had muscled out Vivian, who had managed to get Parmenger to put down his book. Vivian now sailed straight by Melrose — apparently on the way to someone more interesting.

"Turning your blue blood red, is she, sweetie?" said Vivian, well into her second brandy.

Parmenger was doing a marvelous job of ignoring Beatrice Sleight once again. Having displaced Vivian, who seemed to interest Parmenger, Beatrice was now draping herself more or less about his chair, thinking the proximity would make him lose his place. Parmenger didn't even look up from his page as he said something to her that detached her quite quickly from the chair arm. Melrose smiled. Rude bastard, he supposed, but likable for some reason . . . perhaps for his very refusal to —

"He's doing my portrait, in case you're wondering why he's putting up with us."

The voice interrupted his reflections. Grace Seaingham had come back from her prayers. She was one of those, apparently, in whose presence it was dangerous to think. "I can't imagine anyone would call it 'putting up with' *you*, Mrs. Seaingham."

The laugh was as pure as the voice. "Come now, Mr. Plant. You're no flatterer."

"I know. That's why I said it."

Pleased, she colored slightly. There was altogether too little color in that pale face, and the tinge of pink against white seemed almost to have drawn itself from the Christmas rose she had plucked from the centerpiece, upsetting its delicate balance. It had been a pleasing, childlike gesture of gratitude toward Susan Assingham for bringing the flowers. A gesture typical of Grace Seaingham, he was sure. If there were any troubled waters, she would be the one to anoint them with oil.

It was very difficult, he thought, looking at her, to avoid this ecclesiastical turn of thought. On the other hand, as with her taking the rose, she reminded him of nothing so much as one of Rackham's fairies, beating delicate wings over Kew

Gardens, a sprite so transparent one could see through her. "I'd like to see this portrait. Is it finished?"

"Yes. It was Charles's idea," she added, with a slight shrug, as if to say she was not guilty of such self-indulgence. "Charles thinks the world of him. He's not a portraitist, ordinarily. I've no idea how Charles talked him into it."

The devil she hadn't. Seaingham was simply not a man one refused. He'd got MacQuade out of that garret, hadn't he? Lord, he'd even got Vivian here, and Vivian never put herself forward.

She excused herself when Susan Assington beckoned. As she moved toward her other guests, he wondered if she were simply too good to live.

TWELVE

1

"ACONITE," said Cullen. "The Queen Mother of poisons. Had your lunch?" he asked, passing the autopsy report across the table to Jury like a plate of food.

Jury had found Cullen and Trimm in a tiny restaurant in old Washington called the Geordie Nosh. Trimm was shoveling in huge portions of meat and vegetables. Possibly, because it was after three o'clock and late for lunch, there were no other diners.

"I ate on the train, thanks." A pleasant-looking woman came over to the table. Jury asked for coffee.

"Ah, man, that's not *food*. How's London?"

"The same. Tell me more."

Cullen did so around mouthfuls of food. "Deadly stuff. Medical examiner says as little as a fiftieth of a gram could kill a man. Greeks used to smear it on javelins and darts." He paused. "Ever see *I, Claudius*? It's how one a the owld buggers got it —"

"I don't mean its history," said Jury, ignoring Trimm's look, which might itself have been smeared with the stuff.

Cullen went on. "Numbness, tingling, burning, heart fibrillation — those are the symptoms, the M.E. said. In other words, she'd've known something was wrong, only didn't have time to do anything about it — and the stuff can work fast. One socko dose —" Cullen drove a fist into Trimm's shoulder. The constable went on eating with great concentration, working his way right round his plate — mash, stewed steak, vegetables — as if all consciousness of the world beyond his plate were gone.

Jury was reading the medical examiner's report. "Could this stuff have been ingested accidentally?"

Cullen shook his head. "No way. Comes from the root of monkshood. Looks kind of like turnips, or something."

Trimm was in the process of eating his mashed turnips or swede and didn't miss a beat.

"Wolfsbane, some call it. Wolves dig it up in winter when they've no food." With a fist wrapped round his fork, he sawed away at his meat, which was obviously tender enough he could have cut it with his finger. Releasing his aggressions, perhaps. He stuffed a large bite of steak in his mouth and pointed to the report with his fork.

"I seem to remember some case or other — can't this stuff be turned into a crystalline powder?"

Mouth full, Cullen nodded, "Aye, it could. Could even kill you if it got into a cut."

Jury pushed the sugar bowl toward him. "Looks like sugar?"

Cullen frowned. "Don't know. Sort of sweetish taste, the M.E. said."

"Helen Minton said she'd occasionally give some visitor tea."

"This visitor puts it in the sugar bowl? Well, that'd take care of a few American tourists." He chewed reflectively. "Ever see American football? Washington Redskins, like?"

"I wasn't thinking of the bowl of sugar."

The woman came back to the table and took dessert orders. Trimm had sopped up all of the rich gravy with a piece of bread. He laid his knife and fork neatly across his plate, that job finished, and ordered the apple crumble. When Jury refused, Cullen said, "Ah, you got to have *dessert*, man. Everything in here's fresh-made. Best food for miles, and cheap, too. Did you locate this painter cousin?"

Jury shook his head. "I've got someone working on it. He's an elusive chap." Jury went back to the report. "Death was immediate?"

"With this aconite, it could have been minutes; could have been hours, depending on the dose."

"Do you know a pub called Jerusalem Inn?"

Trimm plucked a toothpick from its holder and belched. "Place owt abacka beyont? Spinneyton way. Nowt but fights an lock-ins there."

"There's a kid there named Robin Lyte."

Trimm shrugged. "Means nowt t'me," he said, prepared to be as unhelpful as possible.

Jury turned to Cullen. "Is the name 'Lyte' common around these parts?"

"Not that I know." He gave a short laugh. "If you're looking for whoever killed Helen Minton at *that* place, I could believe it. Only all around Durham there's been more snow than here. Spinneyton's been snowed in, from what I hear." Cullen looked gloomy. "Match with Sunderland was called off too."

"No one could have made it to Washington in the snow, then, that what you're saying?"

"Not unless they skied here," said Cullen, catching himself before he actually laughed. "Think it was someone there, do you?"

Jury shrugged. "I don't know what to think. There's a hotel near here called the Margate — "

"Sheels," said Trimm. "Soonderland coast." He punched his thumb behind him as if the coast of Sunderland were on the curb.

"South Shields," said Cullen, translating. "I know the hotel. Kinda run down; used to be a nice place. Oh, your sergeant called. Wiggins, that the name? Man kept sneezing, I couldn't make it out, quite. You're to call Scotland Yard."

"Thanks. You going back to the station?"

"Um. Come on Trimm; not got all day, we haven't."

Constable Trimm spooned up the last of Cullen's custard and let the spoon clatter into the bowl. "Doon," he said with the satisfaction of a man who's completed a trying task.

2

"SHE was pregnant," said Wiggins. The crackling sound might have been a bad connection, or just Wiggins removing the cellophane from another box of cough drops. "Of course, the school couldn't keep her, said the headmistress. The old headmistress, that is. Took me a long time to track her down. Place is near the sea, too." There was a pause during which Jury was meant to commiserate.

Jury didn't. He could almost hear Wiggins's sinuses whining. They seemed to have taken on a life of their own.

Sergeant Wiggins went resolutely on. "According to Maureen — oh, I went back to the Minton house for a bit of a chat. I know you didn't tell me to — "

Jury smiled. He bet Wiggins went back. "No, but I'm glad you did. I think Maureen knows more than she's telling."

"She did; she knew Helen Minton was pregnant. Of course, she didn't want to say, thought it would be disloyal. But since I'd found out anyway, I guess she thought it wouldn't hurt to confirm it."

"What else?"

"Parmenger, her uncle, nearly went berserk. In a muck sweat he was about the whole thing."

Jury was silent for a moment. "Seems something of an overreaction unless he was a real Puritan. Unless — "

Wiggins seemed to be breathtakingly silent.

"Wiggins? What else did she tell you?"

Wiggins cleared his throat. "I'm not supposed to say anything — "

Jury held the cool receiver against his forehead for a moment to keep from yelling into it. Then he said, "I work for Scotland Yard. So you won't feel too disloyal to Maureen, I'll help you out. She thinks the father was Frederick Parmenger, right?"

"Sorry, sir. That's right. She's pretty sure he was the father."

"That certainly would explain it better. Still . . . did he believe some old wives' tale idea of cousins intermingling?"

"Don't know. And we located Parmenger, sir."

Jury was lighting a cigarette. "Thank God for that. He certainly keeps himself to himself. Where is he?"

"Place called Spinney Abbey — it's up near where you are. About ten miles from Durham."

The match nearly burnt Jury's fingers. "Spinney Abbey? Is there a Spinneyton on that map in your mind?"

"That's right, sir. Owned by a man named — just a tic — Charles Seaingham. He writes things — "

"I know. He's one of our leading critics. Go on."

"Well, it seems Frederick Parmenger went up there weeks ago to do some painting. Got a commission from this Seaingham to paint the wife's portrait."

Jury was silent, thinking, for some moments.

"Sir?"

"Thanks, Wiggins. You did a great job."

Ordinarily, any compliment from Jury would have cleared

Wiggins's sinuses in one second flat. But he seemed more concerned with imminent tragedy. "You want me up there, sir?" The tone clearly implied no burning desire to join his superior.

"Sure."

Silence. "It's Newcastle-upon-Tyne."

"I know that."

"Coal country. You know that old saying, 'coals to Newcastle.'" Wiggins's feigned laughter strangled him. "On the train? You know how I hate train stations." Since Jury was saying nothing encouraging, Wiggins added wistfully, "As I'm not on duty tomorrow, I was going with Maureen to Stevenage to visit her brother."

"Okay. Since I'm full of the Christmas spirit, you can take the train from Stevenage." Jury let Wiggins rattle on about smoke, coal and grime, as if the sergeant were himself a toy train on a track, and then said, "Right. Well, I'll expect you tomorrow. Take a fast train."

"You got to be careful of those. The suction's so bad it can pull you right onto the tracks."

"Stand behind the yellow line."

THIRTEEN

JURY looked down the strand to the Margate Hotel — a long, white, blank-faced building — luminous on the wet, gull-starred sands like the skeleton of a ship picked clean by the tide where snowdunes mounded against a rocky promontory. There were no signs of life, except out there beyond the rocks, a man and woman walking, arms wrapped round one another, both turned to black shadows by the sun setting over the sea.

On the Margate's porch, scattered rocking chairs creaked with wind or the ghosts of old guests. The porch had been deserted by the living. One could hardly expect a seaside resort to be a hive of activity in midwinter, he supposed; but there was something about this hotel that made him wonder if even its summer days were gone. Hard to imagine colorful bathers out there, the high-pitched squeals of children with sand pails, the bright bathing caps.

Only the fact that the large front door stood open told him that the place was not closed for the season. And then came other signs: raised voices from a point at the end of the shadowed hall; the opening and shutting of drawers from a room behind the front desk; and when Jury looked to his left, through a door ajar, the figures of two or three elderly people sitting still as effigies. All he saw of one woman was the twined gray braid above the top of a chair. Another must have been asleep, head drooping. And then there was the fluttery movement of a hand as it turned the pages of a magazine.

A girl came out of the back room with a sheaf of folders and stopped suddenly, surprised, apparently, at winter custom. She herself must have been the youngest thing around, in her late twenties, pretty in a sullen sort of way. Probably thought it wasn't worth going to the trouble of paint and powder around here. But now her eyes raked over Jury and then strayed to a piece of broken mirror propped in a corner of the desk. She bit her lip and ran her free hand over her hair. "Wanting a room, were you?" She slipped a registration card in a little holder and shoved it toward him. Her smile was both flirtatious and ruined by bad teeth.

Jury let her hang onto her illusion for a moment that he might be a customer. "Not many people this time of year, are there?"

Disgust was written all over her petulant face. "Aye. And the ones that come, they're these old-age pensioners. They all got something the matter with them, but Mrs. Krimp — that's the owner — let's 'em live here on the cheap." She shrugged thin-bladed shoulders. "Might as well . . . no other custom." From her bag, resting on the counter, she drew a wand of lipstick and started making up. Then she got out comb and nail varnish as if Jury had stopped by to pick her up for a night on the town. She settled down for a natter. "Anyway, gives me a job, it does, so why should I complain? Though I'm a trained steno, just try to get a job up here. I can tell by the way you talk you don't come from here."

"I'm from London."

"London." It might have been Atlantis. "Never been there. Aren't you lucky?"

Jury smiled. "It's got its drawbacks. No sea air, for one thing."

"In the summer I guess it's not all that bad. There's a few places in Shields that's a bit of fun." She left it to Jury to imagine what sort of fun she had in mind. "Then there's places in Washington New Town, in that new shopping center. There's a disco there called the Silver Spur that's got rock groups. Ever been?" Jury shook his head. 'Don't like disco music, that it? Kiss of Death's on tonight."

"What?"

"Oh, *go* on. Kiss of Death. That's one of the best groups around. You're not *that* old."

"Unfortunately, I am."

Cupping her chin in her hands and smiling her unseductive smile she said, "You don't look it. Anyway, I like — "

Older men. He finished it for her. "As a matter of fact, I don't want a room. I want information."

It was as if they'd had a long-standing affair and he'd just thrown her over. Beneath the paint and powder, her face hardened into sullen lines. "What sort?"

Jury took out the snapshot of Helen Minton. "This woman: she's been here a few times, I think. You recognize her?"

But the girl didn't even look at the picture. Her eyes narrowed. "You police, or what?"

"Yes." Jury laid his card on the desk, which she frowned over. "Scotland *Yard?*" What he had lost in the romantic arena, he had gained in the professional. Her face was all wonder at the idea that the Margate Hotel had awakened the interest of New Scotland Yard. She looked down at the picture, started to shake her head, and then looked again. "Oh, aye. Been here two or three times, maybe."

"When was the last time she was here?"

"Don't remember exactly — maybe a week ago."

"How long did she stay?"

She shrugged. "Couple of days."

"Was she friendly with any of the guests?"

"You must be daft. Who's to get friendly with? Wait a bit, now, I'm a liar. . . . She did seem to talk to Miss Dunsany sometimes. But mostly she just liked to go out and walk up and down the beach. I guess she liked the sea air." She leaned across the reception desk, and there was a sharp glitter like broken glass in her otherwise empty eyes. "Why do police want to know about her?"

"Did you ever see her with a man? I mean, did she ever come to the hotel with one?"

"No, not when I was here. You never get that sort of thing here, not in this broken-down place. Any man ever brought *me* to a place like this for a weekend — "

Jury interrupted before she could get into her own amorous adventures. "So she came alone and pretty much stopped here alone and took long walks. Didn't you think it a little odd?"

She shrugged. "Beats me why anyone that young — I mean young compared to them — " She nodded toward the parlor. " — would ever come to the Margate."

She unscrewed her small bottle of nail varnish and started painting her little fingernail blood-red. Since Jury wasn't going to make free with any salacious information about Helen Minton, she had lost interest in her, alive or dead.

"You said that she was friendly with one of your other guests."

"Aye. Miss Dunsany."

"And where is Miss Dunsany?"

"In the parlor, I expect. Maxine'll be along with their coffee about now. They like it in there after the evening meal. Think the place was the Ritz in London, wouldn't you?"

At that moment, a slatternly girl in an apron — Maxine,

presumably — came down the corridor with a tray. " 'Ot water, 'ot water," she said, as if she were hawking it, one of the old London streetcriers. "Makes me sick, Glo, the way I got to run back and forth for 'em." Apparently, she was addressing the desk clerk, who must have been used to the complaints of Maxine, as she didn't bother to look up from her glistening thumbnail. All she did was shrug as the other girl toiled into the parlor.

"Would you mind pointing out Miss Dunsany to me?" asked Jury.

Glo made no move to rise from her stool-perch. "You'll see her. She's the one always sits in the chair by the fire."

Miss Dunsany might have been occupying the fireplace seat, but it was doing her no good if she were seeking warmth. The grate looked as if it had not been lit in recent history. The logs piled up there Jury took at first to be a display piece, unlightable.

The room appeared chillier yet in the dusky light playing across the clumsily arranged furniture, the sofas and chairs of murky brown, some slipcovered in faded linen.

The old lady, perhaps with a young woman's memory that fires were lit and parlors warm, sat in a wing chair by the hearth. She was dressed in dark blue crepe de chine with a shawl round her shoulders. As Jury approached she was picking up her cup with both hands to steady it. There were two other people in the room, a birdlike woman and a wheezing man whose stomach hung over his belt. He was inspecting his fresh pot of hot water. None of them spoke to one another.

"Miss Dunsany," said Jury, sitting down in a lumpish chair opposite her. "My name's Richard Jury, I'm with Scotland Yard C.I.D." When she looked at him, startled, he added quickly, "and an acquaintance of Helen Minton."

That did not reassure her. "Helen. Something's happened, hasn't it?"

"I'm afraid so, yes."

She looked at the cold grate, a woman used to bad news. "Would you like a cup of coffee, Mr. ——? I'm awfully sorry. My memory isn't quite so good as it used to be."

"Jury. But call me Richard."

"My own name is Isobel. What is it that's happened?"

"An accident. Helen's dead."

She looked away from Jury, her eyes traveling about the room with a brittle look that suggested this was just the sort of news one would expect in the Margate. "I'm terribly sorry. I liked Helen. What happened? I know she took medicine for a heart problem. But you wouldn't be here for that?"

"We're not sure what caused it. Her neighbor said Helen knew you."

Isobel Dunsany stared into the cold grate. "I thought it, you know, very odd that Helen would come to a place like this. It's rather awful, isn't it?" The face was old and lined, but the smile was young. "I suppose I stay here out of habit. It didn't always use to be this way. Of course, I could afford something better."

For a moment Jury thought this was defensive, in the manner of the old who resent their reduced circumstances, relegated to lives of slender means — the awful furniture, indifferent service, empty rooms telling them, *This is what your lives have come to; this is what you deserve.* But observing her clothes — the quality of the crepe de chine, the fine wool of the shawl — to say nothing of the silver brooch and the rings on her hands, it was obvious that she was telling the simple truth. She could easily have afforded better.

Fiddling with her empty cup, she went on: "I remember this place from when I was a young girl. My parents brought me here. You'd be surprised how very popular it was then. And how gay." Her eyes — that sort of blue which a younger person always finds surprisingly bright in the old — roved the room. "The furniture in this room was Louis Quinze, burgundy and gilt . . . there are still one or two small chairs over there," — Jury's eye followed hers to the faded side chairs set between two windows — "and in the middle of the room was a large circular couch on which I loved to sit. Pretend I was waiting for my young man to come and claim me. There were dances. There is a ballroom in the back. Closed off now. Too hard to heat." She drew her shawl more closely about her shoulders and looked at the cold hearth. "But how I *do* wish they'd light that fire, at least."

"That's easy enough," said Jury, taking matches from his pocket. The paper and kindling caught and in another few minutes the logs began to spark.

This totally unexpected event caught the attention of the room's two other occupants, who now rose arthritically from their chairs a distance away and claimed other chairs nearer the fireplace. They all sat rather still, as if paying silent homage to this marvel, this blaze in their cold chamber.

The warmth inside the parlor must have leaked out into the hall, for it had caught the attention of Mrs. Krimp — if this was Mrs. Krimp, the manageress — who came churning through the doorway to see what in heaven's name was going on, and which of her guests she could blame for this infraction of the rules of the house.

From the look of her, Mrs. Krimp carried her own heat with her. Over electric blue pants she wore an orange jumper. Her newly permed hair was red, and lay close to her skull in fiery little licks. Her odd, yellow cat's eyes flared with indignation. "Here now! Mr. Bradshaw," — as if he had been the fire-lighter — "you know the fire's not lit after the evening meal. Too near your bedtime to make it worth it. Miss Gibbs, I'm surprised — " Seeing a stranger stopped her. Perhaps it wasn't good business to be castigating her old guests in front of a potential new one. She shut up and licked her lips slightly at the thought of a new infusion into the old blood of the hotel. There was something mildly vampirish about Mrs. Krimp.

Her illusions were, however, soon smashed by Glo who, apparently having heard the beginnings of a row (and any action was better than none at all), came up behind her and whispered in her ear, while the two of them looked at Jury.

"Police!" said Mrs. Krimp. "Well, that don't give you the right to come into *my* hotel and upset routine — "

Slowly, Jury rose from his chair. He never strained much for effects, but he had cultivated a way of getting up that seemed to stretch his six-feet-two another couple of inches; and of softening up a voice already disarmingly soft, which could sound simply deadly — the shadow that followed you down the street and up the steps. Mrs. Krimp took a step or two backward when he said to her: "You know, Mrs. Krimp, that there are certain standards hotels must maintain. That fire — if it's been lit in a *week,* much less after breakfast, I'd be surprised." He took out his notebook, thumbed over a couple of pages (as if he'd already made voluminous notes on the horrors of the Margate), and added a few squiggles. "Granted, I'm not an hotel inspector. But I intend to get one out here" — he smiled charmingly — "bloody quick."

The old man, Bradshaw, wheezed with strained laughter. Miss Gibbs, the tiny woman, cocked her birdlike head at Mrs. Krimp, as if asking her, Well, how do you like that, you old she-devil?

In a kind of spontaneous combustion, Mrs. Krimp's face reddened. Her mouth worked speechlessly.

Seeing her advantage, Miss Dunsany put in, in the manner of one used to speaking to servants: "Yes, Mrs. Krimp. And whilst we're about it, could we have something other than *tinned* tomato soup for our dinner?" Then in a grand way she added: "And we would all like a glass of port."

"*Port?* Whatever do you mean? The bar's not stocked in winter —"

"My dear woman, I'm speaking of *my* port. The case of Cockburn's that I left in your care, to be put in the cellars."

The Cockburn's, Jury bet, had been keeping Mrs. Krimp contented for some time, judging from the cobweb of tiny red veins on her face. Cockburn's and gin.

Mrs. Krimp fumed and flamed, all of her separate parts — the orange jumper, red hair, yellow eyes — blazing but not blending. She marched from the room like a tiny patchwork hell.

In a few minutes, Maxine, stepping a bit quicker, and looking at Jury as if he might slap the cuffs on her there and then, appeared with a tray containing mismatched glasses and a bottle of Bristol Milk.

Miss Dunsany smiled. "Her private stock, I daresay. I can imagine what happened to my Cockburn's."

During the next half-hour, they all had two glasses apiece (though Jury saw Bradshaw cadge another while Miss Dunsany gazed at the fire) as they sipped and talked in turns. Bradshaw and Miss Gibbs eventually nodded peacefully off as Miss Dunsany reflected about her old life here at the Margate Hotel. The boardwalk (long since gone), the bathing machines, the ladies with parasols and gentlemen in white trousers and striped coats. As she talked, Jury could hear the wind roaming about the building, slamming a distant shutter, creaking an unlatched screen door, seeking a way in. As she spun out her past, the room rattled with memories.

"Helen Minton," said Miss Dunsany, finally, having put it off as long as she could. "She wasn't the sort of person you'd expect to find here at the Margate."

"What sort was she, then?" Taking out his packet of cigarettes, one of which Miss Dunsany accepted, he lit them.

"An unhappy one. I believe she found out far more about

me than I ever did about her. She hadn't much family, I know that. A cousin she saw little of, an artist, I believe. I don't know exactly what happened to her parents. The father, I gathered, was caught out in something rather unsavory. Embezzlement, perhaps?" Her eyes questioned Jury, as if he might deduce the facts in the case from whatever meager evidence she offered. "Anyway, the mother died shortly thereafter, as though the scandal had killed her. She must have been a weak type if that were true. My own husband — well, we needn't go into *that*. Helen went to a boarding school that she hated. I daresay it would be hard to take the deaths of one's parents and then wake up one morning and find you'd got nobody. She said that it never fails, when people find out you're alone, they'll set about making you lonelier. The way she talked about school, you'd think she'd dreamt it, rather than lived it. The other girls were cold; the corridors a confused tangle. And then when she was sixteen or seventeen she was suddenly taken out. By the same uncle who put her in."

"Why was that?"

"I don't know."

Jury thought for a moment. "You say she wound up knowing a good deal about you? Did she ask a lot of questions?"

Isobel Dunsany looked a little puzzled, as if she hadn't thought of it that way before. "Helen was certainly not nosy. She did exercise a considerable amount of patience when I went on about myself. But then," she added, "so have you." She chucked her cigarette into the fireplace as if it were now hers to do with as she liked.

Behind them Bradshaw and Gibbs were having a minor quarrel over the sherry bottle.

"Could she have come here looking for you, Miss Dunsany?"

Her cool blue eyes regarded him. "It's possible, now I think back. Although it seemed ordinary enough at the time — with my rather tiresome way of going on about the old days, my family, and such — she seemed quite interested in the servants. I had a maid, Danny. Danielle was her real name. Either a French mother or a rather silly one to give her such a jumped-up name."

"How did the girl come to you?"

"She'd been in service for years before she married. Very fine references, and a good girl she was. Her husband had scarpered, as they say, and there was a child to support. As a matter of fact, I think what had happened was that he'd taken Danny's money with him. Money she'd saved. I don't know, and that's why she had to go back into service."

"When was this?"

Her laugh was vague, a bit embarrassed. "I'm not too good on dates. A dozen years ago, more perhaps."

"And Danny, what happened to her?"

"I lost track. I'm sorry." She pressed her fingers to her head, looked up and said, as if the caverns of memory had shown some way out, "Lyte. That was it."

"L-y-t-e?"

"That's it, yes. Danny Lyte. *Now* I remember. It was an old Washington family name. Funny, Helen would be interested in her."

"Do you remember anything about her child?"

Miss Dunsany was, perhaps, too contented with sherry and firelight to remember too much now about her past. "She lived in Washington — I mean the old village. I never saw the little boy but once. Now, what was his name?"

Jury waited, but Miss Dunsany only shook her head.

"Robin?"

She looked at him in some childlike amazement at the second sight of Scotland Yard. "Robin. You're quite right. Now, I remember: named after her father. Robin." The name seemed to call forth a clear vision of brown hair, brown eyes, a slack and aimless look. That was the way she described him to Jury. "It was sad. The boy was a bit, well, backward. Yes, it was sad."

"And Helen Minton. Was she interested in the boy, too?"

Score two for Scotland Yard. "Why yes. How would you know that?"

Jury smiled. "No way, really. Just guessing."

Mr. Bradshaw and Miss Gibbs had so increased their familiarity with the sherry bottle that a little Christmas songfest had taken hold. They each had chosen separate songs, however, a discordance of carols.

Jury thanked Isobel Dunsany and rose to leave. An inspector, he assured her, would be visiting shortly. There might not be dances, but there might be a let-up in the tinned soup. Jury smiled.

"I do hope you find what you're looking for. Good-bye, Mr. Jury."

She turned her face again to the fire, dying in spite of all of their efforts.

FOURTEEN

1

" " I 'm going to have an early night,' said Lady Stubbings."
It was a line that Melrose Plant could easily have dis-
pensed with — weren't they *forever* having their "early
nights"? — but in this case, he found the line especially ex-
cruciating and wished the whole lot of them would have an
early night.

Thus far he had counted half-a-dozen bodies down in the
study or sprawled over the terrace or out in the potting shed.
Melrose yawned and tossed *The Murders at Stubbings* aside.
It was obvious who the murderer was and he was only too
happy she was making an early night of it. . . . Instead of
having their early nights, why didn't the entire cast of char-
acters simply remain in bed in the morning — as he had
managed to do — thereby saving the trouble of getting murdered, the murderer the trouble of murdering them, the
reader the trouble of reading about them and — most important — the writer the trouble of writing about them. He had
gone on this thriller-reading kick ever since meeting Polly
Praed. Each of hers he had read twice, so that he could make
appreciative and astute comments about them in his letters.

These she seemed to fail to appreciate, as witnessed in the last letter to *Mr. Plant* (*Lord Ardry? Your Grace??*). Really.

Melrose pushed the pillows at his back, trying to prod them into a more supportive position. Then he picked up *The Print on the Ceiling* from the stack of books on his bedside table, noticed the name of the author was Wanda Wellings Switt, and put it on the pile of rejects for that reason alone. He did not care how the print had landed on the ceiling, even if it was the bloody foot of a fly.

The Third Pigeon, by Elizabeth Onions. The dusk jacket showed a cloud of pigeons (the smart ones) flying off against a backdrop of dark and snow-threatening sky. And in the foreground, the dumb one who had hung around long enough to get itself shot by the ominous rifle barrel protruding from the bushes into which the third pigeon was dropping like lead. Why was someone writing about murdered pigeons when one had the entire human race to draw upon?

He would have to get up, he supposed. The morning headache he had pleaded could not keep him from the other guests forever — although given Agatha's prognostications, it was always possible. Her gray head had popped in and out of his door like a cork as she ran down the list of possible diseases: they began with the terminal, and, having failed to get Ruthven to call for a priest, had descended to the acute, and lately to the merely chronic.

Melrose got up now to go to the long window in hopes that the gods had pulled off a small miracle of weather-legerdemain, and he could throw his bags into the old Flying Spur and —

Snow.

Snow, snow, snow. Lady Assington had announced it as "ever such an adventure," as if they were all being asked to rub sticks together to make a fire and live on whale blubber, when actually they were being sustained by crackling logs, cigars, Grand Marnier, and Sambuca.

Ruthven entered and inquired if his lordship would be taking afternoon tea with the others.

Melrose studied the ceiling, found it cold, cloisterlike and without so much as a bloodprint, and more or less fell out of bed like the third pigeon.

2

TEA was a singular affair that could have sustained anyone but Agatha for days: smoked salmon sandwiches, partridge pâté, something imprisoning truffles, and, of course, the cake plate, which Agatha was scavenging for fairy cakes.

Since the interesting ones like Parmenger and MacQuade appeared to have taken vows of silence in keeping with their surroundings, the conversation was dominated once again by Beatrice Sleight and Agatha.

Taking a break from the subject of the Ardry-Plant titles, Agatha was now onto the Ardry-Plant money. Having none of her own, she was now busily spending Melrose's: ". . . and one of the finest collections of Lalique at Ardry End. We're going to Christie's next month to the auction. . . ."

Of which Melrose knew nothing, nor would attend. To some vague question, Agatha replied with a laugh that sounded more like camel bells than windchimes. "My late husband, the Honorable Robert Ardry — "

As she piled courtesy titles on top of Christie's, Melrose wandered from the dining room into the hall, but not before he heard her say, in response to a question from Beatrice Sleight —

"I? Oh, no, my dear, not a sou." She laughed artificially. "I'm right down to my diamonds and, ah — *ma devise.*"

Since the diamonds were entirely his mother's, she would at least snatch at her share of the family coat of arms.

3

"DON'T stick your hand in the flames," said Melrose, wandering into the drawing room after luncheon to see Tommy Whittaker sitting by the fire. "You wouldn't be able to play the oboe."

Tommy looked up and smiled. There was not a blotch on his handsome face, yet he seemed oblivious of mirrors, certainly the ornate one above the fireplace. "I *am* dreadful, aren't I? I should practice more."

"Not here, please."

Tom Whittaker's pervasive gloom was broken by his laughter. "Sorry you've been subjected to my music."

"Don't apologize."

"Do you read?"

"I know how, yes." Melrose lit a cigar.

"I wonder if I ever shall again." He looked over his shoulder. "All these writers . . ."

"Ah, but you'd be denying yourself the delights of *The Third Pigeon*, and very possibly the entire Elizabeth Onions canon." Tom looked puzzled, and Melrose said, "Just a thriller writer. Don't worry, the Onions woman won't show up. Mr. Seaingham probably draws the line at thriller writers."

Tommy sighed. "Maybe a murder'd be a good idea. They could make me the victim." Cupping his chin in his hands, he looked like he might commit himself to the flames.

"Such sacrifice is noble, but unnecessary. I understand what you mean, though."

"I'm glad *somebody* understands."

Melrose was not sure he wanted to be thought "understanding." It could lead to all sorts of complications.

Tommy got up. "Look, let's have a walk round, what do you say?"

"Walk? Where?"

Impatiently, he shrugged. "Well, outside. We could walk round the ruins."

"How delightful. Haven't you noticed the snow's nearly to our knees?"

"We could walk about the cloisters, or what's left of them. We could sit in the chapel, or something."

Cloisters, chapel, how jolly. Melrose had simply thought to go back up to his room and be ill again with *The Third Pigeon*.

"I wanted to talk to you about tonight. Where no one can overhear us."

"Tonight? Is something happening tonight?"

"Yes." Tom Whittaker was already going for their coats.

Even the walk down the long gallery, at the near end of which was Charles's study, found the temperature dropping by degrees. The gallery lay in the East Wing of the main building, once the abbot's home, and its end had been converted into a sort of solarium, pleasant enough in summer, Melrose imagined, but a depressing surround of glass in winter. One felt the snow coming up to the tips of one's shoes. The Lady Chapel where Grace Seaingham said her nightly prayers was down a covered walk to their right and the cloister-ruins off to their left. At least the cloisters were covered, what was left of them. Nothing at all was left of the basilica, so from where they now stood, it was a clean sweep of snow to the main entrance, broken only by the narrow road made by the plow over which Seaingham had driven his Land Rover the night before and which was now half-buried again.

The air was fresh, the wind died down, and one could have found in his surroundings a whole creaking history of the Cistercian Order. It simply made Melrose colder to imagine cloaked monks on their way to morning matins.

Melrose's attention was soon riveted, however, not on history but on what Tommy had just said: "*Skis!* You expect me to put on skis and go down to the Jerusalem Inn with you?"

"Oh, *come* on. It's a lark. You could have snowshoes if you'd rather. There's a whole arsenal of sports equipment in the gun room. It's just this end of the gallery, next to the solarium, and Mr. Seaingham's got all that stuff—"

"Hold on! I have never skied, and certainly never snowshoed, in my entire life."

"Neither had I until I got slapped up here. Look, we may be here for the rest of our lives—"

Melrose looked up through a hole in the stone and uttered a mute prayer. "Don't say things like that."

"It's quite simple really, the skis," said Tommy, eminently rational, even if Melrose wouldn't be. "You said you'd read *Skier*. That book is practically a manual on skiing. That's how I figured it out how to work them. MacQuade's an expert cross-country skier. And that's what we're talking about: cross country." Tommy pointed out the country ahead of them, as if Melrose were snowblind.

"Don't I know it. If you feel compelled to set out on this venture, why not get MacQuade to go with you?"

"Because I can't *talk* to adults."

Then what, wondered Melrose, did that make him? "Well, why must you ski around the countryside *anyway?*"

"It's the match. At Jerusalem Inn. You see, I've been playing there for some time; Meares Hall is just the other side of Spinneyton. Didn't you know that? Aunt Betsy and the Seainghams have always been great friends. Well, there's no one else about, is there?"

"The Spinneyton Slasher, maybe."

"I've never heard of him." Nor did he, apparently, hold any horror for Tommy Whittaker, who was interested only in his pool game.

"Not *pool!* Snooker." Tommy frowned as if his new friend

had made some hideous social gaffe. "Anyway, the Jerusalem's a great place. Naturally, I've had to think up ways to get there and the regulars don't know who I am, of course."

"Neither do I," said Melrose, as he turned to go in.

"I can show you about the skis in five minutes. All we have to do is wait till right after dinner. It'll be dead dark and no one will see."

"They will miss me over the brandy," said Melrose, knowing no one would miss anyone at this point.

"Lie and say you're sick. Like you did this morning."

By now they had reached the door to the chapel. "I am not a liar."

"Sure you are. Listen, you've forgotten what it's like, being young, and not being able to do as you please, no smoking, no drinking, no snooker. I'm not permitted to play at home. We've this huge games room, but after Aunt Betsy discovered how much I liked it, she was afraid ... well, to tell the truth, I think poor Aunt Betsy is afraid I'll turn out like Father. Though she'd never say it. It's her one blind spot, really. She's managed to have Parkin — that's our butler — serve up all sorts of reasons for keeping the room locked."

"That does seem a little severe, I'll agree. This is a pretty place." They were standing in the nave. Before the pale blue and gold figure of the Virgin, votive candles burned.

Tom Whittaker was not interested in heaven. "Severe. You bet it is. If I told you what I go through to get my practice in ... oh, well, never mind that. The thing is, I've got to play every day."

"Why on earth do you need *me*, then? If you've been cross-country skiing now for two nights —"

"An alibi."

"What?"

"It's chancy for me. I mean, no one's seen me yet. But if Aunt Betsy were to find out, there'd be hell to pay. This way,

I could just say we were out looking about the ruins, or something. You can make up some good lie."

Melrose looked at the face of Mary, frozen in time, wearing her inscrutable smile. He could have sworn she was smiling at him, egging him on.

"Oh, very well," Melrose said, as crossly as he could, to make sure the young marquess didn't think he was a pushover, and would be calling him out on other harebrained adventures.

As Tom gave him a comradely clap on the shoulder, Melrose had to admit that anything would be better than a night with *The Third Pigeon*, even skiing to Jerusalem Inn.

FIFTEEN

1

ROBBIE was playing Pac-Man and Nell Hornsby was behind the bar. The kitten was back in the straw of the manger, Alice removed for presumably more interesting pursuits.

In Jury's wake, a few of the regulars put in a casual appearance at the bar. Dickie was already there with his leek beside him like a date, still with his teeth out, smiling across at Jury. "Aa'm clammin fer a pint, man. Buy yer one?" Jury thanked him. Dickie was no welcher, that was certain.

Nell Hornsby threw the bar towel over her shoulder and drew off two pints of bitter, set Jury's down, took Dickie his.

"Have one yourself, Nell," said Jury. She turned to the optics and got herself a small whiskey. "You know where Spinney Abbey is?"

"Aye. Through Spinneyton, turn right. You too?" She laughed.

"Me, too? What do you mean?"

"Last night four people were asking for it. From Northants, Joe said. An earl, one of them was. Walked in right in the middle of one of Nutter's — ah, awright, ya fond bugger!" She yelled across the room to Nutter. "Oney got two hands."

"What did he look like?"

"Tall, less than you. Kinda light hair, green eyes. Good-looker," She might have been going to add another "less than you," but stopped herself.

"Who were the others?"

·She shrugged. "Didn't see them meself. Joe said one looked like he might have been the other's valet. And an old lady. A young one, too. Good-looker, he said. Reminded him of that film star — what's her name?"

"Vanessa Redgrave," said Jury, more to his glass than to her.

"That's it. You know them, then."

Jury nodded. "They were going to the Seainghams'?"

"Aye."

He couldn't imagine what Melrose Plant was doing at Spinney Abbey, but he was certainly glad he was there. Jury would be saved a lot of time and trouble. Plant had certainly helped him out before on cases.

Nell Hornsby drank her whisky and asked, "You like snooker? There's a match in the back room. Clive's there."

"Thanks. Maybe I'll have a look." Jury was delaying his visit to the abbey. The later, the more the element of surprise.

And the longer before he'd have to see Vivian Rivington again.

The back of the Jerusalem was one long room, stone-flagged and cold, except for the inadequate heater in the big, cold fireplace. The back was reserved largely for the snooker-matches, the lowlier pool table having been relegated to the front room. The players didn't seem bothered by the cold; neither did their audience, most of whom had moved from the game in progress on the first table to the new frame about to begin. Clive, in tinted glasses, took a sort of boxer's stance for the break.

Jury wondered how he managed with those glasses. Although Jury's knowledge of snooker was about as heady as his knowledge of Italian opera, he still thought Clive's stance a little sloppy. His left hand made a very poor bridge for the cue. But then his fingers were stubby, which put him at a disadvantage anyway. Still, Clive appeared to be resident champion, if one could go by the way people gathered to watch him break. He took a long look at the pyramid of red balls, clipped the top outside red, sending the cue ball off the cushion to angle back above the blue and behind the other colors on the balk line. To Jury it looked like a damned good shot, setting up the yellow for a pot in the middle pocket. Clive potted three more reds and colors in turn before he miscued on a red pinched up against the cushion, the tip of his cue running off the top. But he'd built up enough of a break that he could look pretty smug about it.

Jury walked over to Clive, who was toasting himself with a pint, and showed him his warrant card. "Sorry to interrupt. Mrs. Hornsby told me you talked to this woman in here."

Warily, Clive looked at the snap and shrugged. "Had a drink is all. She said nowt." He looked toward the table. "My torn." He looked a question at Jury, who nodded, and shoved past him to the table.

A voice at Jury's elbow said, "I got the clothes."

It was Chrissie, carrying the big doll now wrapped round in strips of sheeting, looking like an accident victim or something ready for the morgue.

"Fine," said Jury. "Looks much more like the baby Jesus."

She seemed to be waiting for warmer congratulations than that. When none came, she turned to watch the game. "Do you play that?" Her small, bright voice pierced the thick smoke and the air heavy with the smells of different brews.

Clive was negotiating a difficult cushion shot and Chrissie was quickly shushed.

Just at that moment, the back door opened, blowing in wind, snow, and two figures who were stripping ski masks from their faces.

Clive miscued and swore.

Jury had the edge over Melrose Plant, who, seeing his friend Richard Jury standing there, could only stare, open-mouthed.

"What's this," asked Jury, looking from Melrose to Tom. "The Spinneyton SWAT team?"

2

"It would probably be better if I just didn't ask," said Jury.

"Probably," said Melrose. "We left the skis outside."

"Really?"

Melrose was watching Tommy talking to the other players as if he'd lived here all his life. "I, ah, suppose you drove?"

"It's the way I usually travel, myself. If you're one of Seaingham's guests, then you've probably met the person I'm looking for — Frederick Parmenger."

"*Parmenger?* What on earth do you want with him?"

"There was a woman found in the bedroom of Old Hall day before yesterday — "

"What old hall?"

"Washington Old Hall. It's owned by the National Trust . . . don't you read the papers?"

"Papers? Delivered how? Look, you don't know how isolated this Spinney Abbey *is*. They've been snowed in there for three days." Melrose held up his ski mask. "You don't think I get kitted out like this every day, do you?"

"I hope not. Parmenger's the cousin of the woman who was found. Her name was Helen Minton."

"Found how?"

"Dead."

Melrose lit a cigar. "Well, I *assumed* that. I meant, how did she die, obviously? Who found her? The National Trust?"

"Tourists," said Jury, shortly.

"She was murdered, then. Why else would they have got you up here?"

"They didn't, I was up here anyway."

"In this wasteland? Whatever for?

Jury told him about his aborted visit to Newcastle and his meeting with Helen Minton.

Melrose was silent for a moment. He blew on the coal-end of his cigar and said, "I'm sorry."

Jury shrugged and drank his beer. "Nothing to be sorry about. I hardly knew her." A terrible feeling, almost of betrayal, stabbed him as he looked absently at the frame just ending. Clive had won every frame; apparently his opponent merely gave up, good-naturedly.

"What about Parmenger?"

"He's — he was — Helen Minton's cousin. It took two days to find him. He keeps himself to himself, apparently."

"Ha! I'll drink to that if you'll buy. Frankly, he's the only one with any sense: he's not at the abbey for pleasure, but for business. He's done Grace Seaingham's portrait. Though I'm very much surprised he'd put himself to the trouble of traveling all the way up here to the frozen North to do it. Parmenger's definitely not the type to put himself out for anybody. And you wouldn't be going to Spinney Abbey in this beastly weather just to tell Parmenger to go and identify the body of his cousin. So what's going on?"

Jury watched as Clive racked the balls for another game. "She was poisoned." He stared blindly at the three balls Clive was placing on the balk line — yellow, brown, green. "What'll you have to drink?"

Melrose just looked at him for a moment. "The usual."

* * *

As Hornsby drew the Old Peculier and the Newcastle ale, Jury looked over to see that the doll, wrapped in its bandages, had been returned to the manger. It made him feel inexpressibly sad; he thought of Mrs. Wasserman and Father Rourke.

"Is the only way to Spinney Abbey on skis?" he asked, handing Melrose his drink.

"Very funny. No, but it's the quickest. And the only means of escape, if one" — Melrose indicated Tommy Whittaker — "is not supposed to be engaging in such frivolous pursuits as pool."

"Snooker," said Jury.

"It's all one to me."

"Much more complicated." He watched Clive chalking his cue. Unless Jury was mistaken, Clive was going to play this lad who had come in with Melrose Plant. He turned to ask about Whittaker, when he heard Plant saying:

". . . road by now is clear, so I intend to pack up myself, Agatha, and Viv — " Melrose stopped and studied the tip of his cigar again.

"What's she doing here? I thought she married that Italian duke, or whatever."

"Count. No. He's floating in Venice. I suspect she's got cold feet. Wet feet, rather."

"Oh," was all Jury said. The last time he had seen Vivian had been for those brief moments in Stratford-upon-Avon. She had been with him, the Italian. Now, this new knowledge washed over him with an intensity that surprised him. Damnit, why couldn't he go about his business and stop stumbling into people who appeared and disappeared? He stopped thinking about it, pointed his pint toward the second table. "Is he going to play Clive?"

"Clive who?"

"The last winner. What are you doing, anyway, skiing

about the countryside with him? And what was all of that 'marquess' business before he kicked you in the shins?"

"Don't miss anything, do you? I'm humoring him." Melrose's sigh was sacrificial. "I feel sorry for him, though I should really feel sorry for *me*, being stuck in that great, cold abbey, treated to amateur piano-and-oboe recitals. But it's not really his fault. He's got this aunt —"

"Now I understand."

"Yes. Only I must say that *his* aunt is genuinely fond of him. Her trouble is, she can't let him be: she's afraid he's going to turn out like his parents — that he'll be the playboy type and start up another Happy Valley in Kenya and engage in wife-swapping and sodomy and whatever those types do. He's the Marquess of Meares, and she wants him to uphold the family honor."

"Good lord, he's so young to be a marquess."

"Not in here," whispered Melrose, watching Tommy take a drink from his pint. The table was set up, the pyramid of balls in place. "The trouble is, great-auntie is going too far in putting up with the piano- and oboe-playing. He's absolutely dreadful — what's he doing with his damned oboe case, for God's sakes? That must have been what he had strapped over his shoulder."

It was true that Tommy Whittaker had brought his oboe case, from which he removed two wooden cylinders. He screwed them together with a practiced quickness and chalked the tip.

"It's a cue! You're carrying a *cue* in your oboe case," Melrose said to Tom.

Tommy looked from Plant to Jury. Without the hint of a smile he said, "You ever try playing snooker with an oboe?"

V

SAFETY PLAY

SIXTEEN

1

HE certainly didn't play snooker the way he played the oboe.

He was playing against Clive, who was obviously unnerved before Tommy even got to the table. Clive missed an easy pot after running up a break of twenty-four. Now, with the reds positioned around the black, Tommy built his break up to forty on the black-ball game alone. It took an amazing repertoire of strokes to do it. Clive sat down and watched with the others. On the last red, Tommy brought the cue ball down the table to the balk line in position for the colors. He pocketed the yellow with enough screw to bring the white back in position for the green, did the same thing to take the brown, then sent the white up the table with a cannon off two of the cushions, but was snookered on the blue because of a red just barely touching it. He played a safety shot.

By the time Clive got up to the table Tommy's score on the break was 54, the sort of score even a professional would be happy about. But it wasn't the accuracy that amazed Jury; it was the speed. Tom didn't appear to stop and think, yet it was clear he played with a diagram in his mind, seeing several shots ahead, as a chess player can see plays beyond plays. Except that Tom moved more like a tornado than a chess player.

"Where did you learn to play like *that?*" Melrose offered him his cigar case.

"Practice," said Tommy simply, thanking Melrose for the cigar, and going back to the table. Clive had glued the cue ball to the cushion and couldn't get at his color. He tried to lay a snooker on Tommy, which Tommy quickly got out of at the same time he used a stun shot to pocket the remaining red and bring the white back to pocket the pink. That left only the black, and the frame was over.

"Practice! You must have started when you were one."

Tommy smiled. "Five, actually. See, my father liked billiards. I used to have to move a packing case round the table to stand on."

"I've never seen anyone so fast," said Jury.

"Then you've never seen Hurricane Higgins, have you?"

2

"WHAT do you mean, no ride?" Melrose thought with dread of the skis.

Hornsby had begun calling Time a half-hour ago and was barking it now to get a few of the rock-hard regulars out.

"It would be better if we didn't turn up at Spinney Abbey together." He nodded toward Tommy, talking to Clive, who was being a sport about having lost miserably to this boy. "Besides you should see he gets back — "

"*He* could get to the Antarctic if there were a snooker table there. Anyway, you certainly don't have any hopes that our friendship is going to remain a secret once Agatha sees you, do you? She'll have our long-standing acquaintance chronicled like Euryalus and Nisus." He knew Jury's fondness for Virgil.

"I know it won't be a secret. But you'll still be more of a help if we don't appear to be working on this case together."

"Well, what case *are* we working on, then? What do you expect to find?"

"Frederick Parmenger, for one thing. So get your skis on. You'll probably get there before I do. Through Spinneyton, turn right, is that it?"

"Believe me, once you're on that road you can't miss the abbey. It's the only thing with lights for miles around. But isn't it a bit late for Scotland Yard to be knocking up people?"

"Yes. But I do it occasionally. Takes them by surprise." Jury smiled and pocketed his cigarettes. "They'll all be tucked up in bed."

"Probably. Nothing ever happens in the country."

"Don't count on it," said Jury.

3

HE WOULDN'T have admitted it to Tom, but even with the wind in his face, Melrose was actually finding it rather pleasant, slipping along silently in the dark this way, over a ground made of glass. Perhaps it was that Jack London side of his nature, for he fancied himself as the hero of *Skier.* As he was considering Going for the Gold, his thoughts drifted like slow-falling snow to Ardry End, port and fireplace, and he decided, No, he really wasn't like MacQuade's hero.

Tommy's mind was also on the book: "It's really suspenseful; I don't know how he did it," said Tommy. "It must be hard to write a book with just one character and keep up the suspense."

"*Tour-de-force* stuff," said Melrose. "No wonder it took the prizes. Not a bad chap, either, MacQuade."

What there was of a moon had got stuck behind some cloud mass and the only illumination came from the dial of

Tom's compass. "We're all right. The abbey's only another half-mile. I recognize that wall over there. I think it's an old farm, or something."

All Melrose saw was a black outline. "Speaking of walls — how do you manage snooker at St. Jude's? I mean you must have to practice like mad to play the way you do. You'd hardly have time for study."

"I don't study. The tutors occasionally wonder where I am — like a misplaced pipe or spectacles. I don't think they'd miss anyone as long as nothing interfered with the cricket matches. I manage to get over the walls early and down to the games place in the village. And, of course, I read a lot after lights out to try and keep some sort of track of what I'm supposed to be learning. I made myself an authority on Mesapotamia; that way they think I must know a lot about everything else. It's amazing, really, how much people think you must know if you know about something nobody else much cares about. Actually, practicing's harder when I'm home." It was the wind's sigh or Tom's, Melrose didn't know which, across the snow. "You see, Aunt Betsy absolutely hates me playing. It reminds her of Father, I guess, who never paid much attention to me except at the billiard table. Well, she's right, he *was* a sort of playboy type. Never worked, spent a lot of money. Frivolous, she calls him. Them. Though I don't mean she speaks unkindly of them to me, really. When I'm home I have to think up all sorts of ruses to keep my hand in. Piano lessons — that's for limbering up the fingers. Aren't I a rotten pianist though?" He seemed almost proud of the lack of accomplishment.

"Never known a rottener."

Tom laughed. "And the oboe. That's just to get out of the house with my cue stick. I mean, it's not easy to carry a cue stick around without someone's asking about it. Then, also, I'm a crack shot."

Melrose stopped. "With what?"

Tom had stopped too, like Melrose's own shadow. "A rifle, of course. And pistols. We've got a rifle range. Father set it up for practice. But ever since Aunt Betsy's got onto this animal-humaneness thing, there's no shooting on the grounds. Mr. Seaingham tries to reason with her, because, you know, he's a great one for birds. Pheasant and grouse and quail. Everytime the Seainghams visit he sees great balloons of birds rushing out of the brush and bracken — "

"Any pigeons?" asked Melrose, pushing his skis up a small incline. "Wait a minute. What's shooting a *gun* got to do with snooker?"

They started up again, ski poles propelling them beneath a few stars that looked hard as iron. Tom said, "For my bridge arm, naturally. It's exactly the way you use your left arm to support a rifle. It's to train me to keep the arm true. If you moved a rifle — or pistol, for that matter — by so much as a quiver, the bullet could be deflected a couple of hundred feet."

"You go through all of that for snooker?"

"If I could play the way I want to every day, I guess I wouldn't. But when you can't do what you want, well, you've got to substitute, to find a way round it."

His aunt, thought Melrose sadly, had a nephew with the dedication of any writer or painter, and she couldn't see it.

Tommy went on about the pub near his school. "Naturally, none of them know I'm from St. Jude's or that I have this damned title."

They whished along in silence for a moment, until Tom broke it by saying, "Did it bother your family when you gave it up?"

"My mother and father were dead. Lady Ardry is my only relative."

"Oh. My parents died when I was ten."

"Do you remember them well?"

"Yes. Mother was beautiful. I don't think she liked me

mussing her up. Well, she wasn't all that affectionate. Father was kind of fun, especially at the billiards table." He laughed. "Oh, that was a lark! But they were always off and about, usually on the Continent." There was a brief and (Melrose thought) regretful silence. "Wish they'd taken me with them. But I always stayed behind with Aunt Betsy." As if he'd been disloyal to his great-aunt, he added, "Not that I don't love her. In everything but snooker, she's champion. She's the one that's taken care of me. I'd do anything for Aunt Betsy," he said quite thoughtfully. Then he added: "Of course, you were *old* when you got rid of your title."

"I don't think under-forty exactly *old.*"

Tom refused to comment on that. "I would do — get rid of mine — except I just can't see hurting Aunt Betsy. She lives for the honor of the family. Whatever that has to do with it."

"But it's your life and you can't let anyone else live it for you."

As if Melrose, by so saying, had actually given him a push into his real life, Tommy laughed and shot ahead of him toward the abbey that yet remained perhaps a quarter of a mile away.

It was another ten minutes before Melrose, feeling like a walrus on skates, had slogged his way to the little door in the abbey wall. It was just in time to hear a cry and see Tom Whittaker keel over as if he'd been shot in the back.

4

THE skis were angled upwards out of the snow, and Tommy flat on his face in it, when Melrose had finally managed to shove his way up to him.

"Damn all!" cried Tom. "Help me up, will you?"

To Melrose's infinite relief, the snow-muffled voice came quite healthily through the ski mask and the dark.

It was extremely difficult uprighting someone wearing skis, particularly by someone else wearing them, but Melrose finally pulled the boy up. Tommy yanked off his mask and ran his hand over his face where the snow had lodged round the eye- and mouth-holes. "Where the hell did *that* spring from? Felt like a log." He managed to maneuver the skis around so he could bend his knees and feel round with his hands. "Didn't you bring a torch?" he asked Melrose, peevishly.

"No. This is the first time for me in this survival-training course."

"It's like a dead animal, or some — oh, my God . . ."

"What is it?"

"That ermine cape of Mrs. Seaingham's. Here — "

"Don't pick it up," said Melrose quickly. He had finally yanked the buckles from the ski shoes. Here, near the walk, the snow was only ankle deep. He waded through it.

"Why not?"

Melrose kneeled down and felt, very carefully, in the snow. The ermine was dusted with snow, its soft nap tacky with ice. What was under it lay facedown. "Because," he said, finally answering Tommy's question, "you didn't fall over a cape, old lad."

He wondered who in the world would want to murder Grace Seaingham.

5

THE second shock came when, after the alarm was raised by Marchbanks and Ruthven, rousing Seaingham and his guests, that the first person to materialize at the bottom of the staircase in the Great Hall, wrapped in white satin, was Grace Seaingham.

She asked him why they were staring at her so. And what on earth was wrong?

Melrose put it as gently as he could. "I think we'll find, Mrs. Seaingham, that one of your guests is — missing."

It was certainly not Lady Ardry.

She came trumpeting down the stairs in robe and mobcap. Why had they been woken from their slumbers, she demanded? Why was Melrose in that strange getup? Why, why, why?

Lady St. Leger, staring at Tommy, was just as eager to know. "Where — what on earth have you been doing, Tom?"

"Skiing," said Tommy. He hadn't meant it to be funny.

Still, MacQuade laughed.

Melrose did not realize he had been holding his breath until he saw Vivian and let it out. Her hair all awry, her dressing gown several sizes too large; she was not one of those beauties who looked her best when awakened from sleep. She appeared to be drugged. Too much brandy, he thought. Nor would he answer her when she yawned and asked him if he'd made up a new game.

All of the guests, and Seaingham himself, were now gathered in the living room. Most of them made immediately for the drinks table.

Melrose looked around and then said, quite simply: "Beatrice Sleight's been murdered."

Except for Susan Assington, who spilled her drink — and even that seemed to happen in slow motion — they were frame-frozen in various attitudes of astonishment and disbelief.

It was Frederick Parmenger who broke the tension by laughing. "I must say, it's a damned original ruse — whatever it's for."

They all went into motion again, some with nervous laughter, some by dropping into chairs. Agatha sighed and tucked a rag curler beneath the sleeping cap that made her head look like a big mushroom. "Don't pay any attention to Melrose. He's being dramatic."

Only Charles Seaingham had the sense to see that Beatrice Sleight was conspicuously absent. His military bearing wilted as he looked at Melrose. "You're serious. But, my God, what ... where...?" He looked around the room, as if a body might materialize there on the rug at his feet.

"Outside," said Melrose. "Tom and I found her. Near the walk that leads to the Lady Chapel."

The frozen looks returned. "You can't mean —" began Grace Seaingham, and, seeing Melrose and Tommy meant it very well, put her hand on her husband's arm for support.

"You're certain she's dead?" asked Sir George Assington.

"Yes."

"Please — have a look, George," said Seaingham.

Melrose stopped him. "It might be as well to wait for police."

"They'll be hours getting here," said Seaingham.

"Actually," said Melrose, "I don't think so."

SEVENTEEN

1

T HUS, when the enormous brass ring on the door rose and fell twice, they acted as if it were the knocking on the gate in *Macbeth*.

When Jury was led into the living room by Ruthven — who wore an old striped robe as if it were his morning coat — Melrose wished he had had a bit more time to gather his wits about him.

Wit was the least of Lady Ardry's problems as openmouthed she hove herself from the rosewood settee, unmindful of the haircurlers sprouting from her cap, and yelled out, "Good God! Inspector Jury!" When they last met, he had been a chief inspector. And although Melrose had told her many times he was now a superintendent, she wasn't buying it, since she hadn't been in on the promotion. Jury smiled and shook her hand and Agatha, apparently having forgotten there was a dead woman in the snow, seemed about to do introductions all around.

Melrose saw Jury's eye light on Vivian Rivington, whose nervous little smile was as unconvincing as any murderess's.

She quickly stepped back from the firelight into the darker reaches of the shadows beyond.

Melrose cut across Agatha's voice-over, saying, "You'd better have a look outside, Superintendent."

Jury got up from where he'd been kneeling beside the body and knocked the snow from his trousers. "Shotgun." He beamed the torch Marchbanks had found for him around the area where the body lay. "Bloody mess."

"Sorry if the snow's mucked up. We didn't know there was a dead body lying here."

"I'm not blaming you. Where's the gun?" He seemed to be addressing the night more than Melrose Plant.

"Back in Seaingham's gunrack would be my guess." Melrose pointed. "The gun room — that's where he keeps all his sporting equipment — is just inside the solarium entrance." He returned his gaze to the ground. "How long's she been dead?"

Jury shook his head. "Not very long. Face and neck haven't even begun to get stiff, and the cold would help the cooling. Actually, you should be able to gauge time of death better." He snapped off the torch. "When did you last see her?"

"Nineish. Tom and I left right after dinner. They were all going into the drawing room for drinks.

Jury shrugged. "Probably knock off another hour there. I'd guess whoever did it just waited until everybody went to bed. She probably hasn't been dead much over an hour. What do you know about her?"

"That she wasn't popular."

"That," said Jury, "I can see."

From Charles Seaingham's study, Jury called the Northumbria station. Cullen was working the night shift and complaining bitterly about the gang in the shopping center who'd just made mincemeat of some of the furnishings in one of the pubs there. Jury broke the bad news that the night wasn't over for Cullen.

"Lord. Does this kind of thing always happen when you walk in?"

"I didn't shoot her."

There was the briefest of pauses while Cullen seemed to be debating this possibility, and then he said, "Aye. I'll call Durham and have them send their crew; they'll get there faster than I can. Is the bloody road to that godforsaken place plowed?"

"Yes."

"Hell." Cullen hung up.

When Jury told Melrose Plant that they'd have to wait for Cullen, Plant said, "Why? We've got a perfectly good policeman right here."

"Nobody asked for my help. We'll wait for Cullen. In the meantime — which one's Parmenger?"

In the course of the introductions, Susan Assington managed to place herself dead center in Jury's line of vision and instead of merely putting out her hand, put it out with a snifter of brandy. The little-girl timbre of her voice dropped a throaty notch or two as she said, "You need this. It's so beastly, what's happened." Her delicious little shiver rippled the satin dressing gown and sent its delicate sleeve a bit farther off her shoulder. Susan had taken over the spot near the fire which Vivian had lately vacated.

But Jury only smiled vaguely, overlooking gown and gleaming hair, to where Vivian was standing. She was looking down at her own tatty robe sadly, like a child who'd got mud all over itself.

"Miss Rivington, how are you? It's been a long time."

Melrose sighed. *Miss Rivington,* for God's sakes. And, he suspected, it would be *Superintendent....*

"Superintendent Jury," she said, her voice small and tight, as she tried to shove her hair around into some place other than where it was. "It's been years. Well, *a* year. Though you can hardly count that ... I mean, it was only for a moment...."

Melrose slugged back some brandy. They would go on this way in their dotage, he supposed. They were an equation he had never been able to figure. What clichés could they come up with now? Oh, yes.

"... it *is* still *Miss...?"*

Agatha answered for Vivian. "Yes, it is. It certainly is. She's not married that odious Italian yet."

Melrose removed Jury from Agatha's grasp and took him to where Frederick Parmenger was leaning gloomily against the bookshelves, communing with his usual whiskey and soda.

"Could I have a word with you, Mr. Parmenger?" asked Jury.

"Me? Why? Am I wearing more of a murderous look than usual? Granted, I couldn't stand the woman, but —"

"It's not about Miss Sleight."

Even Parmenger couldn't hide his surprise at this: "What else, in heavens name, could there be?"

When they were alone in Seaingham's study, Jury found himself loath to tell Frederick Parmenger about Helen. It was partly because he did not want to face the facts yet again. It was a small room, a sanctuary cozier than Grace's chapel. The wood was dark and burnished; the bookshelves held rare bindings protected behind glass; the desk was covered with news-clippings, magazines, a ship's decanter full of whiskey, a pharmacy lamp; the surround of the small fireplace was inlaid with beautiful tiles; the couch was tan leather, the easy chair dark-brown velvet with a well-worn nap. There were no ornaments but for some hand-carved ducks and pheasant. There was no artful arrangement of anything, just everything falling into perfect place — furnishings, books, paintings — as things probably fell into place in Charles Seaingham's mind.

The paintings were a small fortune in themselves. One Manet, one Picasso print, one Munch. And one Parmenger. That sat on the easel nearly in the middle of the room. Apparently Parmenger had been working on it in this room, which told Jury a lot about Seaingham's relations with his wife.

"It's about Helen Minton," said Jury, finally.

"Helen? What about her?"

Whether the catch in his voice was real or feigned, Jury wasn't sure. Still, he disliked breaking the news and stalled with, "Haven't you read the papers?"

"What papers? We've been snowed in here. What about Helen?"

"I'm sorry to have to tell you, Mr. Parmenger. There was an accident. Helen's dead." Parmenger sank farther into his chair. He made Jury think of someone trapped inside a bell, descending deeper into the sea. For a moment, Jury thought he literally did need oxygen, that he was going to pass out.

But he didn't. He rose and refilled his glass from the decanter on the desk, downing that drink and pouring another. The knuckles that gripped the glass were white.

"Impossible. How could she be dead?"

Jury took the question to be rhetorical. "When did you last see her?"

"Two months ago." Parmenger looked at Jury out of drowned eyes. "How can she be dead?"

"She was your cousin?"

As if the wider communion with his work would release

him from the narrower vision of death and police, Parmenger had risen from his chair and was standing before his painting of Grace Seaingham. "Yes," was all he said.

Jury waited for more.

Finally, Parmenger turned and said, "What the devil *is* all this? How is it some Scotland Yard policeman would be coming here telling me about Helen?"

"I knew her, very briefly. Quite by accident. She was — a charming woman." He watched Parmenger's face as if he expected it to splinter, sending out finer and yet finer cracks like a shattered windscreen.

He seemed to rock back on his heels, but beyond that, there was no more display of feeling. "Charming. Absolutely." He glared at Jury like a Roman who wanted to kill the messenger who'd brought the bad news. Indeed, an old coin might have borne the stamp of his handsome, chiseled face.

There was a silence as they studied one another. Finally, Jury said, "You haven't asked me how she died."

"Her heart?"

"No. She was poisoned."

Frederick Parmenger's response to this was to wheel about and once again take up his study of his own painting. After a few moments he said, "I don't believe it."

Jury looked at his watch. Twenty minutes since he'd called Cullen. It would take Cullen another twenty to get here, probably. He had plenty of time to wait out Parmenger, so he waited.

The portrait of Grace Seaingham showed her in a long-sleeved, ivory gown — quite plain — taking all of its richness from the material itself. Parmenger had done a wonderful job of rendering the texture of watered silk, as he had of winter light pouring through the window and striping the Chinese rug beneath her feet. The light made her look ghostly. Jury half-expected to see the dim outlines of the glass-fronted bookcases through her figure.

Parmenger stood, smoking a cigar, gazing at the portrait as if that was the only business they had between them. Finally he said, "My last duchess. Robert Browning? Well, it will damned well be my last portrait, I hope."

"You see yourself as the Duke of Ferrara, then?" Jury smiled.

Parmenger seemed surprised a policeman would know Browning. "No. More as Duke Ferdinand, I think. *Duchess of Malfi.* The one who went mad with lycanthropy. Thought he was turning into a wolf. Strange play." The look Parmenger had given Jury was almost as dangerous as a maddened animal, but it was a challenge withdrawn as he turned back to the portrait and frowned, seeing, perhaps, some imperfection.

"You don't appear unduly upset about Beatrice Sleight, Mr. Parmenger."

"I'm not. Indeed, I was incredibly relieved that it wasn't, after all, Grace. Grace is a truly good woman, tiresomely pious, but nobody's perfect." He tossed off a good half of his drink. "Beatrice Sleight was, on the other hand, a bitch. To be closeted with that woman for an hour would be enough to make you want to tear her to pieces — like a wolf, perhaps. To be snowed in with her for three days — my God, I'm surprised she lived as long as she did."

"Who had a real motive, do you think?"

"Everyone." He drank off the rest of the whiskey, poured himself another.

"One person in particular."

"Well, not I. Where was I at the time, et cetera? Is that next?" He relaxed in his chair, tilting his head as if to get a better line on his portrait, and answered his own question. "I was in my room," he said, still looking at the painting through narrowed eyes, critically. "There's something *wrong* with the damned thing." He was clearly more concerned with paint than dead bodies, unless it was an act. "In my room, like everyone else; we went up early. Couldn't stick one another for one more evening round the fire."

"You didn't hear anything? No shot, nothing?" asked Jury. Parmenger shook his head, got up, still with his whiskey in his hand, plucked a brush from a glass jar, mixed a little ocher with a bit of flake white, and drew a line so faint that Jury couldn't even see it. Parmenger dropped the brush back into the jar and returned to his chair.

"Nothing. The bedrooms are on the other side of the house altogether from the Lady Chapel. Hell of a wind, too. Don't think you'd have heard a cannon."

"You hadn't gone to bed yet, though," said Jury, looking at Parmenger's suit.

"No. I had to stay dressed in order to go outside and shoot Bea Sleight." He looked at Jury with the same impatience he had looked at his portrait.

"Can you think of anyone here who might have wished Helen Minton dead?"

"Here?" His laugh was a snort. "Good God, no. No one here knew her."

"Anywhere, then?"

Slowly, Parmenger shook his head. "Helen was too decent; she couldn't have had any enemies."

"Except for one," said Jury, getting up when he heard the sound of a car in the snow-muffled distance.

EIGHTEEN

1

DETECTIVE Sergeant Roy Cullen was Sunderland born and bred. As a consequence, although he did not welcome violence, he was not theoretically opposed to it. He preferred, however, to work this out of his system by dealing with disturbances at Newcastle football matches rather than by involving himself in alleged murders involving members of the upper classes. It was Cullen's opinion that most of the people collected here in Spinney Abbey might be considered as unemployed (or unemployable, according to the South of England) as the rest of the Newcastle-Sunderland area, and had got their money (and plenty of it) in ways that Cullen likened to finding stuff that dropped off the backs of vans. Making money by writing books was something Cullen couldn't quite square with his own thankless job and the salary it brought him.

There was the goddamned snow that he'd just waded through; put that together with the body of the woman lying in it he'd just had a look at and the football match that would probably be called this Saturday because of weather, and the murder up at Old Hall, and Sergeant Cullen might be excused for being in less than a good mood. He was seldom in a good mood, but he hadn't been put in a better one, what with that butler, whose nose hung on an invisible wire in air, taking hats and coats as if he meant to delice them.

As for the houseguests collected here in the drawing room: he felt all the friendliness for them he usually reserved for the Newcastle front line. Charles Seaingham made more writing for the papers in a year, he supposed, than Cullen would see in a lifetime; even the nightclothes of the women looked rich; the doctor — Harley Street probably — wore a silk dressing gown; the younger one, middle-aged and sharp-looking, was probably landed gentry with a string of racehorses; the intellectual (he identified anyone with hornrims that way) probably wrote smash-hit sexy plays or wasted his time in some equally well-paying pursuit. There was a kid, too. He looked okay, but definitely not the football type and probably spoiled rotten. And the coup de grace was Scotland Yard. It was not that Cullen was protecting his manor; it was just annoying as hell that Scotland Yard had got here first, almost as if people like the ones he was playing his eyes over now thought they had to have the top of the line: Fortnum's for their groceries; Scotland Yard for their murders.

Thus went Roy Cullen's reflections as his eyes canceled out each of them in turn. He offered them his version of a smile, which didn't make anyone happier, including Cullen, and said, "This is Constable Trimm."

Cullen liked Trimm. He liked him for his small stature, for his innocent and fresh-faced look — deceptive, of course; Cullen liked to carry Trimm around like a baby in a basket to make the unsuspecting subject of interrogation think nothing really horrid would happen, not with Trimm there. Trimm was worse than Cullen when it came to dealing with the *Lumpenproletariat* (the "lumps," as they called the back-street Sunderland scum and the Newcastle supporters — not much difference there) in ways that were not always totally ethical but which got hellish quick results. More subtle methods would have to be used with this abbey lot, the niceties of police ritual somewhat more strenuously observed.

"Sorry we've got to keep you up." Cullen's tone was as scorched as burnt toast. He couldn't help it; they looked so damned . . . *privileged*. "Durham police are going over the grounds. Who found her?"

"I — or, rather we — did."

The racehorse owner. And the kid. The kid would be easy enough, but he wasn't sure about the other one. "Your name, sir?" asked Cullen, elaborately polite.

"Melrose Plant."

"Earl of Caverness," snapped out the old one in the mobcap.

An earl. Cullen was probably right about the horses.

"Melrose Plant." Correction.

Cullen folded a stick of gum into his mouth and asked with a pleasantness he damned well didn't feel, "Which is it? You don't seem to agree."

"Take my word for it, will you?" said the horse owner.

Cullen shrugged. If titles were so thick on the ground they could pick them up and put them down at will, why the hell should he care? "You and the lad found her, that right?"

"That's right," said Tommy Whittaker, spelling his last name for the benefit of Trimm.

And here, the other old lady — more stately-looking than the first — put in, "He's the Marquess of Meares."

My God, thought Cullen. Still wet behind the ears and a marquess, yet.

"*Skis?*" Cullen leaned across the papers brought into Charles Seaingham's study by the Scene of Crimes man and stared at Melrose. He shook his head, smiled his unenergetic

smile. "Are you telling me, Mr. Plant, that you and this — "
He looked at Trimm, who supplied the name. " — young
Whittaker were out there *skiing* to a pub?"

Plant offered his cigar case around, got two turndowns, lit
up himself. "That's what I'm telling you. We were coming
back from the local — Jerusalem Inn, it's called — "

"Aye. Outskirts of Spinneyton. But could we please get
straight just why you felt compelled to *go* there in the first
place?"

"It was the snooker match, you see — so we made for
Jerusalem Inn. It was on our way back we stumbled over
her." Cullen stared at him, eyes narrowed. "Well, she wasn't
there *before*, Sergeant."

"How do you know that?"

"We took the same route. Tommy had it down — "
Melrose stopped. No sense in telling them more than he had
to.

But neither of these policemen were fools. Constable
Trimm looked up, his cherubic face bright in the lamplight
and asked, " 'Had it doon'? What's that mean?"

"Nothing, really. He'd marked the route carefully so we
wouldn't get lost on the way back."

"What time did you leave?"

"Nineish. After dinner."

"And what time back?" asked Cullen.

"When the pub closed. Time was called at eleven, and we
might have hung on for another ten minutes. Twenty minutes
to get back, that made it — "

"Eleven-thirty," said Trimm, as if Plant couldn't add.

"That's it, yes."

"Then what happened?" asked Cullen.

"The tips of the Whittaker lad's skis caught on the body
and he went over. I helped to pull him off."

Cullen shook his head, almost sadly, as if they had been listening to an amateur practitioner of the lying arts fail miserably once more. "Could we back up? You say you and Whittaker just suddenly decided to put on skis" (another headshake) "and go cross-country to the Jerusalem. Why did you get this sudden impulse on *this* night?"

"It seemed a good idea. Something of an adventure, you know."

"An adventure." Cullen looked up from the papers on the desk and said, "It puts you and the Whittaker boy right in the thick of it, doesn't it? More opportunity than anyone else had. The rest of them weren't out *skiing.*" He aimed a quick little dart of a smile at Melrose.

"I couldn't say, Sergeant. Not having had a report from the doctor on the time of death. And what was Beatrice Sleight doing out on the chapel walk at that time — ?"

"I'll ask the questions, if you don't mind."

Just what the inspector in *The Third Pigeon* would say. Melrose sighed.

"She was shot in the back with a .041, smallbore shotgun. The gun wasn't found in the snow. And where would you suppose it was?"

The question was no doubt rhetorical. "In the gun room."

"Which you had to pass on the way out and on the way in."

"You don't think we skied to the Jerusalem carrying a shotgun, do you?"

"Well, I don't know, do I?" Cullen folded another stick of gum into his mouth, smiling thinly. He looked back at the papers on the desk. "You're the Earl of Caverness?"

"No more. Plant's the family name."

"Why don't you use your title?"

"Because I don't want to."

Plant was obviously not conforming to the rules these non-lovers of the aristocracy had laid down for aristocratic behavior. Either that or they might have thought they had stumbled on some dark secret in Plant's past which would illuminate the present proceedings. "Sorry you don't approve."

"Political reasons? Like that communist Benn? You want to run for Commons, or something?"

"No. Surely my title or lack of one seems a little irrelevant, Sergeant, considering you've got a corpse in the snow."

"Are you good with firearms, Mr. Plant? Being an earl, and everything, I imagine you do a lot of hunting? Shooting?" Cullen smiled.

"No."

They regarded him with skepticism. How much more skeptical would they be of the Marquess of Meares, a crack shot?

Tommy, however, seemed to feel he had come through trumps up. "I think they liked me, especially the chubby one."

"Liked you? *Liked you?* My dear chap, I don't think it's a popularity contest; I mean they're not in there marking scorecards. What on earth do you mean?" Melrose felt twinges in his legs. He was sure he would awaken — if they ever let him get to bed — with cramp.

"I explained to them that I wasn't carrying a gun in my oboe case. Just a cue stick. Constable Trimm was fascinated. They're both of them snooker fans. Though I get the feeling they go more for the studied approach. You know, Ray Reardon and that lot. Nothing like Hurricane Higgins. I asked them if they'd kind of keep it under their hats about the Jerusalem, naturally."

"Naturally," said Melrose.

"Sorry if you think it's cold-blooded, me talking about snooker when poor old Beatrice Sleight — "

"Never mind," said Melrose. "If Cullen and Trimm can take it, I can."

2

AFTER five minutes with Charles Seaingham, Jury was glad he wasn't a writer or a painter — or at least one with no talent. Seaingham was a man who almost compelled one to believe him, not only because of his deep convictions, but because he neither embroidered nor evaded; he apparently believed in sweeping away the debris in order to look at the shell of the actual wreck. If the wreck were a badly done book or painting, Seaingham would make no attempt to refurbish the building.

In this case, the wreck was himself and he lost no time in getting down to the fact he'd been having an affair with Beatrice Sleight. "It was stupid of me. Done a lot of stupid things, but never over a woman. I only hope to hell Grace doesn't find out. I'd hate to hurt her. Well, I have no excuses; there it is." He half-raised his arms as if in some attempt to importune heaven, but let them drop again as he himself dropped into his leather armchair.

Stupid, perhaps. But Jury wondered if Seaingham's choice of Beatrice Sleight wasn't in some way to be expected. He bet it was more the grossness of her mind than the voluptuousness of her body that had made him vulnerable, ironically enough. Perhaps he was simply tired of fine-tuning his own mind in order to deal with the really good stuff — occasionally, even, with genius.

They were talking in his small study off the long gallery, dominated now by the portrait of his wife. On the table beside Seaingham's chair was a copy of *Skier*. Seeing Jury glance at it, he said, "MacQuade is the first really good writer to come along in some time. I hope unrequited love will help and not hinder him."

Jury smiled. "Meaning?"

"He's in love with Grace. But then I think rather a lot of men have been. Sometimes I think she should have been living in England in the 'twenties and had a *salon*. She'd have been wonderful. Grace bolsters egos; I don't. Cigarette?" He offered Jury a black leather box. "No, I'm afraid I don't. Sometimes I dislike my job because I'm not really out to 'get' our artists. They'll get themselves sooner or later."

"I read some of MacQuade's book. He could teach a survival course. What do you think of him personally?"

Seaingham's eyes rested on the Manet as if looking for the sustenance of great art to get him through a difficult time. "Likable. No harm in him, certainly. At least I don't think so. I daresay he can handle a rifle, but then so can the lot of us. We do grouse-shooting, pheasant, that sort of thing."

Jury said what he'd said to Parmenger: "Beatrice Sleight's murder doesn't seem to have touched you deeply — "

Seaingham cut in, sharply: "Her *murder*, yes. Her death, perhaps not. She was becoming — difficult. That sounds terrible, but it's true. Trouble."

"What kind?"

"She seemed to think she could hold me hostage somehow — or at least my good opinion about her vile books — by threatening to tell Grace about us."

"And would you have prevented that at any cost?"

"Meaning, did I kill her? Could have done, I suppose. But I didn't."

It seemed to Jury that Seaingham was expecting the next question to be other than it was. "Do you know of a woman named Helen Minton?"

Seaingham got up to pour himself a drink from the whiskey decanter. "Could I offer you a drink?"

He was playing for time, Jury thought. "No, thanks."

"What was the name of this woman — ?"

"Helen Minton."

"No, I don't think so."

"Read the papers today?"

"Haven't read them for days, no. We've been snowed in. Why?"

"Helen Minton was from London, living in Washington. The Old Town. Her body was found in Washington Old Hall two days ago."

"My God." Seaingham looked utterly perplexed. "I don't understand though what that has to do with —" He indicated the gallery, the solarium beyond.

"Helen Minton was Frederick Parmenger's cousin."

Jury thought Seaingham looked for the first time as if he really couldn't assimilate the information given him. He simply shook and shook his head.

"You never heard Parmenger mention her?"

"Well . . . no. Never. But then he talks little about himself. Have you asked Grace? She's more the one to inspire confidences."

Jury didn't answer that question. "My showing up here was not exactly fortuitous — as I imagine Sergeant Cullen would agree." Jury smiled. "I was on my way here to talk to Parmenger. And find, strangely enough, a dead body on your doorstep."

When Seaingham got up to replenish his glass, Jury noticed his hand was shaking. He imagined it would take a lot to unnerve Charles Seaingham.

But much less to unnerve MacQuade — or so Jury thought. MacQuade came near to stammering over answers to obvious questions. No, he had heard nothing that sounded like a rifle shot.

At Jury's elbow was a copy of *Skier*. "I've read reviews and some of the book. You seem to keep getting better." He pointed to *Skier*. "It was short-listed for two other awards."

"And the critics keep waiting for me to fall on my face.

But not on this particular book." He sat back, relaxed a bit. "You certainly are up on the literary scene, Superintendent. Charles Seaingham should have invited you to his party."

"He did." Jury smiled. "You must have loathed Beatrice Sleight."

"I did." The match that struck and flared reflected Mac-Quade's dark eyes like burning coals. "Ever read any of that trash she wrote? A good writer would gun her down — for cluttering up the landscape."

Very clever, thought Jury. Still, he was relieved that Mac-Quade's intelligence had overridden his rather adolescent manner.

"*But*," MacQuade went on, "if Bea Sleight was having an affair with Charlie — that would give me a hell of a lot less motive — " He stopped, apparently realizing he had over-played his man-of-the-world persona; he had strongly hinted here at his own feelings for Grace Seaingham.

But Bill MacQuade had so many personae, Jury was having some difficulty pinning down the real one.

Recovering his poor attempt to appear indifferent, Mac-Quade said, "And I hardly think I'd kill her because she was a penny-dreadful who couldn't write prose. Let me make things easier for you, Superintendent. I could shoot your eye out at a hundred feet and I'm a cross-country skier. I had to do a great deal of research for that damned *tour-de-force*" — he nearly shoved the book off the table — "and I could sur-vive easily overnight between here and Washington. In case that's somebody's theory. Except for Tommy Whittaker — and God knows, *nobody* would be stupid enough to think . . ." He paused.

Jury thought it was quite a dramatic ending to whatever scene or chapter MacQuade was leading the reader on with.

". . . would think *he* had anything to do with it. His aunt doesn't believe in guns — so he probably can't even shoot straight."

"Probably," said Jury. "Who told you about Helen Minton?"

"Parmenger." MacQuade looked at Jury, and another persona, maybe the real one, came through. "I never heard of her before now."

3

JURY walked into the study as Cullen was questioning Sir George Assington, and after waiting for a nod from Cullen, sat down in a chair against the wall. He felt as if he were a guest at a theater performance.

Not that Cullen, and certainly not Trimm, were in any way theatrical. There was, however, a bit of the monologuist about Sir George. Jury imagined Sir George was not unmindful of his reputation. He had certainly been discoursing long enough on hematology and blood types to make even Trimm decide to interrupt. "You coom up here to shoot, do you?"

"You mean pheasant and grouse, I assume, and not people? If you're asking me if I can handle a gun, yes, *Constable*, I can." Sir George emphasized the word just enough to let Trimm know the vast difference in their positions.

Cullen interceded and Trimm leaned back against the bookcases. "You're Mrs. Seaingham's physician, is that right?" When Sir George nodded, Cullen asked, "And what's ailing the lady, might I ask?"

"You mightn't," said Sir George. "I don't discuss my patients' conditions."

Jury watched Cullen folding yet another sliver of gum into his mouth. He was wearing his mild, noncommittal expression. "Not even with police?"

"Do you wish to subpoena my records?" asked Sir George, acidly.

"Not especially. I mean, it'd be simpler just to tell us."

Sir George said only, "Sergeant, I've an important meeting at the Royal Hospital tomorrow — or today, that is. Might I go? Or are we all under arrest?"

"Maybe," said Cullen. "Thing is," he went on, screwing up the gum paper and taking aim a basket, "you want to keep her alive, I expect. I mean that's what you've been trying to do, you being her doctor?"

Sir George sighed. "Mrs. Seaingham is, admittedly, in a poor state of health — "

"Well, she'll be in a hell of a lot poorer if someone shoots her."

"I'm a trifle confused, Sergeant. I thought we were talking about the bullet wound in the body of Miss *Sleight*." There was a distinct suggestion here that the Northumbria police couldn't remember the name of the victim.

Cullen leaned back and stuck his feet on the polished surface of Charles Seaingham's desk. "Oh, but that was a mistake, wasn't it? It was Mrs. Seaingham they meant to kill. That's the top and bottom of it." Methodically, he chewed away.

As if in imitation of Cullen's motion, Jury tipped his chair back against the wall and smiled slightly as the silence in the room was broken only by Sir George coughing before he said, "Grace? Why on earth would anyone want to kill Grace Seaingham?"

"Tell me and we'll both know. But from what I've heard of the Sleight woman, what'd she be doing going to say her prayers? And dressed in Mrs. Seaingham's cape? A bullet in the back on an unlit walk. Why don't you just tell us about Mrs. Seaingham's condition and save some trouble? Right, Superintendent?"

Jury only said, as Sir George turned to stare him down, resentful of this further intimidation, "Probably. I was wondering, though, if I could ask Sir George a question?" Cullen nodded.

"Do you remember a Dr. Lamson? Back in the nineteenth century."

Sir George laughed artificially. "Not quite that old, Superintendent."

Jury's smile was somewhat more disarming than Cullen's chewing gum. "Obviously not, Sir George. Didn't this Lamson poison a young fellow — ?"

Sir George broke in. "That's right. It was aconite. *Aconitum napellus,*" he added, his surprise at this policeman's knowing about the case giving way to his superior knowledge of poisons. "At that time, aconitine poisoning was nearly impossible to trace. Told his victim it was medi——" Sir George stopped suddenly.

"Medicine, that's right. A notorious case. Administered in a gelatine capsule, wasn't it?"

Sir George looked from Cullen to Trimm to Jury and slowly rose. "You are surely not suggesting that any medication I have been administering to Mrs. Seaingham . . ." His face was suffused with blood, as he fisted his hands and leaned on the desk. "Mrs. Seaingham has been unwell for some months now. She has lost weight and at first I was suspicious that she might be anorexic. Though knowing Grace as I do, such a thing seems impossible."

To his back, Jury said, "She hasn't been eating properly, is that it?"

Sir George looked at Jury as he might look at a specimen in formaldehyde. "That's correct. She has told me nothing at all except that she feels vaguely ill."

"Blood tests would surely — "

Sir George straightened, and with his military bearing, was an imposing figure. "Grace doesn't want any tests. Not with all my insisting. Simply says, with God's help, it'll go away."

Sir George stuffed the pipe in his mouth with an aggressive gesture, apparently incensed that Grace would choose God over Sir George.

"Oh, it'll go away all right," said Cullen, with a smile like splintered wood.

NINETEEN

1

GRACE Seaingham was an enigma.

Parmenger had captured it all, had gotten behind that cool, blond detachment to the combination of opposites beneath it: to the chilly beauty, but warmth of manner; to the glasslike fragility, but inner toughness; to the sanguine attitude, but businesslike approach.

It was that with which she confronted Jury's question about her husband and Beatrice Sleight. "I've known for some time, of course."

Her directness was disorienting. It was as if, having locked away the truly valuable knowledge — more than the person she talked to would ever crack open — she could afford to deal in the small change of frankness.

She went on in that mild (and, to Jury, vaguely irritating) manner: "In a way, I could hardly blame him. After I got over being hurt," she added, as if apologizing for a childish infraction of some adult rule.

"Why should you get over it? Why should you even try?" Jury had taken out his notebook but was not really taking notes. He doodled. It helped him think.

Grace Seaingham looked indulgent as she tilted her head and smiled. "Don't you think we should — well, take the longer view, Superintendent?"

He smiled back. "I think you mean the higher view. Forgiving all sorts of things, because God would?"

She moved her head, that pale blond hair that reminded Jury of angel's hair, but her smile stayed in place. "Yes. Because God would."

"I don't know what God has in mind."

She looked away, down at the hands clasped in her white satin lap. It was a handsome dressing gown. He wondered if she always wore white.

Jury went on: "It must have been . . . difficult for you having her here. As a matter of fact, I'm rather surprised you'd want to have a houseparty so near to Christmas, Mrs. Seaingham."

"I didn't want to, really. But Charles is used to London. I love this isolation; my husband doesn't. He's used to having lots of people around. You can't keep a man like Charles . . . locked up, can you?"

Thinking of the high stone walls of the abbey, Jury wondered if that wasn't more or less what she had in mind. It was she, she had told him earlier, who had scouted it out and bought it. Grace Seaingham apparently had packets of money of her own, handed down to her by a father whom she loved to describe as having been "in trade."

"Mrs. Seaingham, why would Miss Sleight be wearing your cape and be walking to the Lady Chapel? From what I've heard, she wasn't an especially devout sort of person."

"I've no idea. She rather coveted that cape, I know. Do you think the, ah, murderer could possibly have tossed it over her — since it was white — to hide her body?" Grace Seaingham looked bewildered. "But I simply have no notion as to why someone would want to . . . murder her."

"She didn't sound very popular . . . but that's not the point.

I don't want to distress you, but after all it *was* your habit to go to the chapel late at night, wasn't it?"

Her control seemed to be cracking just a little: "You're not suggesting it was *me* someone wanted to — ?"

Jury nodded. "Your idea about hiding the body in the snow might be a good one, except the shot went *through* the cape. So she must have been wearing it. That solarium is never used, you said, in winter. It's dark. Someone might easily have been waiting in the dark and seen the person he or she expected.to see, given that long and hooded cape. You. Only it wasn't you."

"I have no enemies, Superintendent. Certainly not amongst *these* people. It's impossible."

"Tell me about them. You've known them for some time?"

"Some longer than others. I just met the Assingtons a short time ago. And Bill MacQuade is perhaps more my husband's friend than mine." From the slight tinge in her cheeks, Jury wondered if that were true. Or if, perhaps, she wished it were. Grace Seaingham certainly did not strike him as a lady who would have a lover — most certainly not under the same roof as her husband. She went on: "He's a marvelous writer. Charles thinks the world of him. And my husband's good opinion is not lightly bought. Not bought at all, really."

"Not even by Her Majesty?" Jury smiled and doodled.

She seemed perplexed. "I beg your pardon?"

"It was just I heard some rumor of a possible knighthood."

Grace smiled. "Her Royal Highness has not, to my knowledge, painted a picture or written a book she wants viewed or *re*viewed."

Jury looked at her. She was certainly nobody's fool. "I only meant that everyone has a pressure point. Push it hard enough, who knows what might happen?"

She simply didn't comment.

"What were MacQuade's relations with Beatrice Sleight?"

"Relations? He didn't have any. I mean, I don't believe

he'd ever met her before this week. Bill's very — " she seemed to be having difficulty finding words to describe him " — withdrawn."

"Um. And the Assingtons? Did they know her at all?"

"Very slightly. I think at one of her book signings they might have met her. But then anyone who keeps up with the literary scene — if you could call Bea 'literary' — " she added wryly, and let it go. "Sir George is rather a well-known doctor, and Susan is his third wife."

"The others — except for Mr. Plant and his party — I take it are good friends?"

"Yes. Vivian Rivington's poetry impressed Charles. He was at a small party her publisher gave. He was delighted to have her bring the others. Charles thinks the more people, the better. Lady Ardry, I understand, is an old friend of Betsy — Lady St. Leger."

Jury smiled. He seriously doubted it. "Go on."

"We've known Betsy for years. She's taken over Meares Hall."

"Taken over?"

"I mean that after Tommy's parents — Irene and Richard — died, Betsy was really the only one who seemed to care enough to keep him. Believe me, she doesn't need either the money or the privilege. The St. Legers have a pedigree as long as your arm. Betsy was sister to Tommy's grandfather. He was the eleventh Marquess of Meares."

"An old family."

She nodded. "And Betsy simply dotes on Tommy. She has no children of her own. Her husband Rudy died a few years ago. He was a painter, too. Though Freddie wouldn't agree." She smiled.

"How long's Parmenger been here?"

"Several weeks. Doing my portrait." She colored a little, as if Jury might think this a self-indulgence. "Charles insisted."

"I've seen it. It's wonderful."

"Freddie's got quite a reputation."

"Do you know any of his family?"

Puzzled, she shook her head. "He never speaks of them."

"Not of his cousin? Her name was Helen Minton."

It was clear Grace Seaingham thought it decidedly odd Jury would know Parmenger's cousin. "No, never. And you said 'was.' Is she dead, then?"

Jury found he had been drawing Father Rourke's square on the pad. He threw it down. "Yes. Northumbria police found her in Washington Old Hall just two days ago. She'd been poisoned."

Grace Seaingham's skin was as white as her gown. She rose slowly from her chair, seemingly more disturbed by this death of a stranger than by the implied threat to her own life. "But that's dreadful. Poor Freddie . . . does he know?"

"Yes. I told him. Since you've been snowed in here, you hadn't got the newspapers. Until the autopsy was done, it was just put down to accidental death." Jury paused. "Has Mr. Parmenger not been away from Spinney Abbey, then, in all the time he's been here?"

Even the small frown did not seem to disturb the placidity of that expression. "Yes, of course he has. We all have. Into Durham, to Newcastle. Why?"

"I just wondered if he'd been to Washington. Seeing that it's so close. And of such historical interest."

"You mean — to see his cousin. I would certainly think he'd have mentioned it, if he had. As you say, it's so close. I'd have been delighted to have had her here."

But perhaps Frederick Parmenger wouldn't have, thought Jury.

2

"It's taken you long enough, Inspector, to get around to us," said Lady Ardry, nodding her head in the direction of Lady St. Leger and Vivian, who pulled her robe more tightly about her and looked everywhere but at Jury. "I'd be glad to give you my impressions —"

"Thank you, Lady Ardry. I'm sure you've kept your eyes and ears open. But at the moment, I'd like to talk with Lady St. Leger."

Agatha had started to rise and sat down, plump, again, obviously unhappy at playing second fiddle to her friend.

Elizabeth St. Leger apparently felt more like getting the business over with than in the protocol of police interrogation. "If you have some questions to put to me, Superintendent, I'd be happy to answer them. Though I'm afraid I haven't much to tell you." As she started to rise, Agatha laid a plump hand on her arm. "No reason Mr. Jury can't take us both together. After all, we've known one another for years. He's well aware *I've* no part in the beastly business."

Lady St. Leger smiled and rose. "That might be true for you, Agatha. Unfortunately, I can't offer a long-standing acquaintance with Scotland Yard as a defense." Her eyes actually twinkled.

"I'm sorry if I seem to be making light of this — business," said Lady St. Leger, once settled across from Jury in Seaingham's study. "To be honest, I'm more concerned, I think, about Tom's — my nephew's — involvement than about Beatrice Sleight's death. I'm not sorry she's dead, and, as they say up here, that's the top and bottom of it." Elizabeth St. Leger smiled slightly and tapped her stick on the floor. It was silver-knobbed and resembled Melrose Plant's, though Jury doubted it was a sword-stick.

"You didn't much like Miss Sleight."

Elizabeth St. Leger seemed to want to choose her words carefully. "I couldn't stand her." A brief smile accompanied this. "So if you're looking for a motive" — she tapped the stick — "look no further."

Jury smiled too. "If 'dislike' were enough of a motive, we'd be picking up dead bodies on every corner. No, you'll have to do better than that."

He was amused at Lady St. Leger's slight frown, as if she were, indeed, *trying* to do better by way of convincing Jury. And then it occurred to him that that might indeed be the case. How far would she go to protect her nephew, who had been found on the spot? He broke into his own reflections. "If you're worried about your nephew, it doesn't appear he could have had much opportunity. For one thing, he was with Mr. Plant. And I know Mr. Plant. Have done for years."

She looked him up and down as if reevaluating his credentials for the job, given his admitted friendship with this rather trying guest who seemed to be causing nothing but trouble, what with turning up dead bodies and, as if it might be the source of the trouble, giving up his title: "Mr. Plant is a pleasant, but distinctly iconoclastic, young man."

"Oh, he's that, I suppose. But he's also an alibi for Tom. So don't be too tough on him."

She smiled. "Yes, he is that. Well, as for me: I went up with the others not long after dinner."

Jury had his notebook out. "What time would you say?"

"Um. Ten, ten-thirty. Ten-thirty, yes. I remember hearing the clock chime the half-hour. We none of us wanted to linger too long, and I myself am really supposed to be in bed earlier." She tapped her breast. "Touch of angina. The doctors want me to have my rest. Or I might not be lingering too long myself," she added, with a somewhat macabre touch. "My bedroom's at the other end of the house. All the bedrooms are."

"You didn't hear anyone moving about? I mean, doors opening, closing, that sort of thing."

"Yes, of course. We don't all of us have private baths. The abbey isn't completely modernized. So I did hear footsteps, yes. But paid no attention. As a matter of fact, I myself came downstairs to get a book. Shouldn't have done. My doctors don't like me using the stairs too much. I came in here."

The library was across the large entrance room, next to the dining room.

"What time was that?"

"A bit after I went up." She seemed to be counting on her fingertips. "Fifteen minutes later, perhaps."

"See anyone? Any servants, even?"

"Narry a soul, Superintendent." She spread her arms. "So there you are — no alibi. Tom — " She stopped, her look worried.

"But he has one."

"I would like to know what on earth he was doing out on skis — with your friend, Mr. Plant." Again, that seeming reassessment of Jury.

Jury smiled. "Winter sports. I couldn't say. How long have you known the Seainghams?"

"Ages. Since before the marquess — Tom's father and mother died. The Seainghams were friends of theirs; they — I mean Charles and Richard — did a lot of shooting together."

"And you, did you join them?"

"How very astute. If you want to know whether I can shoot, yes, I can."

Jury noticed she seemed trying to grip her walking stick in such a way as to hide the arthritic twist of one or two of the fingers.

Not the crack shot she once was, perhaps. But Jury was

impressed, not only by lady St. Leger's self-possession and —
élan was perhaps the word — but by her determination that,
if the Marquess of Meares's alibi fell through, she was going
to be there to catch it.

Her gray eyes glittered back at him; they reminded him a
little of Helen Minton. Jury wondered if he would ever inspire the sort of love in a woman that Tommy Whittaker obviously did in Lady St. Leger.

"I wonder if you'd ask Miss Rivington to step in on your
way to bed?"

3

BUT for the fact that she was sporting a flannel dressing gown
several sizes too big for her, and that her hair was uncombed,
Vivian Rivington looked exactly as she had the first time he
had met her, years ago and in similar circumstances. And
seeing her now in her unflattering getup, their last meeting
(more of a collison than an accident, with Vivian on the arm
of her Italian fiancé) might never have happened. Then she
had walked in looking like something turned out by de la
Renta. Right now, in her drab bathrobe, she looked more like
something turned out of the house.

A log in the fireplace split and spilled sparks. For some un-
accountable reason, he was taken back years and years to his
childhood and his favorite book, where Mole and Badger sat
together in a hollowed-out tree. What an unattractive image
for the two of them, he thought, smiling — add Melrose
Plant as Ratty, and he'd have the three of them. He stabbed
an arrow through a heart on his pad and then stopped smiling. Instead, he felt an unbearable longing for something he
had never had — unsure, even, what it was.

She looked so damned human standing there in that bathrobe and those old carpet slippers he wanted to reach out and
hug her. And, he suspected, rather more.

"Hullo, Vivian."

"Hello. It's Agatha's, in case you're wondering."

Confused, but laughably confused, he smiled and said, "What?" It was wonderful, in a way. It was as if they'd met, not once in the last several years, but every day on the corner, with only the immediate to talk about, having told one another everything else.

"This bathrobe," she said, narrowing her eyes. "You're staring at it. I forgot mine so I borrowed one of Agatha's. She always brings enough in her cases for three." She smiled briefly, warmly, and then apparently thinking smiles not suited to the occasion, frowned.

"It suits you. Sit down."

Again, he wanted to laugh, she looked so cross. She sat perched on the edge of the chair Grace Seaingham had recently left. This the two women seemed to have in common, some desire to punish themselves for as yet uncommitted sins. There were many more chairs in the room and more comfortable ones. But Vivian had never been one to make a pleasure-trip out of anything, not even Italy (he bet), and certainly not murder.

As he pulled his notebook toward him he saw her surreptitiously try to comb her hair with her hands. When he looked up, she stopped. Her principal vanity was worry over whether she might appear vain. "I don't know why you want to talk to me about all this. It's awful, of course. But you know perfectly well I didn't have anything to do with it." Although she extended her own arm along the beautifully carved arm of the chair in what was meant to be a graceful gesture, the grace was lost in the shortness of the sleeve. Agatha's arms were quite stubby.

"You sound doubtful." Jury drew another fat heart and was now stabbing it with another arrow.

"Oh, don't be silly. We only just got here yesterday — I mean, now it would be day-before — we none of us knew

anyone here until then. Except I knew Charles Seaingham."
He leveled a look at her and she added quickly, "But only a
little. I only saw him the one time."

"Um. Okay. What I want is your impression of these people. Such as: who do you think did it?"

She scratched her head, which didn't help her hair, and
said, "I'm absolutely — I can't get over it. She was sitting
across from me at dinner. Now she's dead."

The sad and lingering look of the old Vivian seemed to
etch itself on his face, as if she were drawing her own likeness
there. Jury looked back at the fresh page of his notebook.
"It's rotten, I know. I'm sorry." He put the notebook down.
"Maybe it's just as well your not knowing them. At least you
can be objective."

Relaxing a little — but not overly — she sat back in the
chair and crossed her ankles. Her carpet slippers were also
several sizes too large. "She wasn't very nice. Well, why not
say it? She was pretty awful."

"Beatrice Sleight?"

"Of course. She was the one that got murdered."

"I know. But she was wearing Grace Seaingham's cape."

Vivian lurched forward in her chair. "You're not saying
someone wanted to kill *Grace Seaingham*?"

"It would appear so. Beatrice Sleight was shot in the back
wearing that ermine cape and on the walk leading to the
chapel."

"My God," said Vivian, weakly. "But Grace is so . . . good.
Almost saintly."

"Maybe. You didn't hear anything, then? No pistol shot?
No commotion, no scream, no anything?"

Vivian shook her head. "The bedrooms are way away from
that end of the house. I can't imagine Beatrice outside the
house in the snow. Definitely a comfort-loving type."

"You all went to bed at about the same time?"

"Yes." She was silent for a while, twisting the tasseled belt of the robe. Then she shrugged. "It's too much to take in, really. I didn't get any vibrations at all about Grace Seaingham. I mean, that anyone disliked her. I'd have thought the opposite to be true. She really *is* the perfect hostess. When Beatrice Sleight was going on and on about titles, and especially Melrose's — these are his slippers," she added inconsequentially, " — it was Grace who simply put a stop to it. I'm stumped. But, of course, it's Melrose you should be talking to. He notices things. Well, *you* know that. He's helped out before."

"To say the least. Thanks, Vivian. You should get some sleep."

But she sat there, clearing her throat. "Aren't you going to ask me?"

"What?" He stabbed a new heart with a new arrow.

The single, unconcerned syllable irritated her to death. "Why I'm not married." She blinked and returned her attention to the tasseled cord.

Innocently, Jury asked, "Is it germane to the murder?" Though why he had this urge to pay her back for untold injuries which she had, actually, never done him, he didn't know. *Sadist*, he thought. But he still wanted to laugh when she rose and tried to make a queenly exit in her outsized robe and slippers. "Seemed like a nice bloke to me. Of course I only met him the one time."

He was delivering the last of this little speech to the door which had nearly, if not quite, slammed.

3

THE others were off to bed, Cullen having finished his questioning and the team from Durham having taken the body away. "I'm knackered, man." He yawned and sank into a chair in Seaingham's study. "Trashed. So what've we got,

Trimm?" He looked halfway over his shoulder at his constable.

Trimm was examining the shotgun taken from the little room next to the solarium that was the abbey's storage space for sporting equipment.

"This." He broke the single-barreled shotgun, peered inside as if the barrel might offer up some new clue, snapped it shut again, and laid it on the desk.

"Run it through ballistics."

"Got to be it," said Trimm. "No other .410 in there. Only a couple of ten bores and some rifles — "

"Nothing's got to be *anything*, Trimm. Run it through ballistics."

"They've nowt — "

"Hell," said Cullen, staring at the ceiling. "Run it — "

Jury broke into the family squabble. "What did the scene of crimes man figure was the range?"

"From the way the pellets scattered, over two feet at least." Cullen picked up the report. "Maybe four, five feet. Wound was pretty big. There was some tattooing. Of course, the cape was thick." Cullen shrugged.

"Straight shot?"

"As a dye."

"The killer could have stood inside the door of the solarium. But no one heard the shot. Even with the rooms being way on the other side, still — "

"Silencer," said Trimm, not offering more than he had to.

"*What?* Why the hell would there be a silencer for a rifle lying about?"

"This Seaingham said he was having trouble with poachers. Said his gamekeeper found it" — Cullen indicated the short cylinder lying on the table — "where the bloke must have dropped it." Cullen sighed and chewed his gum. "None of 'em really got alibis. Motives are fuzzy. . . ." Cullen closed his eyes sleepily.

"Anyway, we can discount Plant, Lady Ardry and Vivian Rivington —"

Cullen's eyes opened. "Oh, aye? And why's that, man?"

"Because I know them, have done for years." He didn't add that Plant had helped him out with several cases. Jury didn't imagine amateur sleuths went down a treat with Cullen.

"So maybe they've changed." He closed his eyes again.

Jury ignored the comment. "And the Whittaker boy — he was with Plant. . . . Why are you shaking your head?"

"Ten minutes, that's why. Ten minutes when he skied on ahead and your friend wasn't with him."

"Well, Roy, if you can tell me how a man wearing skis could get into that gun room, arrange for his victim to be conveniently waiting on the walk wearing someone else's cloak, shoot her, put the gun back, and then fall all over her still with skis on . . ." Jury left the sentence unfinished.

Trimm finished it for him. "Means nowt."

4

IT WAS nearly six but he knew he wouldn't sleep. Jury stood in the mysterious purple light of dawn looking down at the place where the body of Beatrice Sleight had lately lain, only the deep imprints of the shoes of Cullen's men to bare witness to what had happened. He walked the short distance to the chapel and pushed open the heavy door.

The draught blew the tiny candle flames, snuffing out one or two of them. He thought of Grace Seaingham coming here every morning, every night, like someone keeping an assignation.

Jury sat down and studied the plaster figure of the Virgin and thought that somehow Grace Seaingham had taken on that pellucid look in the way that one takes on the look of another human being one is used to being around.

He thought of Father Rourke's paradigmatic square. What the priest had described was a net of belief of such intricate weave that Jury couldn't begin to understand it. Was it all supposed to be such a mystery? Wasn't it supposed to be simple? *Contradictions,* the priest had said, *opposites.* From his back pocket he drew out the cover torn from the journal on which Father Rourke had drawn his square, that square which was universal enough to account for everything. He looked at the *H* in one corner. He added to two other corners a *D* and an *R*. Helen, Robin, Danny. He thought of the pert, blond young woman in Robbie's picture who bore no resemblance to him; of the Bonaventure School that took children who had nowhere else to go.

She had given him the only name she knew to give him, since he wasn't hers to begin with, Jury was sure.

He looked at the square. It was the fourth corner he wondered about now: the murderer?

How long he sat there he didn't know, but when he finally walked out of the chapel it was light. In the near distance, out there across the long sweep of snow and the broken wall, there was one thin strand of pale gold and the snow looked a deep lavender as the light crawled slowly across it.

5

"GET up," said Jury, preemptorily, handing Melrose Plant a cup of tea.

Pushing himself up from his pillows, Melrose looked about him like a victim of snowblindness. "Up? What are you talking about. I only just got down. My God." He turned his head toward the windows. "Dawn. It's only dawn." He sipped the tea. "This stuff's cold. Cold tea at dawn. Is the firing squad ready?"

"You've been spoiled by Ruthven with his scones and hot tubs. Come on. We're going to the Jerusalem Inn."

Plant sank back, trying to burrow into the pillows. "You're mad. I always suspected it. Snooker at dawn, is that it? Right round the twist you are. Don't you realize you and those two you brought along from the Spanish Inquisition kept us up until nearly five, and now it can't be more than six. Besides that, you bring me cold tea. And I'm paralyzed."

"Only from the mouth down. Come on. It's after seven."

"I am *not* getting out of this bed without my tea." Melrose pushed himself up, leaned over and yanked the tapestry bell-pull. "I shall have a fresh pot. Then I shall consider rising. Anyway, how is it your mind's working after everything that happened last night? What'd old Vivian have to say, anyway? I hope they supply toast with my tea."

Jury smiled. The question about Vivian was slotted into the conversation like a man sticking coins in a machine and walking away hoping he'd hit the jackpot.

" 'Old' Vivian? She's a good ten years younger than either of us."

Testily, Plant said, "Well, but I've known her for a hundred years. Don't you wonder why she's not married to the 'odious Italian,' as Agatha calls him? You met him in Stratford. The one with fangs."

"Yes." There was no point in rushing Melrose Plant, who would lie there like a boulder until he'd had his tea.

"You're a fount of curiosity, aren't you? She won't tell *me*. I don't think she's going to marry him."

A knock on the door brought a pretty between-stairs maid with a tray. Seeing two of them where she expected one, she said, "Oh, I'm sorry, sir. I'll just get another cup."

Jury moved away from the french window and took the tray and smiled at her. "Don't trouble yourself. Mr. Plant doesn't need one."

The girl looked up at him — it was a distance — and she couldn't seem to help her hand straying up to her white cap. She smiled. "Very well, sir. Thank you, sir."

Said Melrose Plant, after she'd scuttled away, "Funny. Give me my tray."

"Sure. And ten minutes to drink your damned tea." Jury picked a slice of toast from the silver rack and munched it, leaning against the window.

Having drunk his tea in testy, morose silence, Plant put down his cup and looked at Jury. "Jerusalem Inn. Is that what you said? For Lord's sakes, it doesn't open until eleven."

"I know. But Robbie'll be there. He cleans the place."

"Robbie? Robbie who?"

"Robin Lyte, the one Helen Minton must have been looking for. I think he was her son. Well, it must have been a shock, mustn't it?" Jury looked across the snow to the chapel and still wondered about the fourth letter.

TWENTY

1

THE little village of Spinneyton, perhaps because it was Christmas Eve, was sleeping in; not a soul did they see save for one grimy child building an equally grimy snowman that listed sadly in front of a falling-down terraced house, as if trying to match the house's bout with gravity.

Spinney Moor was desolate and veiled in mist, remnants of which floated away and across the road leaving rents in the diaphanous cloth of the fog.

Looking at this bleakness, Tommy shivered and said, "I'm glad to come along, but what good will my talking to Robbie do?"

"Well, you said you were teaching him the game, and I imagine he trusts you. Maybe he remembers more than he thinks he does. Maybe he'll tell you," said Jury.

"I doubt it. Poor Robbie . . ." Once more he looked out at the moor, and said, "Looks haunted, doesn't it?"

"Probably is," said Melrose, sleepily, from the back seat.

"Still as the grave," said Tommy.

"The village is probably empty because they've all gone

down in the peat bogs. Bloated corpses will rise from the bogs, stalk about greenly and strangle us all in our sleep. As long as they get Agatha, I won't complain."

"You're in a jolly old mood, aren't you?" said Jury, as he braked in the courtyard of the Jerusalem. A slant of sunlight dazzled the snow that was lying so neatly on roof and eaves they looked iced like a wedding cake. Frost shone like separate stars on the mullioned panes, behind which Robbie's face appeared, distorted by the wavering old glass into something gargoyle-like. When Jury knocked, the face disappeared for some time before he finally opened the door.

"Hullo, Robbie," said Jury. "I know it's not opening hours yet, but we need to talk with the Hornsbys. Police business, see." Jury showed him his warrant card and said to the slightly scared look, "Just routine stuff, Robbie."

The brown hair, which the boy shoved up from his forehead, the pale brown eyes, the face, which before Jury had seen nothing in, perhaps because it was malleable, like putty — in it now Jury thought (or did he merely imagine it?) traces of Helen, like a face floating under water.

Nell Hornsby appeared through the curtained alcove at the rear of the bar. "Well, *hullo!* Something wrong?"

"Nothing wrong, no. I just wondered if I could have a word with you."

"Aye. I'll just be getting Chrissie's porridge." She disappeared through the curtain.

Robbie — big, rawboned, clumsy — went on slowly sweeping. Robin ... a common alias for the criminal, the outcast, the disenfranchised. Jury saw his face brighten up a bit when Tommy said something to him about playing a frame.

Lighting a cigar, Melrose said, "What's the connection? I mean between this gangly lad and ... everything else? What's the connection between your Helen Minton and all of it?"

"Frederick Parmenger, for one thing."

"*Parmenger?* Why?"

"I think he's Robbie's father. According to a servant who's been with the Parmengers for years, Edward Parmenger went wild over Helen's pregnancy. He must have known, you see. And he didn't like the idea of his son and Helen —"

"That's not surprising. At their age, and in the circumstances. One does tend to bridle a bit when one finds one's charge in a family way."

"If *one* had a way of seeing everything in a totally Victorian way. But this isn't the turn of the century we're talking about. And why *then* — I mean, later on — this attack of conscience where Edward leaves Helen the house, instead of leaving it to his own son? First he wants to get rid of Helen; next, he pulls her back. I think it's pretty strange."

Nell came back to the bar. "There now. What are you wanting?"

"Old Peculier," said Melrose, slapping down a pound note on the slick surface.

She looked confused. "It's not opening time yet; afraid I can't give you drink . . . that is, unless —" She looked at Jury.

"I'll turn a blind eye to the licensing laws." She drew off the dark ale for Melrose.

"Tell me about Robbie."

She stopped suddenly in the act of wiping dripping foam from the glass. "Robbie? What about him?"

Jury smiled, offered her a cigarette. "I don't know. That's what I'm asking you."

The smile seemed to stop her briefly in the act of lighting up, and she colored a little. "Aye. Well, he started working for us, for his keep. His meals, I mean, and some pocket money. Poor boy. Came here when he left school, like I told you. And he's such a good lad. So we took him in. He lives with us, now."

"Bonaventure School?"

"Aye."

"There's a Robert Lyte buried in the cemetery of the Catholic church in Washington. Could that have been some relation?"

Early as it was, Nell Hornsby didn't say no to a drink. As she turned to the optics, she said, "Robert? Well, it could be. I don't know. But why're you so on to Robbie? Done something wrong? Not him, I can't believe it."

"No, of course not."

Melrose, the Old Peculier having coaxed him into a better humor, let Jury have his talk with Nell Hornsby as he himself wandered into the cold back room to watch Tommy Whittaker and Robbie. Robbie held his cue stick with much of the same awkwardness as he had held his broom, but with a great deal more delight. Tommy made a safety shot, leaving a long shot on the red for Robbie. Not too easy; not too hard. Robbie missed.

Tommy was too good a player not to lose sight of everything else, and that meant Robbie, at least for the moment. He potted the red with just enough topspin to bring it back in a perfect position to pot the black.

Melrose was concentrating on Tommy's play, when a voice at his elbow said, "He should just hit the black one."

He looked off and around and could not find the source of the voice until he looked down. The owner was holding a doll almost as big as she was. A child. He bounced a glance with plenty of reverse spin off the little girl, hoping she'd go away.

Not only did she not go away, she insisted upon her point. "Why doesn't he *just* hit the *black* one, instead of doing it with that white one, if that's the one he wants to get rid of?" She frowned at Melrose, as if he were responsible for this ridiculous going-the-long-way-round.

Melrose considered. She couldn't be more than five or six and here she was with her huge dumb doll, rewriting the rules. "Be*cause*" — acid dripped from the syllable — "there are rules. Run along, now, and dress your doll."

"She *is* dressed," said the little girl, who apparently took his comment as an invitation to join him and slid herself up on the bench, adding, inscrutably, "or *he* is." Her look at the doll was doubtful.

He tried to watch Tommy's play, but could only revile himself for adding that comment about the doll. She had scouted out interest; she would take full advantage of it.

"Her dress is pretty, isn't it?"

Despite the sweetness of the voice and the bare glimpse he had got of luminous eyes, Melrose was not falling for her. He kept his eyes on Tommy's cue stick — Robbie had stood back, forgotten like a broken-armed statue in a formal garden — and refrained from answering.

"The swaddling clothes underneath make him bunchy."

If he could stand Agatha's non sequiturs, Melrose thought, he could certainly deal with this smaller and, admittedly, far more attractive version. "I am confused," he admitted freely, lighting another cigar, hoping nicotine would deliver him from a brain swimming in the currents of early-morning Old Peculier. "I *thought* the doll was a girl-child."

"She is," said Jury, who had come in from his talk with Nell and with a pint of her best bitter. He sat down on the hard bench, thus pressing the little girl closer to Melrose. "Her name's Alice."

"Tell me, Alice. Why is there this confusion about your doll?"

The brown eyes regarded him with total disgust: "Not *me!* Her!" She shoved the doll in his face and then added in her cryptic way: "Or him. I'm *Chrissie.*"

Making a break of 147 would have been nothing compared with understanding Chrissie. Her mother really should tell her the difference between the sexes, he thought, settling back to watch the *Wunderkind* run a break up to fifty before he seemed to realize he had forgotten his friend, Robbie. Tom missed an easy shot (quite deliberately) and then stood back so Robbie could have a go. Robbie missed an easier. They were now lighting up cigarettes from the packet Tommy had cadged from Jury. They were talking, or, at least, Tom was having a sort of one-sided chat with his friend.

"Whatever do you expect to learn?" asked Melrose of Jury, as Chrissie began removing her doll's dress with no regard for modesty.

"I don't know. I don't know how much he remembers about Danielle Lyte. She died years ago, according to a friend of Helen Minton's."

The doll, Melrose saw, was wrapped in what looked like torn-up strips of sheeting. Probably she meant it to be underclothes. Chrissie set about neatening the strips.

"I still don't see the connection with the murders. Even supposing he *is* the son of —" Melrose looked down at Chrissie, always operating under the assumption that children heard everything and filed it away to blackmail you with at some later date, and said, circumspectly, "— you know, those two. Assuming he is," — Melrose's head inclined toward Robbie — "why would she have to die for it?"

"Maybe she was just bad," said Chrissie.

He *knew* she had been sitting there absorbing every word. "When I want your opinion, I shall ask for it," said Melrose, pretending not to notice the small tongue suddenly stuck out in his direction. Her limpid brown gaze turned to Jury. "I guess I'll have to put him back."

Jury nodded. "You really ought. Mary and Joseph probably miss him."

Mary and Joseph? Melrose refused to have anything to do with this runic conversation. Chrissie took up the doll and pushed past Jury and ran out of the room.

"I've got to go to Newcastle Station to collect Wiggins. Care to come along?"

"Sergeant Wiggins! Up here in the frozen North? Does he realize what he's headed for?"

"Afraid so, yes."

Tommy came up to their table and handed Melrose a cue stick from the rack. "Why don't you have a go? You might stand a chance."

"Thank you very much," said Melrose, icily, taking the stick and going over to the table.

"He doesn't really remember much about his mother. She died when he was pretty young, he's not even sure how young. He has a picture —"

"I've seen it."

"He's very vague about it all." Tommy looked sad and sighted down his cue. "I suppose I should consider myself lucky." His tone was doubtful, though.

"It's not a case of 'should,' is it?"

"The trouble is I'm the last Marquess of Meares, unless I get married and have children. I think Aunt Betsy's already got her eyes on the daughter of a duke — one of them. It doesn't make any difference; they all look like trolls. But I shouldn't complain. No one tells me what to do except for Aunt Betsy and fourteen solicitors." There was no irony in his tone. "So you might say I've plenty of freedom to do what I want."

"Doesn't sound to me like you've got all that much."

He defended his aunt: "You can't blame her. I'm already disgracing the family name at St. Jude's Grange by failing everything except Mesopotamia, which doesn't come up all that often, anyway. I cut tutorials to play snooker and I'm hoping if they think I'm stupid, they'll let me off. Otherwise, I'm sunk. It'll be Christ Church College — that's where people like me end up —"

Jury laughed. "You make it sound like the high-security lock-up outside Durham."

Tom balanced the cue stick on the palm of his hand. Per-

fect control. "Oxford is such a gritty old town. All they have
is bookstores and haberdasheries where they sell scarves with
the school colors and I'll probably be expected to try for a
rowing Blue. I loathe rowing. There isn't a pool hall in the
whole damned place. I've looked."

"You're going to drop that stick if you're not careful." Jury
pocketed his cigarettes and checked the time.

"Me? I don't drop things. Do you know Aunt Betsy's told
the butler to keep the billiard room stuff locked up? The way
some people would lock up the liquor if they had a flaming
drunk in the family."

"That's going pretty far."

"Well, I guess I see her point. If I'm obsessed, I'm obsessed."

"It's not exactly as if you're possessed by demons." Jury
smiled.

Tommy let his stick fall into his other hand and sighted
along it like a rifle. "You know how I get in the billiard room?
It's during the tours. We have tours see, mostly of the gardens, which are quite fabulous. I put on an old coat and hat
and glasses. The guides wouldn't know me from Adam anyway. And when the last tour's on, I just hang round the edge
of it, slip in the closet and wait for them to leave. I can get in
an hour or so's practice that way. No one else ever goes in the
games room. Then I just slip out the french door and go
round. No one's figured out why the french door isn't locked
some mornings."

"My God, what determination." Jury laughed.

Somehow, Robbie had managed a safety shot that landed
the cue ball up against the cushion. Melrose chalked his cue
tip. If he didn't miscue — and he probably would — he could
pot the black —

"Get your chin down," said Tommy, standing behind him.

Melrose straightened and sighed. "I don't need an audience."

Jury smiled. "If you're going in for championship play, you've got to get used to it. Hurry up; I've got to get to Durham."

"Then let me concentrate."

All he needed now — and there they were — was a pair of brown eyes just at cushion level staring at him.

"Go away," said Melrose.

Chrissie did not move, nor did her eyes.

There was nothing for it, except to try. He lapped his bridge fingers on the edge of the table —

"Straighten them out. You can't make that bridge for a cushion shot."

Oh, *damn* them all! He felt as if his arm were frozen in place, and he was rather ashamed of himself for wanting to show off to Whittaker, who, once again, told him to get his chin down to cue level.

"And stop looking at the pocket. Look at the ball."

How did *he* know Melrose had let his eye stray to the pocket? He looked from the cue ball to the black, a perfect shot if he didn't miscue. Just as he drew the que back and thrust it forward, the small voice said,

"It'd be easier just to hit the black one."

He cursed. The tip of the cue slipped right off the top of the white ball, and she, apparently having accomplished her purpose of making him miscue, went off, carrying Alice.

Jury smiled. Tommy sympathized. Melrose stared at the white cue ball and the black object ball. He straighted up and looked at the empty door Chrissie had just gone through. "I'll be damned," he said. "It really *was* Beatrice Sleight."

Maybe he couldn't play snooker, but he could get a thrill by wiping that smile off Jury's face.

2

THEY were standing outside beside Jury's police-issue Granada, Melrose hunched down against the cold in his fisherman's sweater. "It was done so no one would think *Beatrice Sleight* was the intended victim. A mantle of confusion thrown over the whole thing — quite literally: Grace Seaingham's white cape. The murderer potted the black with the white. It's quite simple. Except of course, getting old Bea to cooperate. That must have taken some pretty fancy play."

Jury was leaning against the car door, looking toward the windows of the inn. "You don't need fancy plays with a shotgun in your hands."

"You mean someone got Beatrice down to the solarium and told her to put on the cape."

"I imagine it was done a bit more smoothly than that, but, essentially, yes."

"So you think I'm right?"

"Dead right. It makes a good deal more sense than explaining the otherwise strange behavior of Beatrice Sleight, surely the last person to go to chapel — and in Grace Seaingham's cape. So someone is going to great lengths to keep police from looking for connections between these people and Beatrice Sleight."

Melrose pulled his sleeves down to cover his hands. The sky had turned a miraculous and dazzling blue; sun was melting snow; the wind had calmed. "Nobody liked her. And if the lady of the house wasn't the intended *victim* . . . well, Grace Seaingham had a hell of a good reason for murder."

Jury shook his head.

"Oh, come on. You believe she's so good, you're overlooking the obvious."

"It's not that," said Jury. "Even if she wanted Beatrice

Sleight dead, what reason would she have for killing Helen Minton?"

Melrose stopped the little jig he was doing to keep warm. "Who says it had to be the same person?"

Jury tossed his cigarette butt onto the hard ground. "I do." He looked up at the marble-hard blue of a cloudless sky. "A lot of poisons are very unreliable — they might just make you sick. Which is how aconite can act on the system, if one doesn't get a fatal dose. The murderer apparently felt that with Helen there was time to take a chance, at least, on when she'd *get* that fatal dose, so the poison could have been put in her medicine by someone visiting Old Hall and death might have looked like a result of her heart problem; then Helen Minton found out something about Robin Lyte. But it doesn't get us very far, does it?"

"If he's Parmenger's son — ?"

"Um. Parmenger's the other reason I think the same person killed both of them. Parmenger knew them both — Helen and Beatrice. He's the connection."

"Could Helen Minton have threatened his reputation by telling the world?"

"It doesn't seem in character for either of them. For her to tell, or for him to mind. Parmenger's above it all. Who else have we got? Lady St. Leger? A little hard to believe you'd shoot a commoner because she hated the peerage —"

"There's always Lady Ardry," said Melrose, hopefully.

Jury went on: "William MacQuade? Sort of a dark horse, that one. He's certainly a survivor, but I see no motive."

"He couldn't stand Beatrice Sleight. She loved making snappy little comments about 'literary' writers. What about the Assingtons? They seem to be standing out on the edge of this whole thing. No motive at all. He's just the Great Physician and she seemed all impressed by the trash Beatrice Sleight wrote. Proper featherbrain. Just the sort of murderer

Elizabeth Onions would have running about in *The Third Pigeon.*"

"What?"

"Nothing. I don't think it's fair to have mental incompetents as murderers do you? They're not responsible."

Jury climbed into the car. "I'm going to Durham. I'll take Grace, you take Susan." He smiled and started the engine.

"Thanks. I'd sooner take cyanide." The car idled as Jury looked past him for a long moment. "What are you staring at?" Plant turned to look at the tiny windows. Chrissie had her face plump up against the glass.

"A pair of brown eyes," said Jury, waving to her, before he drove away.

Melrose saw the eyes quickly disappear below the sill where the melting snow dripped and ran like rain.

TWENTY-ONE

‹·❦·›

1

O N A day like this, seen from a distance and through the fog, Durham Cathedral appeared to float magically above the peninsula where the River Wear made its sharp, hairpin turn.

The chapel in which Grace Seaingham knelt was off to the right. How long could a woman stay on her knees? Jury wondered. It wasn't a long time standing, but on your knees, it was like forever.

Jury studied the geometrical quarry-markings on the columns, and watched her. Finally, she rose, made her way across the empty pew, and came out upon the aisle. Her glance downcast, she didn't see Jury until she was a few feet away from him. When she did, she caught the collar of her white wool coat about her neck as if Jury were a stiff, unwelcome wind. She did not smile.

"Sorry, Mrs. Seaingham. I'm not shadowing you." His smile felt artificial, as it usually did in her presence. "You said you'd be here, and I wanted to tell you something. . . . Look, I'm sure you'd rather talk somewhere else."

Her own smile made him feel cheated; of what, he didn't

know. "I don't mind. Do you? If we're talking about death —" She gave him a slight shrug. "— why not here?" With one of her elegant, Edwardian gestures, she indicated they might walk about. They might have been going on a tour of Spinney Abbey.

Jury felt, here in the cathedral, at a disadvantage. Though why he should want an advantage over Grace Seaingham he wasn't sure. He turned to look at her and saw that serene profile, the pale hair. She had stopped before the fresco of St. Cuthbert. "Freddie Parmenger should see this. Only he doesn't much like churches. Did you know the monks carried St. Cuthbert's bones about for hundreds of years? First from Lindisfarne, and then Chester-le-Street. It's not far from here. This was the final resting place." Her face still turned toward the fresco, she asked him, "What was it you wanted to tell me?"

"It wasn't you, Mrs. Seaingham. I made a mistake there. The intended victim really *was* Beatrice Sleight."

He felt her indrawn breath almost as if she were robbing him of oxygen. The whole massive Norman structure made him feel like a mountain-climber, a clumsy back-packer, out of his element, as he looked up at the rib vaulting, the transverse arches. He felt a sort of lack, a need to be reassured, like some fractious kid. He felt ridiculous.

And it was obviously in his own mind; it was nothing she was doing or saying, for her sudden turn on him was merely surprise and relief. "But why in heaven's name would Bea have on my cape?"

"Whoever killed her wanted everyone to think it was you they meant . . ." He didn't finish. "Just how the killer got her to wear the cape and go outside, I'm not sure. Perhaps some plausible story of having a little 'talk' where they couldn't be seen — in the chapel, maybe —"

Her eyes were luminous, whether with relief or the beginning of tears, Jury couldn't tell. "Then it wasn't —" Abruptly she stopped, turned her head toward the painting of St. Cuthbert.

"Wasn't what? Or who?"

She didn't answer.

"Your husband, you mean. I doubt very much that it was your husband in any event."

"You don't think he killed her?"

Jury didn't answer this. He only said, "If she was his —"

Her smile was chilly. "Go on, say it. Mistress. Might he have been concerned that Beatrice was going to tell *me?*" Her voice was taut.

"Blackmail?"

"Charles didn't know I knew."

Jury let that go by. It was her first suspicion that was more interesting. "You were relieved at first that someone wasn't trying to kill *you*. Again, your husband?"

"No, of course not." She said it too quickly.

"Mrs. Seaingham, when you found out about the murder of Beatrice Sleight, you assumed it might be you someone wanted to kill. No one else did, except police." And Melrose Plant, but he didn't add that.

"Well — the cape . . ."

Her tone wasn't convincing. "You turned out to be right. But I think your assumption was a little strange at the time. Why do you always wear white?"

She was taken aback by the question. "Why . . . I don't know; I suppose I never thought much about it." She looked down at the coat.

"You shouldn't. It only increases the pallor; it accentuates how pale you are. You should wear colors. Pastels, something like that. It's obvious you don't want people to think you're ill. And you are ill, aren't you?"

Perfectly recovered and utterly cool, she said, "I'm dying, actually."

"Of what?"

Only a small muscle twitched in her cheek as she shook her head, "I don't know. Neither does Sir George. He can't make it out. The tests show nothing."

"You're lying, Grace. There haven't been any tests, have there? You won't let him make them."

The porcelain skin did take on color at that as she gave him a long look. "If you already knew that —"

"It's because you're afraid it's your husband, isn't it? That's the way some poisons work. Small doses, just a bit at a time. Arsenic. Aconite could, except you'd have known immediately something was wrong. There's numbness, tingling —"

"Don't be stupid! How can you imagine —" The voice was strained.

Jury put his hand beneath her arm. "What you've been thinking about Charles isn't true."

She obviously did not know what to say to this and reverted to the subject of the saint on the wall. Jury thought she looked almost luminous against the dark background of stone, the ghost who never stops searching. "He didn't like women, you know, St. Cuthbert. That chapel I was in, the Galilee Chapel it's called, was built for women because he didn't want them approaching his shrine. He didn't like women at all."

Jury smiled. "Nobody's perfect. Let's go outside."

The princess had come down from entrapment in the tower to have a peek out of the front door at a world that she hoped was real. The coil of hair, silvery in the sunlight, had loosened and strands escaped, feathering her temples. In her cheeks, there was some real color, and her skin looked almost amber in the watery light trapped in the close, girded on three sides by the buildings used by Durham University.

With the defenses pretty well stripped away and even the mannerisms changed — she was chewing at a corner of her mouth, taking off the pale lipstick she wore — she put Jury in mind of a pretty, nervous young girl. The long strap of her purse slung over her shoulder, her arms were tightly folded across her breast and she was telling Jury about her bouts with nausea, her refusal to eat more than would barely sustain life, her careful monitoring of whatever she drank. "Do you like old movies?"

"When I get a chance to watch."

"Remember *Suspicion*? I've felt like Joan Fontaine — you know, when Cary Grant is walking up the steps with that glass of milk." Her smile was genuine; the violence of her bout with tears coming out of the cathedral seeming to have rinsed her face of all traces of its old anxiety. "Weren't people afraid it really was him, the husband? But, of course, no one could *really* think they'd let Cary Grant be guilty. Because he was so charming; because he was Cary Grant." Sadly, she looked at Jury. "My husband isn't Cary Grant."

"No. But he's not trying to poison you."

"How can you be so certain?"

"Simple. He loves you."

Her look, for her, was almost coy. "Now, just how do you know that?"

"For one thing, he said as much. For another, he didn't love Beatrice Sleight. For yet another, there's the way he looks at you. And, absolute proof: I can't imagine a man like your husband, whose study must be absolutely holy to him, letting a painter in there and you in there to sit for a picture, unless it was terribly important to him."

She looked at him with something like wonder, a vulnerable, youthful look, and then she laughed. "You're either a wonderful detective or an awful romantic."

He smiled. "Oh, I'm both." He took her arm. "Come on; let's have lunch."

* * *

In a tiny, luncheon-jammed restaurant in the middle of old Durham they ate some marvelous food — mushrooms as drunk as lords in winy, cheese-crusted dish; a casserole whose main constituent was Old Peculier; Stilton and gooseberry tart. Jury made sure that Grace ate everything, and she didn't need much coaxing. While they ate, she told him about herself and Charles: how she had simply been hoping the "thing" with Bea was a sort of middle-aged-fling business — she laughed — old middle-age; how she had always wanted children, but it had never happened. "And yet, there was Reeni — Tommy's mother — who thought children were a bit of a bore." She ate her cheese and tart and grew quiet for a moment. "I used to watch Tommy with her. He adored her; she was so beautiful, but no character, really. Neither Irene nor Richard had much of it, to tell the truth. They were fun, charming, rich, and —" She shrugged and changed the subject. "There's an old junk shop near here I like to root round in. It's where I found this" — she raised the pendant she always wore — "and later found out how much it was worth. The poor, old man had no idea: he sold it for a pound. It's worth a thousand." She let the necklace fall. "I was wondering, could we go there for a few minutes?"

"Sure." Jury paid the bill and they left, walking up the cobbled street toward her shop.

"I'm glad to hear you're not perfect, Grace."

"Meaning?"

"The junk dealer. You took him for a thousand quid." Jury laughed.

She stopped dead. "Really, Mr. Jury. I went back and gave him the money."

"Oh, hell. And I was just beginning to think there was hope for you."

She smiled broadly. "Meaning — I split the difference with him. I'm not perfect, after all."

"You could have fooled me."

They both laughed.

But as they entered the secondhand shop, Jury did not feel really happy at all. If her husband wasn't trying to poison Grace Seaingham, who was?

TWENTY-TWO

1

"WHAT do you think, Ruthven?" asked Melrose. His butler paused in the act of brushing Melrose's jacket and appeared to be contemplating a universal enigma.

"Had you noticed, sir, how Mr. Marchbanks decanted the claret last evening?"

The circumstances of last night might have provoked some other response, he thought, from anyone else. But given Ruthven's unyielding concern with the proprieties, Melrose supposed he oughtn't to be surprised. "Didn't let it breathe, or something?" Melrose was scrutinizing himself before a cheval mirror, a scrutiny that had nothing to do with vanity, but rather with seeking out signs of decay and premature death, and wondering, as he often did lately, if he couldn't trap some unwilling beauty into sharing Ardry End. He sighed, thinking of Polly Praed and her idiot letter. ("*Your Grace??*") "I was thinking, Ruthven, more along the lines of what happened to Miss Beatrice Sleight, *not* about the butlerian maladroitness of Marchbanks."

"Indeed, that is terrible, my lord. I barely slept a wink, thinking of it." But the apologetic tone suggested the murder of Beatrice Sleight was merely an addendum to the awfulness of claret sediment.

Melrose picked a microscopic bit of lint from the jacket Ruthven had just brushed and put it on, wishing that his butler would stop that milord form of address. He had given up correcting Ruthven long ago: the Earl of Caverness once, the Earl of Carverness forever. It must really stick in Ruthven's throat that earls were one down from marquesses. Teenage marquesses, at that.

Ruthven, bringing up the polish on boots that had been polished once by the Seaingham's footman, sighed and murmured something about "poor Mrs. Seaingham."

Surprised, Melrose turned from the mirror, unsuccessful in his attempt to plaster down the lick of hair that stood up on the crown of his head, yank it about as he might, and said, "What about Mrs. Seaingham?"

"These boots were not done proper, my lord."

To Melrose they looked like burnished copper. Patiently, he repeated, "What *about* Mrs. Seaingham?"

"Why, she looks quite ill, sir. And perhaps you wouldn't notice how she scarcely touches her food. I've seen her plate come back, without hardly so much as a bite taken. Not too much of a surprise, of course, when you come to think on it. We, being used to Mrs. Ruthven's cooking —"

"Martha's. She's been cooking for the family all of my life. No need to stand on formalities."

"Yes, sir. Thank you, sir. But what I wished to say was that, knowing *superior* cuisine, it is not at all surprising that Mrs. Seaingham might indeed lose a bit of appetite here. I mean, *really*, sir. The Cumberland sauce merely disguised a rather overcooked joint." Ruthven's otherwise granite-still face came close to a smirk. "And the béarnaise —"

"My dear Ruthven. I really do not think that what has happened in Spinney Abbey should be put down to a choice of sauces."

"No, my lord. You're quite right," he said, his own line of thought undisturbed. "It's more the people, isn't it?"

"I should think so, Ruthven." Melrose lit a pre-luncheon cigar and watched Ruthven place the boots on the floor, giving a sad little headshake over them, as if they too were destined for an early grave. "They'll never be the same, sir."

"The boots? Or the guests? I take it you approve of neither?"

"It's not for me to comment, my lord. But it's clear that, well, some of them just won't do. I mean, sir, did you see Lady Assington with the Stilton?"

"Threw it on the floor, did she?"

Briefly, Ruthven shut his eyes, bearing up patiently under his young (forever young would Melrose be in Ruthven's eyes) lordship's making light of a serious matter. "She used a scoop, sir. I allow as how these jumped-up lower classes use them, but —"

"Surely, you're not calling the Seainghams 'jumped-up,' and if they supply scoops — Ruthven, *why* are we talking about cheese scoops? Tell me something more to the point: what do their servants think of the Seainghams in general?"

Ruthven looked simply shocked. "*Really,* my lord. I would not lower myself to reporting the common gossip below stairs."

In the distance a bell tinkled like a cow in the pasture. "Time for luncheon, Ruthven. Come on, give —" Melrose aborted a sneeze with his handkerchief.

"I do hope you've not caught a chill from being out last night. You have simply not conditioned yourself for winter sports, my lord."

Ruthven was, if anything, a master of undersell. "I haven't conditioned myself for *any* sports. I am one of the idle rich."

"That is not at all true. You have your professorial duties at University."

"You must've heard something. You haven't been spending all of that time amongst the forks and knives and Branston pickle without hearing something."

As Ruthven set to rebrushing Melrose's already perfectly brushed jacked, he said, "Only that the Seainghams had had several rows and that *he* wanted a divorce. Well, of course, Mrs. Seaingham, being High Church and all, wouldn't hear of it." He paused, reflectively. "Did you notice Mr. MacQuade, sir? Last night at dinner, I mean?"

"Notice what? He does seem interested in Mrs. Seaingham, certainly."

"Well, I wouldn't know about that. But he didn't *slide* the port, my lord. He lifted the bottle."

And with that startling bit of news, Ruthven swanned out of the room.

2

MELROSE found Susan Assington, in a dark green lawn dress, adrift in the library like a leaf fallen far from its branch, unused as she appeared to be to books: given the vague surprise she registered while turning pages, Gutenberg might only have come along yesterday.

"Looking for something to read, Lady Assington?"

He had taken her by surprise, that was certain, as she quickly stuffed the volume back into the bookcase. "It's just something on gardens."

Hard to imagine her with a hoe in her hand, but Melrose went on, holding up *The Third Pigeon*. "I can definitely recommend Elizabeth Onions, if you like a sort of Scotland-bird-shooting mystery milieu —"

That was obviously no recommendation to her. "I hate

thrillers. Anyway, I don't see how you can make jokes about it. . . ." She was definitely on the verge of tears. "Proper mess, I call it." Lady Assington's idiom seemed to have removed itself from Hampstead Heath to the stoops of Lambeth, reestablishing the shopgirl Susan as the real owners of both.

"Sorry. Guess I wasn't thinking. Would you like a cigarette?" Melrose extended his gold case, hoping she would sit down in one of the old leather chairs for a cozy conversation.

"I don't mind," she said in a pouty way, and did sit down.

Melrose took the twin of the chair opposite, lit their cigarettes, and watched her toy with hers more than smoke it.

"Stuck up here . . . feel like I'm in prison, I do. When do you suppose they'll let *all* of us go? There's George gone off to London to one of his meetings and left me here. . . ." Above the well-shod foot Susan Assington was nervously swinging, Melrose thought he recognized one of those plain little Laura Ashley dresses, probably in the hundred-pound range, a dress designed to make its wearer look simple and countrified, as if she'd just come in from milking silver-plated cows. Susan was definitely not the milkmaid type.

"Did you know her well?"

"Who?" She flicked cigarette ash into the cold grate.

The woman really was featherbrained, or doing a good job of pretending to be in the face of a bloody murder.

"Beatrice Sleight."

"Oh," she said, as if the murdered woman were of no more account than one of the Onions pigeons. "Well, we saw her round and about. Proper bitch is all I've got to say, though George didn't seem to think there was any harm in her. 'No harm?' I says to him. 'Look at those books she writes.' Well, of course, *I* don't read trash like that," she added quickly.

From the music room came the cacophonous sound of a piano being disemboweled by Tommy Whittaker.

Susan Assington held a hand heavy with emeralds to her forehead. "Oh, I *do* wish that boy'd stop it. Why his aunt ever thinks he's musical, I don't know." She was flipping through a glossy fashion magazine and held it out to Melrose as if he might be her hairdresser. "What do you think of this do?"

Patiently, Melrose took out his spectacles and studied the "do." The model's hair stood up on end and with her darkly outlined eyes, Melrose assumed she'd either come upon the Thing from Spinney Moor or else was It. "Not for you, Lady Assington. The way you're wearing it now is much more becoming."

Delicately, she ran her hair over the smooth, dark helmet of hair, and said, "You oughtn't to wear glasses. You've got smashing eyes. Green," she added helpfully, in case he'd forgotten.

Melrose thanked her and pocketed his glasses. Haut coiffure forgotten, Susan had levered herself a bit forward in her chair, displaying embellishments beside her glossy hair, and was looking into the eyes she admired. "Funny you being a bachelor." Hematology and murder seemed to be going the way of all flesh.

"Not really. Just haven't got around to marriage, I expect." He listened to Tommy going down the scales at the same rate as Susan's Hampstead accent. Trying to work the conversation back to murder, he said, "I'd think you of all people would appreciate what's happened." That got him a puzzled frown. "You were saying at dinner that all of us here together at a country house party seemed ripe for a murder."

"Well, I was only teasing, wasn't I?" she said with some fright.

"Of course, of course." Melrose's tone was soothing. "How did you happen to meet Beatrice Sleight?"

"You sound like police," she said, surprising Melrose that she could come anywhere near the mark. But her tone was casual. "At one of those autograph-signings. In a bookstore. George thought it'd be fun to go along and get her to sign one of her books. He knew her, you see. In a casual way."

"A casual way" was how Sir George had put it to the Northumbria police. His wife seemed to accept this rote description without qualification. "But it's Grace Seaingham, isn't it, they meant to kill?" she said, glancing at Melrose with surprising sharpness. "You know where you usually start looking when there's that sort of trouble — the husband."

"The Seainghams strike me as a very well matched couple, very fond of one another."

"Can't always go by looks, can you?" said Susan. "What I don't understand is, they act like it was one of *us*. When it's obvious it was just someone trying to break in or just some tramp and Beatrice must have seen them, or something." She flung down her fashion magazine, having exhausted every new gown and "do" before she got up to leave.

Susan Assington could certainly fly in the teeth of the evidence. Melrose decided to break the news gently. "Well, that would seem to be rather unlikely because of the snow." She actually managed to appear bewildered. Melrose embroidered: "We've been snowed in, you see."

She looked at him as if he were a bit dim. "That doesn't mean everyone else's been snowed *out*, does it?"

3

"DO BE dummy, Melrose," said Lady Ardry, slapping down a card as Melrose wandered into the games room. Agatha, Lady St. Leger, and Vivian were having what looked like a game of three-handed bridge. "We don't expect you to do anything. You've never been good at cards."

Noticing a copy of Debrett's lying on the table beside Agatha, he thought perhaps they should have been playing at Patience and Peers. "Your invitation to join the party is irresistible, Agatha, but no thank you. Anyway, if you're playing three-handed, you don't *have* a dummy."

"We could," said Vivian with that gritty little smile she'd lately affected. She scooped up a trick.

"You seem to be taking the events of last evening with iron self-control. I applaud you."

Under her dusting of rouge and powder, Lady St. Leger blushed a bit, as if they'd been caught out like bad children. "It's just to take our minds off the whole — nasty business."

When he entered, she had been taking her mind off the nasty business by extolling the virtues of the marquetries of Miln and Abbisferd over the earldom of Dunleith, a bait to which his aunt now rose.

"Perfectly *hideous* places," said Agatha, sitting in close proximity to the tea table. "Monkeys climbing all over the cars — if you're not going to play, why must you be about, Melrose, whilst we're trying to concentrate?"

Monkeys? wondered Melrose. "I thought I'd left my book in here. I'm merely waiting for Superintendent Jury." He picked a cue from the rack and walked about the table to get a better look at Agatha's hand. He'd played cards with her before.

Cards fanned out against her bosom, the expression on her face made it clear she would rather he do his waiting elsewhere. "It's not for me to say, of course," she said, slapping a trump on Vivian's king, and sweeping in the trick, "but why should Jury be here? What's the death of Beatrice Sleight got to do with Scotland Yard?" She grimaced as Elizabeth St. Leger led with a diamond. "After all, it's not as though the Northumbria police asked for his help, is it?" Vivian a deuce of clubs. "I don't see —"

"What did you mean, 'monkeys'?" asked Melrose.

"What are you talking about?" Agatha was suddenly overcome with a fit of coughing and drew a handkerchief from her long sleeve, whereupon Melrose noticed, sighting along his cue, that a king of hearts quietly landed in her lap. Agatha coughed gently, replaced the handkerchief, and said, "We were merely speaking of the rather resourceful ways in which some of the peerage were keeping up their estates." She slapped the king of hearts over the absent fourth's queen. "Of course, a place as small as Ardry End doesn't present the problems of an estate as large as Meares Hall."

It was the first time Melrose had ever heard *her* call Ardry End "small."

"Oh, I don't know," said Melrose, fascinated with his aunt's shuffling of the deck. At least two cards had thus far come off the bottom. "It's not so big as Spinney Abbey, but —"

"That's scarcely a comparison!" She fanned out her cards, looked them over, and led with a jack of diamonds. Then, apparently remembering that she, as well as her nephew, had some vested interest in the family seat, said, "Still, Ardry End is one of the finest smallish manor houses in the country. And it might be added, we needn't keep it up by selling tickets to coach parties and having grubby-fingered children make free with the lawns and gardens."

Melrose refrained from pointing out *she* needn't keep it up at all, since it wasn't hers. He was more interested in what would be the final disposal of the ace in her lap.

Elizabeth St. Leger was not to be baited, however. She merely played her card and said, "You are very fortunate, then. Most of us" (Melrose smiled, knowing that Agatha would never be included in that "us") "really must do something to defray expenses. And I rather like it, somehow. I like people enjoying the gardens; I really am quite a gardener myself . . . is that *another* ace, Agatha?"

Agatha didn't answer this direct question, but said, "Oh, we've fine gardens, too. But we enjoy them only *ourselves*. It's such a pity that the peerage has had to *stoop* so. Just look at Woburn Abbey. Chockablock with tea tents and antiques people and all manner of trade. And Bath." Lady St. Leger played her last trump — a five of clubs. "That's where the monkeys are," she said to Melrose, "at Longleat. And lions and so forth. The place is a *zoo.*" While she was addressing Melrose, she had another brief coughing fit and trumped the five with a jack. "But of course I sympathize," added Agatha.

That should make news, thought Melrose. . . .

"There are times when one must take desperate remedies for the sake of one's good name. Melrose would agree, I'm sure."

"Most certainly," said Melrose, watching Agatha sweep the last trick from the table before she reached for the cake-plate.

Elizabeth St. Leger had either grown tired of cards altogether or of her friend's playing of them and had now seated herself by the fire in the drawing room, at work on her embroidery.

Melrose, waiting for Jury to call, did not even try to hide his astonishment when Agatha drew from a workbasket — one she had probably scrounged from her hostess — an embroidery hoop.

"You, Agatha? I've never seen you do embroidery."

"Certainly I do. But then you have never asked, have you?" she said with typical Agatha-logic, accompanied by a typical Agatha-sigh. "I'm doing your Christmas present, if you must know."

That was even more astonishing. His aunt had not, in living memory, ever given him a gift. She had, instead, given him excuses. He came to look over her shoulder. There had been little stitching done, and that was crude at best. "It looks like a mouse."

Stabbing her needle through the cream background, she said, "Don't be silly. It's a unicorn."

"It looks like the ear of a mouse to me."

"It's a unicorn's *horn.*"

"Well, anyway, why are you embroidering unicorns?"

"*If* you must know and spoil the surprise —"

There would be no earthly way to keep her from spoiling it for him, since she had, he knew, every intention of impressing Lady St. Leger with her intricate handiwork. She started to speak, but Melrose forestalled her.

"No, no, Agatha. I'd much rather it be a surprise," and he frustrated her by turning the topic of conversation to the first thing his eye fell upon — one of the bowls of Christmas roses. "These are lovely flowers," he said, now addressing Elizabeth St. Leger, the gardener among them. "It's nice to have white flowers at Christmas." He did not know why, particularly, but it kept the subject off Agatha's embroidery.

"Aren't they?" said Lady St. Leger. She looked at the bowl of flowers. "*Helleborus niger,* the black hellebore. Strange name for a pinkish-white flower. I suppose it's because of the root. That's black and extremely poisonous." She snipped a dark green thread with her scissors. "Sweet of Susan to bring them, all those flowers. She doesn't strike me at all as the sort who would think of it, frankly."

Sweet of Susan, yes. Melrose stared at the flowers, and came back from his reflections when Elizabeth St. Leger put her hands to her ears and said, "Oh, dear. He's started up again." She looked at Melrose. "I don't suppose you could distract him from his music for a while, could you, Mr. Plant? I'm sure everyone would appreciate it greatly. I know I would."

Melrose thought for a moment and then said, with a smile. "I'd be delighted if he'd go with me into Durham, now the roads are open."

Lady St. Leger threaded another needle and said, "Where did Superintendent Jury take him this morning? All I could get out of Tom was something about routine police business. And are we permitted to leave? I mean with police every-where —"

Not exactly true. There were only two constables outside

still going over the snow around the chapel. He was glad she'd asked the second question so that he could avoid the first. "We're not under house arrest, Lady St. Leger. I'm sure we're free to leave. So long as we don't leave the country, I guess." He had moved again behind Agatha to watch her progress on the unrecognizable unicorn.

"Durham?" said Agatha. "Why do you want to go there?"

Safe in the knowledge that Agatha would much rather sit here cozily with her great friend than visit a great cathedral, Melrose said, "Because it's beautiful. I want to see the cathedral."

"Very well," she said, as if he needed her permission. "I shall sit here and work on this. It's taking a great deal of time." He was expected no doubt to thank her for the time she would spend in place of the money she wouldn't. He didn't, and she went on. "If you must know, I'm doing the Caverness coat-of-arms."

He blinked. "Christmas is tomorrow, dear Aunt. You expect to have an entire coat-of-arms finished by then?"

"Given the difficulty, I should think you wouldn't mind waiting. 'Two lions ermine, one unicorn armed and unglued.'"

Elizabeth St. Leger bit her lip.

"'Unguled,' Agatha."

He then went off to the music room to tell Tommy Whittaker that he could stop playing the Whittaker rendition of what used to be Chopin, get his togs on and start playing the real thing.

Tommy nearly broke his bridge hand, slamming down the cover over the keys. "Jerusalem Inn? You're kidding. Aunt Betsy —"

"This afternoon Jerusalem Inn is Durham Cathedral."

TWENTY-THREE

1

A CHRISTIAN mustering courage before the Romans opened the gates could not have looked with firmer resolve at the slavering lions as did Detective Sergeant Wiggins look at the Newcastle station before he detrained. It was no worse, though certainly no better (only smaller), than Victoria, King's Cross, St. Pancras. Interesting architecturally, it still hadn't the allure (although Sergeant Wiggins would scarcely have used the word) of St. Pancras, perhaps the headiest of all stations.

The Newcastle station had the usual consortium of tracks, tramps, smoke, and sausage rolls, the last served up in a seedy-sad-looking railway cafe. It had always been Wiggins's feeling that train stations were one giant dustbin, something to be avoided. That went double for the London Underground, which was, unfortunately, unavoidable as it was the quickest way from his flat in Lambeth to New Scotland Yard. Jury recalled how relieved Wiggins had been to discover, over a year ago, that a specially equipped car prowled the tunnels, systematically cleaning them. He had to take the Bakerloo Line and Wiggins always contended that the Bakerloo and Northern were the dirtiest. Jury (his sergeant had often reminded him) was stuck with the Northern.

But Wiggins had little resistance to anything without his afternoon cuppa, and thus agreed to having it on a crisp-bag-littered table in the cafe. He cleaned the table first, of course, with paper napkins.

It was only after certain rituals had been performed in obeisance to the Allergy God, that Wiggins could be enjoined to give out. And Jury never hurried him in this direction as it only unnerved the sergeant who was, taken all in all, a store-house of information with a skill at note-taking that surpassed Boswell. He crammed in details so small (and often useless) a high-powered telescope couldn't have picked them out of a night sky thronged with stars. But certain facts were invalu-able, and Jury had learned to pluck them from the Milky Way of Wiggins's conversation.

Right now, Wiggins had his notebook open beside his un-appetizing slice of soggy-crusted apple pie. "Annie Brown," he read. "Born Brixton, 1925 — a long time before the riots, of course, but still a right run down old place." There fol-lowed a thorough account of the old Brown abode and Brix-ton itself. "Schooling slim — took her O-levels but never went any further." Jury was treated to as thorough a going-over of Annie's schoolwork as any headmistress might have undertaken. Fortunately, the rest was dished up more rap-idly. "Got an assistant's post at a comprehensive; moved to Dartmouth and started out with first formers in a girls' school called Beedle — more brawn than brains there. Finally ended up at Laburnum School." Wiggins wiped his mouth with a paper napkin. "According to the headmistress, she was 'satisfactory,' but I got the impression only just. Then she trots along one fine day and resigns, saying she's got a better post."

"We'll just trot along ourselves and get the rest of it from her. You did a great job Wiggins, digging out that information with the dread sea air to contend with." Jury looked at the awful pie. "Hope you live to tell Maureen about it."

2

THEY were admitted to the Bonaventure School by the same rawboned girl, one of whose duties it must have been to greet visitors. Though Jury could find little of what might be called "greeting" in the whole visit.

This certainly extended to the posture of Miss Hargreaves-Brown, sitting at her desk with that injured look of Time Wasted. She did, however, rise as Jury introduced Detective Sergeant Wiggins. Wiggins was greeted with no more enthusiasm than Jury had been two days before.

She wore the same heavy wool dress, the dab of white handkerchief showing at the wrist, dark hose and blunt-nosed shoes. Her eyes were hard and flat like well-rubbed pennies.

But underneath her cool detachment, Jury thought he noticed a certain tension. That there were now two policemen instead of one might have suggested to her they were getting down to business.

Jury did: "It's about Helen Minton, Miss Brown, and your relationship with her. It is just plain Annie Brown, isn't it?"

Her hands tightened their clasp, but she said nothing, only looked off to her left, toward the high wide window on the open court. There were no sounds of children's voices.

"The children," said Jury, "I suppose are at their lessons. What children there are." Slowly, she turned her head, the dull look replaced by a feverish one. "You would have liked to turn this into another Laburnum School, I imagine. But up here—" Jury shrugged. Still she said nothing. Jury took out his packet of cigarettes, lit one, and motioned to Wiggins.

Sergeant Wiggins, his notebook open, read off, with his usual lack of expression, the information he had given Jury in the cafe, the name, the dates. ". . . and you left Laburnum the same time Miss Helen Minton did, to the day. Parmenger's solicitors, with a bit of prodding by police" — Wiggins smiled his thin smile — "indicated that a yearly bequest of some thousand pounds had been made to Bonaventure School. Not much for a big place like this. Heat alone must cost you something fierce." As if this called up visions of viruses, Wiggins took from his pocket-chemist supply a box of licorice cough drops and unzipped the tiny plastic strip.

Jury continued for him: "Edward Parmenger found you this post. Or bought it for you. My guess is there was a good deal of money changed hands to do something with the school. But more to keep you quiet."

She tried to muster the old Hargreaves-Brown manner, but the starch had gone out of both her and her name. "I've done nothing illegal," was all she said.

"Depends, doesn't it?"

"I don't know what you mean."

"I was thinking of Robin Lyte."

"Robin? What about him?" Her face was like a Greek mask, expressionless.

"My guess is he's Helen Minton's son. You were the teacher Helen told, worse luck. I assume you told Edward Parmenger. And Parmenger was a Puritan and protective of his son. It would have been bad enough in any circumstances to have his ward get herself pregnant. But pregnant by her own cousin —"

There was a convulsive sound. Annie Brown was laughing.

"Cousins!" she said. "It was rather more incestuous than that, Superintendent. They were half brother and sister." That she had tripped up Scotland Yard seemed to please her immensely. "I see you don't know *everything*, then."

"We'd be happy if you'd tell us."

With elaborate calm, she studied her nails. "You are quite

right about the money, the school, and the confidence. That is, the confidence that both Helen and her father placed in me —"

Feeling perhaps the confidence misplaced, Jury asked: "When you say 'her father,' I assume you mean Edward Parmenger."

"Of course. Neither Helen nor the boy — Frederick? — knew of the liaison between Edward Parmenger and his sister-in-law. But, good heavens, I imagine you can see why he'd be in a state."

"Parmenger told you this? But why?"

"Mr. Jury, I am not a fool —"

"I don't doubt that for a moment," said Jury.

But she either didn't notice the ice in his voice or didn't care, now she was so thoroughly sure of her advantage. "When I notified him about Helen —"

"You 'notified' him."

"Why, yes, of course. The girl could hardly stay at Laburnum School, could she? The family had to know."

"Shouldn't that have been the job of the headmistress, though, rather than one of her staff?"

She seemed to be turning this over. "Naturally, I considered that. But in the end, well, one wants to save a young girl any possible embarrassment —"

"One wants," said Jury, "to get on in the world." He forestalled the obvious objection she might make about this assessment of her motives by asking, "And Edward Parmenger told you about Helen's and Frederick's true relationship? I'm surprised."

Annie Brown merely shrugged. "He was — caught off balance, perhaps. And I am the sort of person in whom one confides. Helen did."

Apparently, Helen had. Jury could only assume that Miss Brown was protean; if it suited her purposes, she could fawn. "My impression of Mr. Parmenger was that he only wanted to be rid of the problem. I did not get the impression of a man of great strength of character. He went into quite a rage, really. I've a feeling it was his son who had the character, in a way. I mean the determination to get what he wanted." She sat back in her old, creaking chair. "You see how well he's done."

"I do indeed, Miss Hargreaves-Brown," said Jury diplomatically. "But it's not going to do you a damned bit of good if you're thinking of putting the bite on Frederick Parmenger. He's the publish-and-be-damned type"

Her eyes hardened again. "I beg your pardon?"

"Go on about Helen."

"Well . . . I had always wanted the post of head of a school. All I was asked to do was keep Helen here until — the child was born, see that the baby was adopted, and send Helen back."

Like a rejected parcel, thought Jury. "No wonder she came here."

"I was most distressed, I can tell you. The understanding was that she would stay away. Right afterwards, Mr. Parmenger sent her on a world tour."

"The world can look like a nutshell if you're miserable."

Miss Hargreaves-Brown shrugged. "She was a stupid girl. Ought to have married and settled down and had children."

"She had one already. You wouldn't tell her anything, I take it?"

"No. You think me some sort of monster for my involvement in all of this. Would it have been a kindness — no matter the ethics — to let her know her child was, well, backward? There was some sort of genetic damage. With that close blood-tie —"

"An old wives' tale."

"Old wives' tales are sometimes true," she snapped.

"What about Danielle Lyte?"

She started. Jury felt he had regained some advantage. "A

young woman — and her husband, who was a drunk, I discovered too late — who was willing to take Robin. Again, for a — fee."

"That's where she got the money the husband scarpered with? And you took him back when Danielle died. Kids certainly get passed around up here, don't they?"

She rested her chin on her folded hands and smiled slightly. "As I told you, I'm not without feeling. Of course, the school took him. Who else would? When he was old enough to get by on his own, we could no longer keep him. Sixteen is our limit, unless the circumstances are extraordinary."

"Funny, I'd think that boy's circumstances just that."

She rose. "I'm really very busy. Is there anything else?"

"Not at the moment," said Jury.

"Let's have a drink at the Cross Keys," said Jury, as they approached the iron gate. "I need one myself to take the chill off."

There was a buzz and the gate opened when, from behind, came a light rustle of branches.

"Good-bye," said the Tree. "And God bless."

"What's that?" asked Wiggins, looking everywhere.

"The trees up here aren't like the ones in London. They talk." From his pocket Jury took a small bag, screwed the top tightly, and called to the Tree. "Catch!"

Wiggins huddled down into his scarf and regarded his superior-gone-mad who watched the white bag disappear in the branches.

"Good-bye and God bless."

Having all but bounced the two sallow-looking young women from the coziest table near the fire, Wiggins, his bunty sandwich and buttered beer before him, seemed happier. "I can't think," he said, "from what you've told me, anyone who'd have a better motive."

"To keep Helen Minton from spreading the word? Well, I'll tell you: Miss Brown is probably quite capable of murder if it would benefit her. But in this case, she might simply try on her look-what-you-owe me approach instead and put the bite on Helen. Blackmail, perhaps. But to keep the word from who?"

"This is a good sandwich," said Wiggins. "Chips in a roll; whoever'd've thought? You don't think it was Frederick Parmenger?"

Jury assumed he was talking about blackmail and not bunty sandwiches. "She might have tried; he wouldn't have paid. I know she was lying about part of it; Danny Lyte didn't just happen along. I'm going over to the Minton cottage and I want you to go back to the Northumbria station and check up on that woman. She worked for an Isobel Dunsany. Miss Dunsany said she was a good worker and had excellent references. I wonder if they came from Edward Parmenger."

Wiggins took this down in his notebook and went back to his sandwich. "Aren't you eating, sir? Some food'd do you good."

"I only eat mushy peas," said Jury, drinking off his pint.

TWENTY-FOUR

1

I T WAS turning dark and there was a dull light showing in the downstairs window of Helen Minton's cottage. The door was standing open.

Frederick Parmenger, drink in hand, was looking at the picture of Washington Old Hall. When Jury spoke, Parmenger looked around at him as if he'd either been expecting him to come, or didn't care, now that Jury was here. He nodded toward the space above the mantel, "She took my picture down."

"Maybe she didn't like looking at herself."

Parmenger was silent for a moment. "What," the man asked dully, taking in the room with a wave of his arm, "am I supposed to do with all this?"

Jury got another glass from the cabinet, sat down on the chair opposite him, and said, "Have another drink, I suppose." He poured out a measure for each of them. But Parmenger was not the type to sit and make a boozy confession to police. The silence descended like winter dusk out in the blighted garden where cold had turned the dahlia stems to

sticks, and thrown a membrane of frost across the field flowers. The old clock ticked for a minute while neither of them
spoke. Parmenger's silence was more draining than his-
trionics would have been: a quick gesture of his hand suggesting he'd like to throw his glass at the substitute painting.
In breaking the silence, Jury could almost hear the sound of
breaking glass. His comment was deliberately mild: "You
really liked her, didn't you?"

· "Liked her? Yes." His tone was wooden. He drank half of
his whiskey and fell silent again.

"But you didn't make a point of seeing her often?"

"Helen was not terribly interested in seeing me." He
reached for the bottle and slopped out more. "Helen did not
really like me." Then he looked at Jury and smiled slightly.
"You think I'm drunk — which I am, I often am — and that
in my besotted state I am going to let all sorts of cats out of
bags, tell you all the secrets I've kept buried for so long?" He
slid down in his chair. "I will give you this: your technique is
more soothing than Sergeant Cullen's."

Jury said nothing.

Parmenger fixed Jury with his still very clear artist's eye.
" 'Patience on a monument,' eh? You won't sandbag me;
you'll just wait me out." He took another drink.

"I would do, maybe. If I knew what I was waiting for."

"We none of us know that, do we?" It was said rather simply, without rancor, and without Parmenger's usual irony.
"Amateurish work." He nodded toward the picture of the
Old Hall. "I could never make Helen out, not really. Although *I* was supposed to be the smart one. *I* am a genius."
He took another drink. Yet Parmenger seemed to be getting
soberer, not drunker.

"You say that as if you didn't care much one way or the
other."

"I say only what the critics say." He looked at Jury, smiling
slightly. "And if Seaingham doesn't know who is and who

isn't, how the bloody hell should *I* know?" His tone changed as he added, "Nice chap, Charlie."

"Helen Minton seemed to appreciate your painting." Jury was looking at the abstract on the opposite wall. "It's surprising that anyone who's so good at portraiture would be appreciated mainly for his abstract —"

"You don't know sod-all about painting, Superintendent," said Parmenger, quite matter-of-factly. "Neither do most of the people I know, even some of my fellow-artists."

"Your father was a friend of Rudolph St. Leger, his wife says. Did you know him yourself?"

"I remember him. He was an ass, thought of himself as another Whistler, lugubrious scenes of trees and meadows and cows. Sentimental imitations of the late-nineteenth-century romantics. He hated my stuff. Tried to keep me out of the Academy. Upstart crow, he thought I was. Or cow. He couldn't paint a *real* cow. He couldn't have done much of anything if it hadn't been for *her.* I mean, she was the one with the money, the position, the contacts. She financed his shows and bullied the critics not only into coming but into at least passable reviews. Except Charlie. He remained as silent as Thomas More on the marriage of King Henry. Rather tactful of him, I thought. To be fair I have to admit old Rudy had some technique, which prevented his work from being *absolutely* embarrassing. I mean, I suppose he could paint a cow if you held a gun to his head. People like you — no offense — would naturally look at the cows and horses and think it was a quite decent painting. But Elizabeth St. Leger really thought the man was talented. I'm not sure it's good to have that sort of reinforcement. People who love you always lie to you, don't they? Maybe not deliberately. It's just they don't know the difference. Why am I going on like this? I haven't thought of old Rudy in years."

"I'm interested."

Parmenger looked at Jury with an artist's practiced eye. "I

bet you are," he said. "I feel a little sorry for the boy. I know what it's like to have someone after you— Want some more?" He held up the bottle of whiskey, seemingly unaware that Jury's glass hadn't emptied very much. Jury held out his glass to be topped up. Parmenger went on: "My own father did everything he could to prevent me painting. Even threw out my paints once, in a tearing rage. Wouldn't give me money to go to art school— probably just as well. What he did want was for me to follow in his footsteps, or at least do something more than dab and daub— as he put it— at a piece of canvas." Parmenger smiled ruefully. "He went into one of his tempers once, threw my paint and brushes out."

Jury smiled. "I imagine Tommy Whittaker can hold his own. You did."

"Had to. But if my father couldn't control *me*, he could Helen. After all, what did she have to fight him with?" He set his drink on the floor beside the armchair he had sunk into.

"He left her a good deal of money and the house, though. He must have felt guilty."

Parmenger avoided the question of guilt, saying, "Who's talking about money? Helen had a lot of creative energy, but it never found a form. I taught her all that I could about technique. We used to go up in the attic to paint. I was always an artist, from the time I could hold a crayon." He seemed to be explaining all of this more to himself than to Jury. "Even if I'd *wanted* to do something else, I'm sure I couldn't've . . . but that's stupid. The desire and the talent must go hand in hand, mustn't they? That attic —" And he looked at the ceiling as if it might still be there, a couple of floors above them, preserved through time here in this cottage. "— that attic on some afternoons when there was enough sun was light-flooded. We'd sit in front of the window. It was an arched window, sort of Gothic like a church window, and round the top little panes of glass were set in, like red stained glass. When the sun shone through, our faces and arms would be dappled with red. I often watched Helen as she tried her painting, sitting there, very concentrated, her pale face blood-patched. We painted what we saw out the window, the tops of the trees in Eaton Square, the gardens, the people down there sitting on the park benches." He stopped. "It was a long time ago."

Jury let him have his silent look back into the past for a few moments and then said, "You said she didn't like you. It doesn't sound like it."

Parmenger finished off his drink, put the glass on the floor beside him. "That came later. We quarreled."

"Over what?"

"Does that concern you?" Parmenger got out of his chair and went over to the french doors, where he stood, gazing out at the frost-hardened garden.

"Over something unpleasant that she found out. Perhaps you know the headmistress — Miss Hargreaves-Brown?"

Frederick Parmenger was a little slow in his denial. "Never heard of her. And what's all this in aid of?"

"She didn't want to ask direct questions, is my guess. In case she might embarrass someone. An interesting speculation."

"Not to me, particularly."

"I think she found the person she was looking for."

"What person?"

"Her son."

He turned slowly from the window. There was a volcanic force in the man, even with his senses dulled by whiskey. Watching Parmenger's expression change, Jury thought of a storm coming on, a sky turning to lead. Parmenger looked frightened.

"He was yours. I know. Go on, sit down before you fall down."

Parmenger slumped in the chair. He had his fingers laced,

covering his face. "I didn't know it, not back then. Helen was —" Unable to bring it out, he stopped.

"Your half sister. I know that, too."

Parmenger got up, went over to the drinks cabinet, saying, "You know bugger-all, Superintendent."

"Miss Hargreaves-Brown — or let's say Annie Brown — told me."

Parmenger's face was white. "That bitch. My sanctimonious father paid her well to keep her mouth shut."

"I can't say I like her, either. How did you find out about the relationship between your father and his sister-in-law?"

"From one of his granite-faced colleagues who was instructed to give me the good news when my father died. I suppose to scare the hell out of me, in case I had any plans for some future with Helen —"

He broke off. He seemed to be looking around the room, into the deepening shadows, baffled. "My sister —" There was in the voice a sharp edge of hysteria, cut off, as Jury imagined Parmenger could repress, very quickly, any emotion he had to.

"How can you blame yourself? You didn't —"

"Sod off! Don't give me your police condolences. I ruined her life."

"You ruined her life? Or could she have ruined yours?"

The implication of that sobered him. "What's that supposed to mean?" he asked in his bullying way.

"Would you have wanted this to come out?"

His look at Jury was pure contempt. "Don't be absurd. Helen wouldn't have told it, and anyway, I don't worry about my 'reputation.' Let the critics do that; it keeps them off the streets." Drink in hand, he was up and prowling the room, picking up first one and then another of Helen's small possessions, reluctantly putting them down, as if they might be an extension of their owner. To hold on to them was to hold on to her.

"Someone's trying to murder Grace Seaingham," said Jury.

"Then someone's making a damned sloppy job of it." Parmenger downed the rest of his drink.

"I'm not talking about the presumably mistaken attack on Beatrice Sleight. That was no mistake. Call it a sort of 'safety play.' Beatrice Sleight was the intended victim all right. But someone is still trying to kill Grace Seaingham."

Parmenger laughed. "Ridiculous." But his expression changed quickly. "Why? You're not suggesting Charles?"

"Are you?"

"No. Only I know that Grace wouldn't divorce him."

"So it's common knowledge that Seaingham was in love with Beatrice Sleight."

Parmenger stopped in his walk about the room. "No. I know it. But then I'm observant — And how the devil have you deduced that, anyway? Nothing's happened to Grace."

Jury didn't answer this directly. "Helen Minton, Beatrice Sleight, Grace Seaingham. . . . Helen wasn't — as far as I know — acquainted with either of the other women."

" 'Helen'? Were you on a first-name basis then?" His face clouded over.

Jury thought of that earlier reference to Ferdinand, the insanely jealous brother of the Duchess of Malfi, who would see her dead before he'd see her happy with another man. "I knew her for an afternoon. Is that important now?"

Parmenger didn't answer. His eyes were fastened on the painting of the Old Hall, as if its amateurish execution were a source of secret pain.

"Helen had a visitor a week before she died." He pulled out his notebook, flipped the pages. " '. . . terrible row.' That's according to Nellie Pond, who lives next door. 'The voices would die down and flare up again.'. . . It was you who came to see her, wasn't it?"

"A cunning deduction. No."

"Nothing cunning about it. You asked why she took the

picture down. How did you know your portrait had ever been hanging there? I mean, if you hadn't seen her for months —?"

His eyes remained on the picture. He sighed. "Very well. Yes, I did see Helen. And, yes. There was a row. I wanted her to stop."

" 'Stop'?"

"Searching. I knew she'd come to the North. Maureen — she's Helen's housekeeper —"

"I know."

Parmenger turned to look at him, but the rancor had left both his face and his voice. "Is there anything you *don't* know, Superintendent?"

"Lots," said Jury, lighting up a cigarette. Parmenger shook his head when Jury held out the packet.

"Well, don't expect *me* to enlighten you. Maureen told me she'd come up here. That was weeks ago. You don't really think I'd have been staying at the Seainghams' all of this time to paint a portrait, do you?"

"Go on."

"There's nothing to be going on *with*. Helen had undertaken this search and I wanted her to stop."

"Why?"

Parmenger paused. "I was afraid," he said, simply.

"That you'd have to take your share of the responsibility?"

"Oh, don't be so bloody sanctimonious. Maybe I was afraid of what she'd find. I mean, of what the child would be like."

If Parmenger knew about Robin Lyte, he wasn't about to tell Jury. "Isn't that superstitious, Mr. Parmenger? The close blood-tie, the deranged child — Antigone was hardly deranged."

Parmenger feigned surprise. "A Greek scholar, too. My, but your talents are endless." His tone changed, and he said, "Helen felt guilty enough as it was." He shook his head slowly, as if it were full of the dust, the cobwebs up in that old attic by the window where they'd sat and painted the trees in Eaton Square. . . .

Jury watched Parmenger, who had got up now to prowl the room. He thought of Father Rourke's study of the Gospels. He thought of Isobel Dunsany, of Annie Brown, of the paints Edward Parmenger had flung out, and especially of Jerusalem Inn

TWENTY-FIVE

NELL HORNSBY was wiping down the optics when Jury walked in. She gave him a big smile, drew a pint of Newcastle for him, and said, "Happy Christmas."

"Thanks, Nell. Not many people in here this evening. I'm surprised."

"Oh, aye. We've only just opened. They'll be in later. Christmas Eve's a big night."

There were only the elders on the bench. Marie and Frank nose to nose, and the chap in the anorak with his book and his nervous whippet. "Where's Robin?" asked Jury.

"Robbie? Last I saw him he was in the back room." As she gestured with the hand that held the bar towel, Jury saw a flash of skirt disappear through the door to the living quarters upstairs.

"Chrissie!" called Nell. No answer. She sighed. "The bairn just *won't* leave that doll alone."

Jury smiled. "She'll bring it back. Probably gone to give it a wash."

Nell shook her head and turned to wipe the beer pulls, and

Jury took his glass over to the table near the fireplace. All he wanted, for the moment, was to think.

He didn't know how long she'd been standing there with Alice all wrapped up in a blanket to which bits of hay were still stuck. "After tomorrow, I can have her back, Mam said."

"That's good. Are you glad to see Christmas come, then?"

"Aye. I'm getting Smurfs and a Barbie Doll and coloring books and a new dress." She sat down and adjusted the blanket more firmly around Alice.

"You know everything you're getting, then?"

She nodded. "I looked. It's all upstairs in the closet. I wrapped them back up again." Her gaze at Jury was clear and straight. "You going to tell?"

"Do I look like somebody who'd tell?"

She shrugged. "Maybe not." She looked him over carefully. "Mam said you was police."

"True. We've all been taught to keep secrets. People don't get things out of us easily."

Her hair, recently washed, matted damply about her small face like dark leaves. Her brown eyes stared into Jury's. "I took off the swaddling clothes. They got dirty. And I pinned him into this blanket. Do you think that's okay?"

Chrissie took these sudden sex changes in stride. "I'm sure it is," said Jury. "I don't think Mary and Joseph will mind, as long as the baby's put back."

She cocked her head. "Are they so dumb they don't know it's Alice?"

And with that sacrilege, she slipped off the chair and hunkered under the rope to stuff the doll in the crib.

Jury sat there for a moment looking at the creche. He wondered how it was he could have heard the same thing over and over and paid no attention —

Melrose Plant put his hand on Jury's shoulder, shaking it. "Where've you been? Tommy's back there" — Melrose nodded toward the back room — "beating them all blind in less time than it takes me to do a crossword. He just laid several snookers on Tattoo that you wouldn't believe. I'm thinking of being his manager. You're not listening. . . . Why are you staring at the Nativity scene?"

"Am I so dumb I didn't know it was Alice?" He got up and started for the telephone beside the bar.

"What are you talking about?"

Jury turned back. "I'm going to call Grace Seaingham. I'm going to ask her to invite me to dinner. I shall, of course, be careful what I eat."

Having finished his telephone call over which Plant thought he had taken an inordinately long time, Jury came back to the table with the remainder of his own drink and a pint of Old Peculier.

"Thank God they've got Old Peculier on draught," said Melrose. "Much stronger. What're you drinking? Lye?"

Jury smiled. "Newcastle Brown Ale. Same thing in strength."

"I did as you said, and had a little chat with Susan Assington. I've been reading up on poisons."

Jury still stared at the shabby little Christmas scene, thinking of skis and priests and paintbrushes, and said, "What did you find out?"

"I was thinking of this business of being snowed in: you know, that the Minton woman's murderer couldn't have been one of *our* happy band. Then I hit on cross-country skiing. MacQuade. Who could live in the wilds for weeks with a rifle —"

"You mean his hero could."

Melrose shrugged and raised his glass. "Here's to life: it's only a story." He went on. "But after reading up on the properties of aconitine, it was pretty clear that whoever poisoned her, number one, could have been doing it over a period of

264 ~ JERUSALEM INN

time, and, number two, didn't have to be there when she took the lethal dose."

"I know. I've been talking to Cullen."

"A nonlethal dose passes out of the system very quickly. Maybe that's what was giving her those side effects. It could, couldn't it, have been in the medicine?"

"That's the way a chap named Lamson disposed of his victim. It's what I thought too, at first. Go on."

Melrose drew damp rings on the table with his mug. "So scratch MacQuade. No more opportunity than anyone else, no motive." Turning ash from his cigar, Melrose said, "Now there's Grace Seaingham. According to her, you say, someone's trying to poison her."

"You think she's lying?"

"She won't let Assington do any tests, will she?"

"A good point. But she *is* ill."

"People have been known to administer little doses to themselves — God knows it would divert suspicion. But let me go on —" Melrose shoved his cigar in his mouth, put the book on the table, opened to a page that he had marked with a little pinkish-white flower. "As the American poet Frost might say, 'What has this flower to do with being white?' *Helleborus niger,* the black hellebore. The Christmas rose with the fatal root. Extremely poisonous. A whole houseful supplied by Susan Assington, how about that? Our little Mary-Quite-Contrary gardener."

"And you're saying that since the source of aconite is also a flower — ?"

"Well, I'm only saying what I'm *saying*. Sir George and Beatrice Sleight. Sir George and, possibly, Grace Seaingham? Or, at least, in little Mary's book. Or garden, perhaps."

"But what have you decided Susan Assington's connection is with Helen Minton?

"I haven't. But she's exactly the sort Polly Praed would

have chosen. All of that featherbrained, dopey little shopgirl act hiding an absolutely pathological personality."

Jury smiled. "I'll reserve judgment, for Polly's sake." He picked up his glass and said, "Let's go back and see how Whirlwind Whittaker's doing."

"I had a long talk with Father Rourke," said Jury, watching the player with Tommy address the ball with a dithering style that wasn't going anywhere. "He's the priest in Washington Village and he knew Helen Minton. Rourke is a structuralist —"

"Really? I'd rather be a manager."

"— and he was going over various interpretations of the Gospels. Fascinating. I wish I'd paid more attention."

Plant lit a cigar. "I'm glad you didn't or we might be here till the snows come up to the sills. But go on."

"What I remembered later was what he'd said about the 'psychological' interpretation: he was talking about the story of the Prodigal Son and its Oedipal implications." Tommy's opponent made a traditional break on the reds, but didn't place the cue ball near a color.

"The Prodigal Son. Ah, yes. The tale that always makes you think you'd be better off leaving home."

"It's not that so much as his mention of Oedipus."

"Oedipus was definitely *not* better off leaving home, poor fellow. He should have stuck around."

"Didn't have much choice in the matter, did he?" said Jury watching Robin Lyte, who was hanging about the table with a cue stick, a look of anticipation on his face.

Looking at Robin, Plant said, "That's a very sad case. It's hell she had to find out — Helen Minton, I mean."

They were silent for a moment as they watched Tommy pot one of the reds and stop the green dead with a stun shot, putting it just where he wanted it. "Imagine how devious that kid had to be to get in the practice he's done," said Jury.

"Devious? I wouldn't call him devious," said Plant defensively.

Jury smiled. "I didn't mean it that way. He's a very clever lad, though. I should have seen it straightaway."

"Seen what?"

"I was thinking again of Oedipus: they had to get rid of him, didn't they? The King of Thebes could hardly keep somebody around who was going to wind up murdering him."

"First it's Alice, now it's Oedipus. I'm confused."

"Save it for now. I've got myself and Wiggins invited to dinner this evening." Jury looked at his watch.

"You *were* having an ungodly long conversation with Grace. I think you know, don't you?"

Jury stubbed out his cigarette in an old tin ashtray. By now, the table was cleared of reds. "I think our murderer is going to try to lay, as Tommy would say," — Jury nodded at the table — "a dirty snooker on someone."

"Who?"

"Grace Seaingham."

Plant said, watching Tommy negotiate an incredibly difficult massé shot, "I rather thought that."

Jury looked at him. "Why?"

"Because of the method."

"Which method do you mean?" asked Jury. "Poison or shotgun?"

"I supposed that *poison* was the chosen method, and the gun only used because Beatrice Sleight had to be shut up immediately. Poisons are a bit chancy, unless you use cyanide or another one that's calculated to put your victim out of business rather quickly." Plant opened the book to another page marked with a match and pointed to a small picture. "Such as this."

Jury stared at it. "I'll be damned. With *that* you don't have to worry about poisoning the whole casserole and littering the house with bodies. How damned clever." Jury read the two paragraphs beneath the picture and shook his head before handing the book back to Plant.

Tommy Whittaker pocketed the last ball, the black, and stood back, tugging down his waistcoat.

"He's cleared the table; you've cleared my mind. Thanks," said Jury.

"Aren't you going to return the favor? Who's killing these women? Helen Minton, Beatrice Sleight, and now, you say, Grace Seaingham. Some rabid misogynist? My bet would be Parmenger, if that's the case."

"Do you mind if I don't say at the moment?"

"Yes, but I won't argue." Plant inclined his head toward Tommy. "I've arranged a Christmas present for him. It was almost as difficult as my dear aunt's embroidered coat of arms."

Jury was silent for a moment. "That's good. He's going to need it."

VI

ENDGAME

TWENTY-SIX

1

GRACE SEAINGHAM'S sudden announcement as the cocktail tray was being passed that Scotland Yard would be dining with them prompted Vivian Rivington to spill half her martini down the front of a high-necked, jade-green gown that made her look more like a Geisha girl than a candidate for the Italian nobility.

The others were equally dressed up, it being Christmas Eve: Lady St. Leger in lace, Lady Ardry in a length of unidentifiable cloth, Susan Assington worrying the uneven hemline of some brown, feathery material that put Melrose in mind of a dry wheatfield, perhaps in contrast to Grace Seaingham's newly found color. Indeed, Susan seemed to wither while Grace bloomed.

Upon their hostess's news, they all shifted expressions and positions as if they were being rearranged by a photographer. MacQuade looked quizzical, Parmenger bored. Tommy might have been trying out a massé shot in his mind, he looked so intensely upon Grace.

Charles Seaingham himself was definitely put out by this announcement. "You didn't tell me, my dear."

"No, I told Cook," said Grace, sweetly. She smiled at him, as if making a point of what took precedence. Grace was dressed tonight not in white but in a soft and flattering shade of tea-rose, which Parmenger had gone on about, saying it brought out her color, suited her hair, and walking round her as if he'd like to go back now and do the whole portrait all over again. Grace had thanked him, noticed that her gown just matched the Christmas roses, plucked one from a wide, shallow crystal vase, and stuck it in the neck of her dress. She smiled brightly at Susan Assington, who looked quickly away.

Grace Seaingham seemed to be the only person there who did not display a case of the jitters, except for Frederick Parmenger and the Ladies St. Leger and Ardry. Those two sat solid as rocks on either side of the fireplace with their embroidery hoops.

Melrose was even more certain Grace was up to something when she said, in response to the several *you're looking ever so much better, Grace, dear*'s, "I feel ever so much better. It must have been that marvelous luncheon I had with Superintendent Jury in Durham this afternoon."

"That marvelous luncheon" was described in absolutely sensuous detail: they'd lunched on, of all things, an Old Peculier casserole and soused mushrooms. None of this one-way conversation was going down a treat with her guests, Melrose saw. There were more refillings of glasses than usual, which, with this crowd, was like giving a Rolls-Royce an oil and lube job.

"Nonetheless, my dear," said Charles. "I feel we've all seen enough of police. They're still out tonight with their damned lanterns and torches. I've lived with them long enough. I don't care to sit down to dine with them."

As Marchbanks slid open the large double door, Grace rose with a smile, and said, "Sitting down to dine in this house is no problem; it's getting up that worries me. Shall we go in?"

2

VIVIAN RIVINGTON's mortification at having to sit down to dine in a gown with a largish stain splashed over the front was not relieved in the least by her having been seated next to Superintendent Jury. He had arrived after a double consommé, and been treated to a few looks from the guests which suggested his presence to be less savory than soup.

This didn't bother Jury. He apologized for having been detained at the Northumbria station and tucked into the excellent warm salad of oysters *sabayon*, remarking on the delectable champagne sauce and the Chardonnay. To follow was saddle of lamb, and Jury and Grace held a similar dialogue on finding spring lamb in December.

Indeed, Grace Seaingham and Richard Jury were having a jolly old time talking about food, drink, fish and game. How the salmon were running in Pitlochary, how the pheasant shooting had been rather poor that year, how the St. Emilion stacked up against the Chardonnay, how Rules compared with White's; Brown's with the Ritz; Boodle's with the Turf Club.

None of which clubs, Melrose damned well knew, Richard Jury had ever bothered to go into except on business, and Melrose sincerely doubted there was ever any business going on in them that would interest Scotland Yard. Although the sight of octogenarians in arctic poses behind *Punch* and the *Guardian* might call for sudden visits from the coroner.

So what they were doing — Grace Seaingham and Jury — was making the other diners nervous. No one apparently could understand *why* this *bon vivant* of a Scotland Yard superintendent had sat down to dine with them; everyone looked guilty (except for Agatha, who merely tried — unsuccessfully — to turn the tide of the conversation), especially Vivian, who, these days, was wavering between personae.

Would she walk by or jump *in* the Trevi Fountain? Guilt simply spread from her divided heart to the tips of her long, sensitive fingers.

When the fruit sorbet had been served and eaten, the guests began acting with uncharacteristic rudeness — even for Parmenger, who, without waiting for his hostess to rise, excused himself to have a compulsive look at Grace's portrait;

Charles Seaingham excused himself to see to the decanting of a fresh bottle of rare port;

Lady St. Leger, complaining of a dreadful headache, excused herself to get her medicine;

Tommy Whittaker said he was going to the music room;

Susan Assington, looking slightly ill from the discussion of gardening undertaken by Lady Ardry, wanted to go to her room for a moment;

Leaving only Vivian (who managed to spill another glass of wine), Agatha, Melrose, Jury and MacQuade.

"Well, there it is then," said Jury to Grace.

There what was? Melrose wanted to ask, as Grace rose and they left the table.

3

THEY took their after-dinner drinks as usual in the drawing room near the East Wing, Marchbanks handing around the tray. Jury seemed to be enjoying Charles Seaingham's superior cigar and superior cognac.

The others, Melrose noted, were drinking their usuals: Agatha, her abominable crème de violette; Parmenger and MacQuade, Remy; Vivian, cognac, as she might be less likely to spill anything in a balloon glass; Lady Assington and Lady St. Leger, crème de menthe; Grace Seaingham, her Sambuca de Mosca; and Tommy, as usual, nothing.

Until Grace Seaingham offered him her Sambuca, to the extreme surprise of his aunt. "Oh, let him, Betsy." She smiled. "It's not all that deadly alcoholic."

Elizabeth St. Leger intercepted the transfer of the little glass very neatly, saying, "Tom might be getting up to things at school I don't know about." Her laugh was not very hearty. "But I really think, my dear Grace, he shouldn't be tempted *here*." As she was returning the drink to her hostess, her hand brushed the bowl of roses and the small glass tilted. "Sorry. We all seem to be spilling our drinks tonight." But Jury was very quick off the mark in mopping up the spilled liqueur before Lady St. Leger could reach it with her lace handkerchief.

Grace smiled benignly. "Think nothing of it." She set the empty glass aside on a table. "I'm so sorry, Betsy. My fault." She laughed. "But I honestly can't imagine Tommy 'getting up to things'!" And her smile turned toward Jury, who was replacing his handkerchief in his pocket.

What Melrose admired most of all in that room, where no one really knew what was going on except the four of them, was Lady St. Leger's iron self-control when she rose and announced that she thought she would have an early night.

The cliché barely registered with him, as she added that she would very much like a word with the superintendent before retiring.

4

SHE did not appear to mind that Melrose Plant had been asked to come along to Seaingham's study. Indeed, Elizabeth St. Leger seemed beyond caring at this point.

Melrose felt supremely stupid at having failed to take her more seriously. He supposed it was because Agatha had been so successful in linking arms (metaphorically speaking) with

"Betsy," that Melrose had simply linked them in his mind —
two stout old ladies together, with their hoops and their cards
and their talk of the peerage.

He observed her there, before the fireplace, where she insisted on standing. She would not sit. In her day, Lady St.
Leger would have been spoken of as decidedly handsome.
With her good bones and clear skin, she still retained much of
that quality. The coronet of gray hair wound tightly about
her head was brushed to a luster; her gray eyes had the same
metallic sheen; this coloring was further emphasized by the
gray lace-and-satin gown. Out of Agatha's presence, he had
thought her unique; now he recognized the coldness at the
core. She made Plant think of a commemorative coin struck
off and recalled from circulation when it was found to be
flawed.

"That was an interesting little charade, Superintendent,"
she said, with a small, ironic smile, as if her life didn't indeed
depend on it, or the book, open on the table that Plant had
earlier shown to Jury. Her look grazed it; she shrugged
slightly. "I was rather glad that Susan Assington was such a
gardener." Her look turned from the book to Melrose. "You
did make me a little nervous there, Mr. Plant, with the talk
of Christmas roses. They come, you see, from the same but-
tercup family as aconite. You were rather close on that
one."

"I don't know that it's an occasion for compliments, Lady
St. Leger," said Melrose with a rueful smile. "But you cer-
tainly handled it with panache, turning my attention to
Susan Assington."

Elizabeth St. Leger, shrugged again. "I'm surprised she has
the brains to get rid of deathwatch beetles."

Jury said, unfolding his handkerchief, "Maybe we could
just start with these. Castor beans. *Ricinus communis.* Total
anaphylactic shock could occur from biting into just one.

Pretty deadly stuff. You took a hell of a chance tonight, trying to kill Grace Seaingham."

"Well, desperate remedies, Mr. Jury — you understand that sort of thing, don't you."

"Grace Seaingham is the type to carry secrets to the grave. She'd never have told anyone —"

"It was obvious she was up to something, bringing you here. And for some reason, she'd lost her fear of food and drink. Blooming, really. Please excuse the ghastly pun, with all of this plant lore —"

"And since only *she* took her Sambuca with coffee beans, you made the substitution when you went to get your medicine. Just dropped these on the plate on the tray. Why didn't you imagine she'd *already* told me what she knew?"

"She could have done, of course. But I didn't think so. I thought, though, she would before the evening was out."

"Where did you get the castor beans?"

"They're quite common. They come in various shapes and sizes —"

Her tone was so flat she might have been talking about frocks.

"— some speckled, some gray. Many one couldn't possibly mistake for the coffee bean. The ones growing in the gardens of Meares happened to be the small, dark variety."

Again, as if the gown were a perfect fit.

"I'm sorry, I can't tell you how they taste," she added wryly. "I only know one has to chew them. Swallow one whole and you're safe as houses, oddly enough. But Grace liked the coffee beans."

"Too bad Beatrice Sleight didn't drink Sambuca —"

Elizabeth St. Leger bristled. "That dreadful woman. She was more of a danger than anyone, and I didn't even know her."

"Was it blackmail, then?" asked Jury.

"Blackmail — you mean *money?*" The tone suggested she never touched the stuff. "Don't be ridiculous. It was her new *roman à clef*. You don't think I'd let her get away with that, do you? Not after all the trouble I'd taken with Grace and Helen Minton — and they were less dangerous. Uncertain quantities. But not Beatrice Sleight. Ah, no. She simply put it to me after the others had gone up to bed."

"And you and Charles Seaingham have done a bit of shooting together. Pheasant, grouse, that sort of thing. You were familiar with the gun room, and certainly familiar with firearms."

She nodded stiffly. Her face was drained of color and she felt behind her for the chair and finally sat down. "It was important, of course, that police would not start making connections between Beatrice Sleight's books and . . . someone who might want to stop her. There would, on the other hand, be no reason for my doing away with Grace Seaingham. No motive."

There was a long, indrawn breath. "The child was born on one of Irene's and Richard's trips: this time to Kenya. Oh, don't think those safaris were some dangerous sort of cutting through undergrowth chased by rhinos: they were guided, well-directed, full of sumptuous banquet-style dinners —" Her contempt was evident. "At any rate, Irene called me, hysterical when the doctors told her. She was always a silly girl, could never handle anything on her own. Nor could Richard if it came to that. I told them I'd fix it."

"You fix people's lives rather easily, don't you, Lady St. Leger?"

She colored at that. "I happen to love my nephew. I daresay you think I'm not capable of such a feeling, but it's true."

Jury did not reply to that. "How did you run into Helen Minton?"

"A visit to Old Hall. She had never met me; I recognized her at once, from Edward's pictures. I couldn't believe it — I mean that it was she. And I could think of no reason for her being there, except she was trying to get information about her child. I . . . befriended her —"

The chill in the air could not possibly have matched the chill in Jury's voice. "What a very odd way to do it. Was the aconite the common garden variety? Wolfsbane? Monkshood? And sometimes called Blue Rocket. What a name. The root looks like horseradish. Or turnip. Helen was fond of hot condiments like horseradish."

"I know. I brought her some, on one of my visits."

"So it wasn't her medicine."

"Oh, no. Nor was it with Grace. Aconite has a sweetish taste which turns acrid. Grace used one of those powdered saccharines. The difficulty there is, of course, the dosage. Very undependable. But with Helen Minton, I used another variety which I picked up in my travels in India. Nepal, I believe . . ." She looked off as if merely remembering the pleasant days of travel. "Yes, Nepal. *Nabee,* they call it. It contains pseudoaconitine. One of the very deadliest poisons known. Pardon the lecture on toxicology —"

"Quite all right. I can get used to anything, almost. And Helen Minton suffered from ventricular fibrillation. You might have got away with death from natural causes if she hadn't died in Old Hall."

Elizabeth St. Leger didn't comment, except to ask with mild surprise, "You knew her, then?"

Jury was uncapping his pen, taking some sheets of paper from his pocket, "I knew her, yes."

"I'm sorry." She said it with simple and complete sincerity.

To this extension of sympathy, he merely said, "I'm willing to strike a bargain, as it's Christmas." He smiled bleakly. "If you'd just care to sign this, perhaps we can wait until after the holiday. Pretty hard on Tom, it's going to be."

"Thank you." He might have been passing her the drinks tray. With the help of her pince-nez, she read it over quickly, looked at Jury with a tiny smile, and signed. Jury recapped his pen and said, "I'll have to send someone along to Meares Hall from Northumbria police to — you know — keep an eye on things."

Her smile was as bleak as his. "I quite understand."

"Police protection. As far as Tommy will be given to understand."

"May I retire now? I promise you, I won't slip out the window and down the ivy. There is no place I care to go." Her voice was suddenly very old.

"Of course."

She had to lean on her cane a bit harder than usual. "You're a very clever man." Her gaze took in Melrose Plant. "Both of you. May I ask what it was gave you the notion about Tom?"

"Frederick Parmenger," said Jury. "His character, his dedication. His determination, when he was young — like Tommy — to fly in the face of everyone. . . . Well, you knew his father — "

"Indeed. To stand up to Edward would *require* determination."

"To stand up to you, Lady St. Leger, would require much more."

With the tip of her cane she traced the figure in the carpet. Then she looked up. "Good-night, Superintendent. Mr. Plant." She left the room.

5

"I'll be damned," said Melrose, after the door had closed on her. "*That* was all that nonsense about 'Alice.' The original child got broken, and another was put in its place."

"They couldn't have poor Robin Lyte as the tenth Marquess of Meares. One child — the mentally defective one — handed over to the marchionness's maidservant, Danielle. No wonder she could supply Isobel Dunsany with excellent references. Another child — Helen and Parmenger's son — handed over to Meares Hall. Edward Parmenger and Elizabeth St. Leger took care of that swap. And the go-betweens were Danny Lyte and Annie Brown."

"You would have thought the headmistress of the Bonaventure School would have been the first one to be got rid of, if that's the case."

"But did she know where Helen Minton's child wound up? All she did was to take it into the Bonaventure School as a foundling. If Danny came along shortly thereafter with a large sum of money and an offer — well, what connection would Danny have had with the St. Legers, the Parmengers, the Meares? Miss Hargreaves-Brown had shown herself to be open to offers before," Jury added dryly. "Oh, she knew all right that something was fishy — she knew damned well Robin Lyte was not Helen Minton's child, but years ago she'd reorganized her filing system, let's say. So it was Robin's file Helen found and took *him* to be her son. It was Robin she found at Jerusalem Inn. And the trusted servant, Danny Lyte, has a softer heart than her employers and goes back and adopts Robin. Like the good shepherd of Sophocles."

"Hell, you'd think they were all shopping at Marks and Sparks, wouldn't you?" Melrose stretched out his legs and his whiskey glass. Jury topped it up. "And now what? I mean what about Tommy?"

"Nothing. He'll go on being the Marquess of Meares, as far as I'm concerned."

Plant nearly choked on his drink. "Hold on for a bloody moment! What do you say to him when Great-Aunt Betsy gets led away by the Bobbsey Twins, Cullen and Trimm?"

Absently, Jury shuffled a deck of cards he'd picked up from

the table. "Well, you see, I don't think that's going to happen." He turned up a card, a queen.

"Not going —? So that was what all of that letting her go back to Meares Hall was about. *'I've no place to go from there, Superintendent.'* "

Jury said nothing, merely reshuffled the cards slowly and looked into the blue flames of the dying fire.

"But look here, I mean, isn't that awfully unethical, or un-political, or un-Yardish, or something?"

"Sure is," said Jury. "Racer would have kittens. If he hadn't already got a cat."

"But what about Tommy? He has to know."

Jury looked up from his shuffling. "God, you're a stickler for the truth, aren't you? You think it would set him up, do you, knowing his aunt had murdered two women and tried to murder a third?"

Plant colored slightly. "Certainly not. But what's the way out? I mean, he *has* to know he's not the rightful heir."

Tonelessly, Jury said, "I don't see why?"

"Well, damn it, *I* do. For one thing, he doesn't *want* to be the marquess. He doesn't *want* to carry on that noble line. He just wants to play snooker."

"No reason he can't."

"You think not? If something ... happened to his Aunt Betsy he'd feel guilty as hell," said Plant, growing more heated with both the conversation and the drink. "He'd probably hang up his guns — or rack up his cues — forever."

Jury fanned the cards out on the table and took a drink. "Don't be dramatic. He's just like Parmenger. Nothing'll stop him. Pick a card."

"No."

"Oh, go on. Make you feel better. It's a trick." Jury's smile fled as he thought of the gates of the Bonaventure School. "Not a very good one, though."

"I just don't see how you can lay that on Tom Whittaker —"

"He's not snookered, not him. Far from it."

Plant was silent, hands wrapped round his glass, staring into the fire and frowning, as though searching for some other line of attack. "I'd think you'd want to see — these women avenged."

Jury's drink stopped in mid-air. "*That* is the bloodiest, stuffiest thing I've ever heard you say. 'Avenged.' From the look on Lady St. Leger's face, I'd say, if I wanted vengeance I'd got it."

"I'm talking about justice."

"With a capital *J*." Jury snorted. He thought they were getting rather drunk. He'd better call Cullen. And Racer. That made him pour himself another drink and slide the bottle toward his friend.

"Perhaps not the Sleight woman. But what about Helen Minton? Will her death go unnoted? I rather thought you . . . well, nothing."

Jury looked down into his whiskey and rolled his glass, making tiny, amber waves. He thought of Isobel Dunsany, living on memories of faded elegance there by the North Sea.

"Her death hasn't gone unnoted. I only knew her for a few hours." Jury felt defensive, as if that should excuse him from any strong feeling. He avoided Melrose Plant's speculative look.

All Plant said, mildly, was, "You were fond of her, nonetheless."

"I've been fond of a lot of women," said Jury, carelessly, hoping that would convey the image of the tough detective plowing his way through bevies of beauties. Of course, it didn't. "Haven't we all?" He looked at Melrose.

"Don't change the subject."

But Jury did, not caring for the subject they were on.

"What puzzled me for a moment was why the marquess and marchioness didn't simply *adopt* an heir — instead of stealing one, you might say."

"Because nobilary entitlement does not work that way. No adoptions, no suspect parentage." Melrose stared at the coal-end of his cigar as if he were the fabled bird hypnotized by a snake. "Ever hear of old Needwood, Viscount Dearing? Tried to claim the child born to the viscountess was not his own. Tried to prove about three dozen corespondents in the case, but since the viscountess was as taut as a telephone wire and had a mouth like a sticking plaster when it came to matters of the bedchamber, the court ruled the issue was either the viscount's or a Virgin Birth." Melrose tossed his cigar into the fireplace grate, and lay one arm across the mantel. "So you see, old boy, one's got to be the real thing, the right stuff, or it's no go." He smiled slightly. "I can't imagine dragging someone's name through the dirt that way, especially one's family, can you?"

Jury looked at him for a moment. "No. I suppose it works the other way round, doesn't it? Where there is adultery, and the family just keeps it quiet."

"I suppose it could do, yes." Plant sat down again, poured himself another drink. "I believe we're getting drunk."

"I believe we are too."

Plant looked at his watch. "Well, we'll have to continue our libations at the pub, because I've got something on."

"What do you mean?"

"Never mind. You call Cullen; I'll collect Tommy. I don't think," he said rather sadly, "there'll be much problem in his aunt's letting him out for one last fling at Jerusalem Inn." Melrose raised his glass. "Happy Christmas, Superintendent."

The glasses clicked and Plant's slid and spilled a little whiskey on his tie. "Worse than Vivian." He brushed at the droplets. "Wonder what that woman — old Viv, I mean —

ever intends to do about Count Dracula." He slid down in his chair. "Now Polly Praed —"

"You're a fool, you know that?"

Plant frowned. "Meaning? Anyway, Happy Christmas once again."

"Happy Christmas, my friend." The glasses clicked.

VII

JERUSALEM INN

TWENTY-SEVEN

❦

1

"WHAT the devil's *that?*" asked Melrose Plant, when the three of them were crowding into Jury's police car, already occupied by a very large and a somewhat smaller package.

"Present for the Hornsbys," said Jury. "Something I picked up today in Durham." He heard paper rattling in the back seat. "It's not for you; don't go opening it."

Tommy Whittaker's excitement at being allowed "on" — he had to use his snooker terminology — for the evening was somewhat tempered by concern for Lady St. Leger. "What's wrong with Aunt Betsy, anyway? She looked bad when she went upstairs."

There was silence for a moment, and then Jury said, "She's an old woman, Tommy. You know she's been having troubles with her health. And after everything that's happened —"

"I suppose so. You any closer to finding out what *did* happen? Does that Sergeant Cullen still suspect *me?*"

"You're not a suspect."

Tommy breathed a sigh of relief.

"Maybe," said Jury. "it's going to be one of those cases we just don't crack."

"Are you kidding?" said Tommy, still enough of the little boy to believe that the Yard always cracks its cases.

"It happens. At the moment what I'm wondering is whether Mr. Plant will get that package open," he said to the small rustling sounds coming from the back seat.

2

THE package had been opened, and the single Wise Man it contained, somewhat faded from years of wear, had been stood beside the other two. And the smaller package, given over to Chrissie, and holding a similarly faded Christ child, placed in the straw.

Chrissie stood, holding Alice, surveying the Nativity scene, its ranks swollen now by two. Her small brows met in a frown. "Yours is smaller than the other two men. And its carrying gold, like him." Alice back in her dress again, Chrissie pointed to the Wise Man next to Jury's smaller one. "I think they're both the same. And we don't have a black one." She looked up at Jury rather critically, as if perhaps he were not as familiar with the Christmas story as he should have been.

Over the voices of the some two dozen denizens of the Jerusalem, who had been revving up for action all the late afternoon, Jury said, "You're right. But he was the only one they had. I found him and the baby in an old shop. I guess they were just the odd lot from someone else's creche." Jury felt he was being very unsuccessful in his attempts to flesh out the scene. He smiled. "Hard to come by a Wise Man —"

Chrissie smoothed Alice's dress down and said, "I suppose so. It was nice of you." This compliment was somewhat grudging. "Only . . . it hasn't got swaddling clothes." Amid the noise around them — the carol-singing, the shouts for drinks — theirs was a little pocket of silence, standing there, looking over the scene. "Do you think Mary and Joseph mind that he was gone?"

"Yes. But now he's back. Maybe that's what counts."

Her small chest rose and fell in a deep sigh of resignation. "I guess I'll just have to *make* some more swaddling clothes."

Melrose and Tommy had worked their way up to the bar, wedging between Nutter and a stranger with blond ringlets, also with a ring in his ear, but in the one which suggested he was definitely not Nutter's type. Had Tommy not just then come between them, the crackle in the air might have charged up considerably.

Tommy shouted their orders to Hornsby, down at the other end, and smiled at Dickie, whose giant leek was tied up with a red ribbon. Dickie grinned and said something incomprehensible. The room was full of people who might have been regulars, casuals, or just the odd Christmas celebrant.

The dark-haired stranger beside him in a storm gray shirt and black waistcoat was smoking a cigarette and drinking lager. The man looked, somehow, like Tommy — or Tommy twenty years hence. He nodded in a friendly way; Melrose nodded back.

"Spirited place," he said, scraping his straight black hair away from a high forehead.

"It is indeed. Buy you a drink?"

"Well, I don't mind now. Thanks." He shoved his glass across the bar, pointed his cigarette at the oboe case stuck between Tom and the bar, and asked, "And what might you have in there? You're clutching it like the devil himself would jump across the bar and snatch it away."

"This? Oh, it's my cue case." Tom looked harder at the man. "You've been here before — haven't you?"

"No. It's a bit out of my way." The man laughed. "You play pool? I wouldn't mind a game."

"Snooker."

"Ah, well. That's my game, too." The stranger put out his hand. "My name's Alex. How about a game, then?"

Tommy, who never dropped anything, dropped his cue case, then quickly retrieved it. He shook his head.

Nutter, always ready to exacerbate any difficulty, gave Tommy a light punch on the shoulder and said, "Go on, then, lad. We don't want any strangers showing us up — and off," he added for good measure, pushing his face a bit closer to Alex's, and obviously irritated that the man just stood there drinking his beer.

"No, thanks," said Tommy, hugging his cue case to his chest and shoving back through the Christmas crowd with his pint. For the first time, Jury thought he looked frightened, sixteen, and alone.

"Anyone care for a frame, then? Say fifty quid a game?"

Nutter's interest in bashing the one with the earring vanished completely at the prospect of managing something profitable.

"Clive. For fifty quid Clive might have a go."

Alex smiled. "Well, now: you don't look like you've got fifty-p between the lot of you."

Dickie seriously started searching his pockets, as Melrose took out his money clip. "We'll let Dickie hold it." He handed some notes to Dickie.

Clive laughed: "I don't care who holds it as long as I get it."

Clive didn't get it.

Clive barely got to the table.

After the toss all he accomplished was to break up the reds, leaving them so widely spaced that Alex made a break of 81 and took fifteen minutes to clear the table.

Clive stood staring at the empty table as if surely some of those balls would roll back again.

Melrose became, not surprisingly, excessively popular as

JERUSALEM INN ～ 293

the back-room big-spender. Now the rest of the crowd came in, and everyone wanted a try.

"They must be crazy," said Tommy, who'd taken his pint and was hanging back in the shadows.

"Why? They're playing with Plant's money."

"Then he must be crazy. Don't you know who that is?"

Within the space of half an hour, Alex had played three frames, running up incredible breaks of 90 and 110, and because there wasn't a hope in hell that any of these pool-players would ever beat him, he finished off Tattoo with a few exhibition shots.

"Who the hell is he?" Jury asked Plant.

"Don't you ever read anything but police files?" Plant shoved the *Guardian*'s sports page at Jury, who looked at the picture, back at Alex and said, "Good Lord."

Nutter was drunk enough to have a go. He intended to smash the pack but got such a top on the cue ball he sent the red over the edge.

Everyone applauded this less-than-brilliant stratagem except Alex, who must have thought it would be unsportsmanlike.

"Ain't no pocket on the floor, lad," said Dickie, who nearly got Nutter's cue stick over the head for that, before Alex flattened his own against Nutter's chest.

Another fifty quid exchanged hands. "Look," said Melrose, "why don't I just give you a thousand and I could stop getting out the money clip?"

Alex smiled. "Well, I wouldn't mind except I'd like to earn it. Now, who's the young fellow — you wouldn't be him, would you? — they've been on about in here just won the local match?" He had, somehow, picked Tommy out of the crowd.

"As a matter of fact," said Tommy straightening up and, for the first time since Melrose had known him, looking down his handsome nose, "I am."

"You're pretty young to be so good. What are you, twenty?"

Tommy shrugged, "About that."

Melrose said, "You see how it is, Whittaker: you're going to have to live for the rest of your life like Gary Cooper in *High Noon*. Remember to sit facing the door."

Alex laughed. Melrose laughed. Tommy didn't.

Tommy won the toss and punched up a break of 23, potting the black three times in succession with the reds, but leaving the rest of the reds bunched together like grapes. He potted the blue, put the cue ball behind the balk line, and now had to try a long shot, intended to smash the pack. He miscued.

A low moan went round the room. Dickie held out both arms: "Thank you, ladies and gen'men — quiet, thank you."

From the expressions on the faces of both players they wouldn't have heard a pack of camels. Alex came up to the table. The white ball was at the other end of the table now but hugging the cushions. It looked like an impossible angle. Alex chipped the red away from the black and sent it in the side pocket, at the same time placing the white in position for the green. He pocketed that and sent the cue ball off three cushions to get down the table to the remaining reds.

Dickie delicately replaced the green on spot.

"Clean the cue ball," said Alex to Dickie.

Dickie leaned over the table, looked at the white ball and shook his head. "Don't look darty t'me, lad."

Alex stared at him. "Doesn't have to look it, man. There was a kick on that last shot. That could cost a lot in money and nerves."

"The marker, Dickie, for God's sake," said Tommy.

Dickie searched round for the little black marker, found nothing, and thumped the leek down where the cue ball had been. Then he went about the delicate business of polishing the cue ball. "Clean as a whistle, it be."

Alex glared and hit the leek off the table.

"Sorry, man." Dickie grinned and once again demanded quiet.

Alex must have had diagrams drawn in his mind as clearly as if they'd been drawn on the table. He potted red, black, red, black so fast that Dickie barely had time to get the black back on spot.

Alex sent the cue ball off four cushions straight back behind the balk colors for a clean shot now at the green. He potted that, leaving the blue a bare inch from the cushion. He didn't seem to put any thought at all into a cannon shot that sent the blue off the far cushion into the open and brought the cue ball off the other three cushions to land up behind the balk line breathing on the pink.

It was a snooker Tommy couldn't get out of. He tried a safety play, but from an impossible distance, especially on a table like this one that didn't run smoothly.

Alex potted the brown with a stun shot and cleared the table then in two minutes.

Nobody so much as breathed.

"Another frame?" asked Alex, chalking his cue tip.

Tommy opened his mouth but shut it when nothing came out. He merely nodded.

Melrose slapped him on the shoulder — a gesture meant to be appreciative of his courage, but which sent the boy, now a bit limp, merely scudding into the table. He chalked his cue. And his features froze into the determined look of a Parmenger whose paintbrushes had just been tossed out of a window.

He lost.

The screw shots, the stun shots, the cannons, the escape plays — the works: Alex was not only a champion player, he was faster than Tommy. Between the two of them they stirred up a wind like a BritRail express blasting through Stevenage.

"Incredible," said Jury. "And to think he just happened to 'pop round' to Jerusalem Inn. How much did it cost you?"

"Few quid."

"A 'few quid.' I'll bet. How much?"

Melrose didn't answer.

"This is your present?"

Alex had cleared the table again. Third frame.

"Some present." Jury drank off his pint. "What've you got for me? A bucket of asps?"

Melrose laughed. "Oh, come on. Tommy loves it. It's taking everything he's got just to get to the table. At last an opponent deserving of him. And especially considering who it is."

"But how'd you ever get him here on Christmas Eve? I mean, the man would surely prefer to be home with his wife and kids —"

Melrose looked at Jury with a pained expression. "Why don't you get married and settle down? He's Irish."

"Oh," said Jury, as if that explained everything. "Northern or Southern?"

"Don't split hairs."

Tommy had left three reds at the balk line, making it virtually impossible for Alex to play safe. The best he could do was to send the cue ball down the table, forcing Tommy to make a long shot. The score was 29 to 30 — Alex one point ahead and looking very intense — with 59 points on the table.

"Poetry in quick-motion," said Melrose, as the terrific spin Tommy put on the ball carried it into the far pocket and brought the cue ball in position for the blue. He pocketed that, then the three remaining reds, the green and the yellow.

There was that last, loose red, down at the other end with the black. He had to size up a position to leave himself on the black.

He overcut, and the onlookers sighed, a few expletives from Marie drawing a shout from Robbie for *quiet*.

The cue ball had left the red at a terrible angle for Alex, who stubbed out his cigarette, moved to the table, and managed to screw the red off the cushion and put so much topspin on the blue that he sent the cue ball off three cushions and clipped the black into the side pocket as easily as if he'd dropped it in with his hand. It was a terrific pot. But he couldn't get back to the balk colors and played a safety.

A few cheers for Alex's playing, from the back of the room, and Nutter picked up a chair and went for the traitors until Clive caught him up.

Eyes shut like a choirmaster trying to order unruly boys, Dickie held out his arms: "Thank you, laidies an' gen'mun, thank you —"

Carefully he picked up the cue ball and went through the ritual of cleaning it and then passed out.

It was as much of a ritual for Dickie as cleaning the cue ball was for Alex.

"Take over, Robin," said Tommy.

Robin Lyte looked confused until Tommy smiled in much the same encouraging way Jury and Plant had smiled at him. "Referee, Robbie. You know the rules."

Robin certainly did, for when Tommy, with perhaps too much concentration, let the cue stick idle through his fingers that single, overlong second, Robbie called.

"Push shot!"

There was a wave of acrimony. Nutter shoved his face in Robbie's, but Robbie was only interested in the Rules of the Game now. He stuck his hand against Nutter's chest and shoved.

Robbie was right, and that left Tommy with a foul and Alex to clear up the colors.

There was a huge round of applause for both of them as they shook hands. Jury looked at Tommy's beaming face —

the truly good loser — and decided that Plant was right. But wrong in another way. Tommy Whittaker might not have been born into the peerage, but the kid was definitely what Plant had referred to earlier as the real thing, the right stuff.

Robin Lyte looked as happy as he he'd engineered the whole show.

The onlookers were all passing them pints, clapping them both on the shoulder, and asking for more.

Alex said, No, sorry, he had to leave.

"When I was your age, lad, I was never so good. I'm twice as old; I've got an edge, now, haven't I? You've just got to watch that temptation to hang on the butt of your cue. That's what happened that last shot. And don't go trickling up behind the ball the way you did once or twice." Alex took out his packet of cigarettes, offered one to Tommy, and lit up.

"Will you be back again?"

Will you be back? Jury thought it one of the saddest questions ever asked.

"Here? I kind of doubt that." He smiled, but he was sizing up his opponent. "I'm sure I'll be meeting up with you again." He got into his coat, turned up the collar, fastened his cue case. Looking at Melrose Plant, he held out his hand. "Pleasure."

"Couldn't you hang around for just a bit?" Tommy's voice was plaintive.

"Wish I could. I've got a match tomorrow. I told you I had an edge. I'm a professional, you see."

"I know," said Tommy simply.

No kidding? thought Jury. Never guess.

". . . and I've got another edge," said Alex, stopping on his way to the door, shouting over the raised voices of Nutter, Tattoo and the boy with the ring in his ear who were singing their boozy version of "Silent Night." Alex laughed. "I'm Irish."

Tommy, his cue resting against his shoulder, stared as Alex made his way through the crowd of Christmas celebrants.

"It was really him."

Jury heard the capital on that "Him."

And Alex waved and walked into the dark of whatever breaks good or bad lay on the other side of the door to Jerusalem Inn.

Headline books are available at your book-shop or newsagent, or can be ordered from the following address:

Headline Book Publishing PLC
Cash Sales Department
PO Box 11
Falmouth
Cornwall
TR10 9EN
England

UK customers please send cheque or postal order (no currency), allowing 60p for postage and packing for the first book, plus 25p for the second book and 15p for each additional book ordered up to a maximum charge of £1.90 in UK.

BFPO customers please allow 60p for postage and packing for the first book, plus 25p for the second book and 15p per copy for the next seven books, thereafter 9p per book.

Overseas and Eire customers please allow £1.25 for postage and packing for the first book, plus 75p for the second book and 28p for each subsequent book.